PARKS PAT MYSTERIES

PARKS PAT MYSTERIES

BOOKS 1-3

P.D. WORKMAN

This is a work of fiction. Names, characters, places and incidents either are products of the author's imagination or are used fictitiously. Any resemblance to actual events or persons, living or dead, is entirely coincidental.

Copyright © 2021 by P.D. Workman

All rights reserved.

No part of this book may be reproduced in any form or by any electronic or mechanical means, including information storage and retrieval systems, without written permission from the author, except for the use of brief quotations in a book review.

ISBN: 9781774681657 (IS Hardcover)

ISBN: 9781774681640 (IS Paperback)

ISBN: 9781774681633 (KDP Paperback)

ISBN: 9781774681664 (Kindle)

ISBN: 9781774681671 (ePub)

ALSO BY P.D. WORKMAN

Parks Pat Mysteries
Out with the Sunset
Long Climb to the Top
Dark Water Under the Bridge
Immersed in the View (Coming soon)
Skimming Over the Lake (Coming soon)
Hazard of the Hills (Coming soon)

Auntie Clem's Bakery
Gluten-Free Murder
Dairy-Free Death
Allergen-Free Assignation
Witch-Free Halloween (Halloween Short)
Dog-Free Dinner (Christmas Short)
Stirring Up Murder
Brewing Death
Coup de Glace
Sour Cherry Turnover
Apple-achian Treasure
Vegan Baked Alaska
Muffins Masks Murder
Tai Chi and Chai Tea
Santa Shortbread
Cold as Ice Cream
Changing Fortune Cookies
Hot on the Trail Mix

Recipes from Auntie Clem's Bakery

Reg Rawlins, Psychic Detective
What the Cat Knew
A Psychic with Catitude
A Catastrophic Theft
Night of Nine Tails
Telepathy of Gardens
Delusions of the Past
Fairy Blade Unmade
Web of Nightmares
A Whisker's Breadth
Skunk Man Swamp
Magic Ain't A Game
Without Foresight (Coming Soon)
Careful of Thy Wishes (Coming Soon)
Time to Your Elf (Coming Soon)
Undiscovered Tomb (Coming Soon)

High-Tech Crime Solvers Series
Virtually Harmless

Stand Alone Suspense Novels
Looking Over Your Shoulder
Lion Within
Pursued by the Past
In the Tick of Time
Loose the Dogs

AND MORE AT PDWORKMAN.COM

STYLE NOTE

Since my largest readership is in the USA, I have chosen to use US spellings throughout this series. That includes the Americanization of centre to center, even where it is an actual place name, just for consistency's sake. I apologize to my Canadian readers for this.

I have chosen, however, to use Canadian grammar, particularly for Canadian voices. If you see what you think is a grammar error, it may just be Canadian, eh?

CONTENT

Contains discussion of Canadian Residential Schools and other other institutional abuses of children. There are no graphic depictions of violence against children or others, but some readers may be sensitive to these topics.

OUT WITH THE SUNSET

PARKS PAT MYSTERIES #1

To the survivors
Strength and peace

CHAPTER ONE

"Mom, you've got to be kidding me! Are you serious?"

Margie winced at Christina's complaint. Up until her phone ringer had shattered their quiet morning preparations, the day had been going well. Bright sunshine streamed in through the kitchen windows of the small house. The rich odor of brewing coffee filled the air. Christina had been blow-drying her long black hair, the hum of the dryer providing a soothing white-noise background as Margie prepared her breakfast and reviewed the day's plans. Everything had been peaceful despite both of their 'first-day' anxieties.

"I know, honey. I didn't plan this. You know I was going to take you to school today and help with your schedule and getting settled in. But..." She gave a dramatic shrug and grimace, "you know I can't control when someone gets murdered."

"Couldn't someone else take this one? You *promised* me."

"They need me. Others in the department will be involved, but this is my first lead, and I can't turn it down."

"You could."

Margie took a deep breath in. Her stomach felt hollow and heavy. She knew she had promised Christina that she would be there for her first day of school. It wasn't fair to expect her to do everything by herself while Margie went off to a murder scene. She was brand new in the Calgary homicide department, and her coworkers would be watching to see how she took on her first case—watching for her to make a mistake. To see whether she was competent, or was just a 'diversity hire' for a department that needed Indigenous representation on the team.

Christina was right, of course; she could turn it down and ask them to make someone else the primary. But what message would that send to the rest of her team about her commitment and ability to handle both her personal life and the rigors of the job?

"Maybe you could start tomorrow instead," Margie suggested. "I could call the school and let them know that you won't be starting today, but you'll be there tomorrow."

"No way!" Christina's response was immediate and emphatic. "I'm starting the same day as everyone else. It's bad enough that I'm the new girl; I'm not going to have everybody looking at me because I didn't start the same day as everyone else. Like I've got some kind of... privilege."

Like Margie's, Christina's black hair, bronze skin, and facial features showed her Cree heritage clearly. Neither one would ever be mistaken for white. But others often saw Indigenous people as lazy, looking for a handout, or expecting compensation for what had happened to them over the generations. Christina wouldn't want to be branded as one of *those Indians*.

"Well, those are the only two options." Margie looked at her watch. "I need to get to the scene. You can go today and get your guidance counselor to help you get everything set up, or you can wait until tomorrow when I can go with you."

Christina slammed the door to the bathroom and started the water running so that Margie couldn't talk to her.

Margie swept her long hair back with both hands and divided it into sections. She deftly braided it and pinned it up into a bun so that it would be neat and out of the way. The coffee machine finished brewing and she poured her coffee into a travel mug.

After making sure she had everything else she would need, including Staff Sergeant MacDonald's directions to get to the site, she knocked on the bathroom door. "I'm going now. Are you okay?"

"I'm fine," Christina snapped. What she said after that wasn't as easy to make out, but it was something along the lines of "Not that you'd care."

Margie sighed. "Love you, sweetie. I'll see you after school. Give me a call if I'm not home and let me know how your day went."

"You're really going to go take this case and make me go to a new school all by myself?"

"I'm sorry. I can't do anything about it."

Christina slammed something down on the bathroom counter. Margie knew there wasn't anything else she could do or say to smooth things over. Christina was old enough that she could manage. She wasn't a shy or anxious child. She was a strong young woman. She would be able to navigate a new school. Margie had actually been surprised that Christina had wanted her to be there. Usually, she was embarrassed by her mother and didn't want her anywhere close to her teenager peers.

"Goodbye. Love you."

There was no answer from her daughter.

Margie picked up her coffee and her shoulder bag and got into the car. She stuck the note with Sergeant MacDonald's instructions on the dash. After starting the car, she waited for the GPS to boot up. She put Fish Creek Park into the GPS, but the route it popped up was nothing like the directions she had been given. She studied the picture on the small screen. The green area was massive, covering many blocks. So there was undoubtedly more than one entrance. She would have to go by MacDonald's instructions and hope that they were detailed enough to get her there.

She pulled out of the gravel parking pad in the back of the house and found her way out to Twenty-Sixth Street. There was a long multiuse path along the ridge above the irrigation canal, or 'the ditch' as it was known as in the neighborhood. There were always people walking dogs, running, or biking along it. Even late at night or early in the morning, she could almost always count on seeing people on the pathway. She was looking forward to taking Stella out to explore and meet other fur-babies. In September, the trees were still green, with just occasional yellow leaves fluttering to the ground, and there were a lot of parks and green spaces throughout the city. The grass along the path was more yellow than it was green. She hadn't realized before moving to Calgary how arid the city was. The summer temperatures were nothing like they were in Manitoba, but it was still hot and dry. She had thought that it would be a lot more temperate in the shadow of the Rockies.

She found her way to Deerfoot Trail and kept one eye on MacDonald's instructions to make sure that she didn't miss any exits or turns.

Despite the traffic, she pulled into the east entrance to Fish Creek Park in under twenty minutes. There had been no need for lights and siren. The man wasn't going to get any more dead.

CHAPTER TWO

There were more cars in the parking lot than Margie would have expected, and she wondered how many of them could be associated with the investigation and how many were typically there every weekday morning, like the walkers on the path along Twenty-Sixth Street. She supposed that if she lived close to a big park like Fish Creek, she would try to get over there as often as possible. She pulled on a face mask, got out of her car and looked around, trying to figure out which way to go. MacDonald had only given her directions to the parking lot; he hadn't told her where to go from there. She had hoped to be able to see the crime scene from there, but all she saw were trees.

"Detective Pat—er—Patter…" A man in a gray uniform shirt, dark pants, and gun belt approached her with his hand outstretched. He had a bandana-style mask.

Margie reached automatically to shake, then drew back and gave him a little wave. "Patenaude," she told him, pronouncing it clearly for him, "PAT-en-ode."

"Oh, that's not so hard." He gave an embarrassed laugh. He dropped his hand to his side. "French?"

"Yes. Métis."

"Sure." He gestured toward her face, indicating her dark skin and whatever he could see of her nose and other features above the mask. "I should have guessed. We don't see a lot of Natives in law enforcement. Sorry."

Margie shrugged it off. "I guess if you know my name, you know what I'm here for."

"Yes," he seemed far more comfortable with this topic. "You're here for our body."

He said it possessively, maybe even a little affectionately. *Our* body. She glanced at his gray uniform. Not the black shirt of a Calgary Police Services uniform. "What department are you with?"

"Alberta Parks. I'm one of the Conservation Officers here. Dave Barnes."

"Okay." Margie nodded. "You know the park well, then."

"Very well. Come on; I'll take you to the crime scene."

She followed him to an electric golf cart and took the passenger seat. Margie looked around her as Barnes drove down one of the bicycle paths, slowing and occasionally tapping his horn as they passed cyclists out for a morning ride.

"The park looked pretty big on my GPS screen. How big is it?"

"Thirteen and a half square kilometers with ninety kilometers of trails."

"Whoa. I'm glad you've got a cart."

"Me too. But we don't have too far to go today. We're just headed to Hull's Wood."

Margie watched the sunlight filtering through the green leaves, creating dappled shadows on the pavement of the pathway. It all seemed so peaceful and idyllic, people walking and running, some with dogs or companions and some alone, the occasional bicycles thrumming along beside them. A paradise in the middle of the busy city. She had been impressed by Calgary's long list of parks, both city and provincial. She liked to walk and bike. She was hoping to be able to ride her bike to work, taking the new bridge alongside Blackfoot Trail, then through Pearce Estate Park and along the Bow River Pathway to get downtown. It would be much better for her than always driving her car. Once she got settled in and more familiar with the route.

"Here we are." Barnes's words drew her attention back to the present and to the not-so-idyllic scene she was there to see.

Tape had been looped around several trees to cordon off the area. Sunlight streamed down on a small clearing. Bright green grass against the dark trunks of the trees. The grass and wild plants had a fresh, sweet scent.

There were more gray-shirted conservation officers and a few dark-uniformed Calgary Police officers hanging around. A crime scene truck was parked outside the cordoned area, waiting for Margie to review the scene and give them the go-ahead to collect forensic evidence.

She dismounted from the cart and looked slowly around before advancing to the crime scene. She looked at the spectators rubbernecking nearby, all hoping to catch a glimpse of something exciting or disgusting to brag about to their friends and family.

No one who seemed out of place. No one who appeared to be anything other than curious as to what had happened. But one never knew. Sometimes killers returned to the scene or stayed around to watch the discovery and investigation go down.

Margie approached the crime scene truck and nodded at the techs who were suited up, face shields on and ready to go.

"Hi. I'm Detective Patenaude. New in town. You guys been here long?"

A couple held disposable cups of Tim's coffee, looking like they had been waiting for her for a while.

"Half hour," one of them commented, thumbing his phone to check the time.

"Okay. Sorry to keep you waiting." Margie pulled on her own protective gear, trying not to fumble or look incompetent in front of them. It wasn't her first rodeo and she didn't want them thinking that she was inexperienced. "While I take a look, do you think you could get pictures of the bystanders?"

One of the men holding a Tim's cup raised an eyebrow. "The bystanders?"

"Yeah. If you could just do that sort of unobtrusively, so we've got a record if one of them ends up being a witness or suspect?"

Most of the observers were not wearing masks, which was lucky. One of the unfortunate effects of mandatory masking policies was the increased difficulty of reading and recognizing faces.

The tech exchanged a look with his coworkers, then shrugged and nodded. "Pictures of the bystanders. Roger."

"Thanks." Margie finished with her protective gear and lifted one of the lines of tape to duck under it. She made her way over to the body with great care, watching for any footprints or crushed vegetation.

One of the uniformed cops nodded to her. He wasn't masked and kept his distance. He had a medium build and a round face, hair thinning on top. "You the primary?" he asked.

"Yes. Hope I didn't keep you waiting too long."

"He might have gotten a degree or two colder while we were waiting, but it's not like he's going to get up and walk away."

Margie chuckled. "No," she agreed. She looked at his name bar. "Officer Smith. You want to walk me through it?"

"Found by a dog walker this morning. As you can see," he tilted his head toward the spectators on the pathway, "there is a lot of foot traffic here, even very early in the morning. Dogs are really good at smelling out bodies. The riper, the better."

"But this one hasn't been here very long," Margie observed. The body hadn't been there long enough for her to detect any decomp.

She gazed down at the crumpled figure. Looked like a male, but he was face-down, so she wouldn't be able to verify until he had been moved. Tall and slim. He seemed deflated beneath the wrinkled jacket and pants. The vegetation in the area had not been trampled down; Margie couldn't see any sign of a major struggle. And there was not a lot of blood and gore. Most of that would be underneath him.

"Has anyone touched him? Moved him?"

"Just to verify that he didn't have a pulse and check for signs of violence."

Margie raised her brows questioningly.

"Stabbed," Smith informed her. "Center mass. Probably too low for the heart, but could have punctured a lung or caught the aorta. Not just a heart attack on his morning constitutional."

Margie stooped briefly to feel for a pulse—never hurt to have it verified more than once—and to evaluate the temperature and rigidity of the body. Someone from the medical examiner's office would be there to take the liver temp and make other observations, such as rigor, but Margie wanted to know for herself as she began the investigation.

"He's been here a while," she observed. "I don't think it happened this morning. More likely last night."

Smith didn't disagree. "The park closes at night. But that doesn't mean someone didn't stick around and avoid being seen. A place like this, you can't check behind every rock. The CO's do what they can to keep anyone from setting up camp here, but still come across homeless encampments now and then hidden in the bush. It's a big park."

Margie looked around. "I guess we don't have the luxury of surveillance cameras like we would if this happened on the street."

"Actually, there are some. I don't know where they all are."

"Probably the parking lots."

"There are wildlife cams too, though. And some of the trails are probably monitored. You can ask the CO's what video they have. Maybe you'll get lucky."

"Not lucky enough to have a video of the actual murder," Margie posited. "That would be too much to expect."

Smith shrugged. "Yeah. You're probably right."

Margie looked around at the ground for anything that was out of place. "Is the knife still in him? If not, did you take a look around for it?"

"Not in him. I kept my eyes open while we were deciding how much area to rope off. I was hoping it might have been dropped close by. But we didn't see anything. We can take another look, now that it's daylight. It was still pretty dark when we got here."

Sunrise had been around seven o'clock the last few days, Margie knew. Of course there had been runners and dog walkers out before that. People trying to get their workouts in before heading to office or retail jobs starting at eight or nine.

So when was their victim killed? During the small hours of the morning before opening? Or late at night when he shouldn't have even been in the park? She hoped they would be able to narrow it down quickly.

"Did you get all of the contact information for the dog walker who found him? And what about him, did he touch the body?"

"Dog might have contaminated it. Owner kept his distance after bringing the dog under control. We got everything we needed from him, down to the dog's name and morning routine. You can give him a call and talk to him or request an interview any time today. He's eager to help."

"Great. Thanks. Do we have an identity for our victim yet?"

"Haven't searched him. He's fully dressed—you know, not for running or something—so he probably has a wallet on him, unless it was a robbery. We figured we'd let the techies do that part."

Margie nodded. It was a good call. They might even have a missing person report on him already if he had a family and should have been home the night before.

She looked around some more without moving her feet, but couldn't see any other clues and didn't want to be guilty of contaminating the scene any further. She looked toward the crime scene investigators and nodded to them.

"Let's get out of the way and let them do their thing," she advised Smith, raising her voice a little for everyone within the cordoned-off area.

CHAPTER THREE

While Margie got out of the way to allow the crime scene techs to do their job, she wandered casually toward the bystanders. She wasn't wearing a uniform but, of course, it would be apparent to everyone there that she was a police detective. They wouldn't have allowed just anyone to get that close to the body. But no one peeled abruptly away from the group or attracted her attention.

"My name is Detective Marguerite Patenaude," she told the onlookers in a friendly, pleasant tone. "I wonder if anyone here happened to see anything this morning? Not necessarily him," she motioned back toward the body, "but anything that's out of the ordinary for the park. Most of you probably walk or run here several times a week?"

Most of them nodded automatically. A few looked away. Maybe they had just been called by their friends to come to see what was going on, in hopes of being able to see something brag-worthy.

"So? Anything unusual? People or activities that you don't normally see? A strange noise or smell? Anything that made you take notice?"

No one stepped forward to offer anything. Most shook their heads and made negative noises. Margie hadn't actually expected to get anything from them. More than likely, the murder had happened many hours before, and the people who walked the park in the morning were not the same ones who walked it in the evening.

"Anybody want my card? In case you think of something or hear anything from someone else?" Margie pulled a stack of business cards out of her pocket and held them out, offering them to each person. A couple people took one. Maybe hoping she'd be able to help them out of a speeding ticket at some point. No one met her eyes or gave her the impression that they would call her later when they could speak to her without witnesses. "All right. Thank you. You can move along, you can't see much from here, and we'll be around for a while. You might as well finish your workouts."

Most of them moved on. Only a few lingered. None of them did anything to make her think that they might know what had happened. No one started asking her questions about the murder. There was no one who appeared to be from the press, though she was sure they would be there within the hour. Even if there were nothing to report, they still had to get some shots at the scene and report that there was nothing to report.

BEFORE LONG, a couple of the other homicide detectives from Margie's team made it to the site. Margie tried to remember their names and what she knew about them. She'd only had one brief meeting with the team so far, when she had been introduced to them and read in on all of the usual policies and procedures. She had filled out her tax forms and been assigned a desk and told when she would be on duty. Even though she had known she would be on duty on Christina's first day, she had made arrangements not to be at the office until later in the day once she got Christina settled at the school. None of them had anticipated that they would be called to a homicide early that morning. That was just the way that it went. You couldn't plan.

Detective Cruz would have played a good Hispanic cop on TV. Olive skin, hair turning to salt and pepper, a short mustache now hidden behind a mask, and a bit of a paunch. But he'd made it clear when they met that he was Filipino, not Hispanic. Margie had been surprised to find such a large Filipino community in Calgary. She had thought Calgary's demographics would skew a lot more white—and redneck—but there was a surprisingly multicultural population. Half of the people in her neighborhood seemed to be either Asian or Polynesian. Cruz was an older cop, probably ready for retirement before too long. Homicide was not an easy job. People didn't stay there for more than two or three years, and Cruz had been there at least four.

Riding with Cruz was Detective Kaitlyn Jones. Margie had been happy to discover that she would not to be the sole woman on the homicide team. She could hold her own; she'd always been able to fit in as "one of the guys," but it was still a relief to know that there was another woman there who would have her back in case of any sexist or harassing behavior. Boys would be boys, but she was not going to put up with any garbage.

Margie filled them in on her arrival on the scene and everything they had done before Cruz and Jones arrived.

"The victim did have a wallet. It gives his name as Jerry Robinson, and his face matches the picture on his ID." She read off the address from his driver's license. "I guess that's not far from here?"

"Deer Run," Cruz said with a nod. "Not far at all. Might have walked in."

"The CO's haven't seen any abandoned vehicles, anything left overnight, so he probably did."

"Any background on him yet?" Jones asked. Her blond hair was pulled back into a bun, and despite the blue mask over her face, Margie could still tell by the cheer in her voice and the fan of laugh lines around her eyes she was smiling. "Wedding ring? Business card? Family pictures?"

Margie laid out what they had. "Union card; apparently he is a welder. Don't know about family or kids yet; his phone is locked. No wedding ring, but that might just be so he doesn't injure himself on a job site. We'll have to do some background and find out if he has a family, make a death notification to the next of kin. I haven't checked social media yet, but that might be a good place to start."

"So it wasn't robbery," Cruz mused. "Everything appeared to be in his wallet? Cash? Plastic? Jewelry wasn't stolen?"

"Doesn't look like robbery. He could have had a watch or necklace or something of value, but we won't know that until we talk to people who knew him. There's no mark on his finger showing that he typically wears a ring, but he could still have one and only wear it some of the time. Cash and credit cards in his wallet. Not a lot, but if the motive had been robbery, I would have expected at least the cash to disappear."

"Okay. Makes sense. Any sign he's been in a fight?"

"We'll have to wait for the ME's report, but nothing obvious. Hands are scarred from working. No split knuckles or broken nose."

"Then what happened?" Jones asked, shaking her head. "Usually, it's pretty obvious. Robbery, fight, drug or gang connection. In a park like this, at night, it could be drugs, but…?"

But Margie hadn't mentioned anything that would give them that idea. "Nothing that I could see. The body certainly doesn't scream drug dealer or addict."

CHAPTER FOUR

Investigating even a major crime like homicide, there was a lot of 'hurry up and wait.' They would have to wait for the video surveillance. For the medical examiner's report. For the techs to crack the code on Robinson's phone if he didn't have a family member who knew it.

By the time they got to the duty room, it was already midafternoon. Phones rang, people banged away at their keyboards and chatted with each other in voices that were a little too loud for Margie to concentrate. Her desk was out in the bullpen, not behind a closed door, and she found it a little distracting.

And she had promised Christina that she would get home early.

"It's my daughter's first day of school," Margie told Jones, hoping she would be the most sympathetic. "Would you mind screening Robinson to see if we have anything on him or if you can find him on social media, and I'll check in with you later? I'd like to pick her up at school or at least take her out for a burger once she gets home. I had promised to go in with her this morning and then I couldn't."

"Sure," Jones agreed. "How old is your daughter?"

"She's fifteen—a terrible age to uproot her and come to Calgary, her first year in high school. I mean, she was in high school last year, but grade nine was high school in Winnipeg, and the high school here starts at grade ten.

So even though she had her first year of high school in Winnipeg last year, she's the little fish again this year. In a new school. In a new city."

"That's tough," Jones agreed. "Which school?"

"Forest Lawn High."

"Oh."

Margie tried to interpret Jones's reaction. She didn't immediately tell Margie what a great school it was, even though the principal had really talked up the school and its programs. But it wasn't like she had badmouthed it either. Maybe she or a friend had gone there for high school.

"Where did you go?"

"Oh, I wasn't in Calgary during high school. Ft. McMurray."

Northern Alberta. Where the tar sands were. Margie nodded. "Cold there?"

Jones shuddered. "Oh yes, it was. No Chinooks there."

"I'm looking forward to experiencing a Chinook wind. We don't get them in Winnipeg. Once it gets cold there, it stays cold all winter."

"One of the best things about Calgary," Jones agreed. "Though it wreaks havoc with the roads. And sometimes the trees, if they think it is spring before it is. And migraine headaches."

Margie nodded, her attention no longer on the subject. She gathered her things. "You have my cell number in case you need to reach me? Sorry to be ducking out early on my first homicide, but I'll be in bright and early in the morning, and you can reach me tonight if you need me."

"Go take care of your daughter. We'll be fine."

MARGIE DIDN'T QUITE MAKE it in time to pick Christina up from school, so she hurried back to the house instead to beat her there and try to smooth things out for when she arrived. She let Stella out to run in the yard for a few minutes, tidied up the living room and kitchen, and tried to decide what they would do for supper. She didn't call or text Christina while she was on the bus, which would probably just irritate her. And she didn't want to inundate her daughter with questions as soon as she got in the door. But she also didn't want to look like she had just been home relaxing while Christina dealt with school and the bus ride home.

Eventually, Christina got home. Later than Margie had expected. Maybe she should have gone to the school to pick her up after all. Christina pushed the door open with a loud bang, then stepped in and slammed it behind her. She ripped off her mask.

Margie kept her temper. Of course Christina was tired and irritable after a long day at school, and she wanted to show her displeasure with her mother for letting her down. Margie forced a welcoming smile. "Hi, honey. How was it?"

If looks could kill, she would have had to arrest her own daughter for murder. Or one of the other homicide detectives would have to, since Margie herself would have been dead. Christina dropped her backpack on the floor and flounced down onto the couch.

"Was it that bad? I'm so sorry. Tell me all about it."

"We should have stayed in the Peg. I don't understand why we had to come here. Your job there was just fine, and I had friends and knew my way around the school and the bus system and everything else there. We should have just stayed. Couldn't we have stayed until I was done school? Three more years? Would that have been so bad? Then you could go wherever you wanted to, and I could go to university or start working. Why did we have to come here?"

Christina was one of the reasons that Margie had wanted to move away from Winnipeg. Yes, Christina had friends there and knew her way around, but that was part of the problem. Margie hadn't liked Christina's friends, and there was a lot of violence and drug culture in Winnipeg. As a cop, Margie knew the statistics about murdered or missing Indigenous women in the Peg. She hadn't wanted Christina to become another statistic.

"What happened?" she persisted. "Did something bad happen, or is it just because it is difficult getting used to a new place?"

"I hate it. Why did you move us to the hood? We had a nice place in Winnipeg. Here, we're in the ghetto!" She kicked at her schoolbag with a thud.

"Ghetto? Calgary doesn't have a ghetto or a hood. This is a nice area. Lots of families and retired couples that have been here for years."

"It's the *hood*. That's what the kids at school say. Forest Lawn is the hood, and everybody who goes to the school is in a gang."

"We aren't in Forest Lawn. We're in Southview. And I checked out the crime statistics before we came. It isn't bad. There is crime all over; you can't escape that. There isn't a lot of gang activity at the school. Maybe some kids there are in gangs, but that was true in Winnipeg too. The crime rate there was *much* higher than here. I don't think you need to worry that you've been dumped into the middle of a war zone."

Christina shook her head irritably. "I should have known you wouldn't listen."

"I am listening." Margie tried to tone it down. Christina needed to know she was being heard; she didn't need her mother arguing statistics. "Tell me more about it. I'll try to keep my mouth shut and just listen to you. I didn't mean to argue. Did you make any friends? Meet anyone interesting?"

"At home, everybody was First Nations or Métis. It's different here. Everybody is white. Or Asian. Or Black. There aren't that many Indigenous kids."

Margie nodded. "I know. The demographics are a bit different. Calgary has lots of immigrants."

"So I'm, like, I stand out. I look Cree, so everyone thinks that I'm… I don't know. Just there for a free ride, or drugs, or to steal their stuff. They look at me like I'm…" Christina shook her head, at a loss for words. "I don't know. Like I'm dirty or a criminal."

Christina threw her head back against the back of the couch in frustration.

"Oh, honey." Margie hoped that Christina was just overreacting and being dramatic. She had found so far that Calgarians treated her pretty well. But she was an adult with tough skin and a badge. Not a sensitive teenager. "I'm sorry you felt so much like an outsider."

Christina nodded vigorously. "Exactly. Like an outsider. I hate it. I just want to go home."

"Is there any way I can help? We're not moving back to Winnipeg, but is there anything else I can do to help make it better?"

"The school is huge. I'm so lost. And everybody already has friends. I don't have anybody."

"Give it a few days. I'm sure other people are new, and people who are looking for new friends. They'll be coming from all different junior highs, so everyone will have to meet new people, and friendships will be changing. Maybe we could look at some clubs or after-school activities that will help you get in with a group sooner."

"I don't want to do sports or photography or any other stupid hobbies. I want to… hang out with friends like I did in Winnipeg."

One of the things that Margie hadn't liked in Winnipeg was how much unsupervised time Christina and her friends had for hanging around, looking for new ways to get in trouble.

"I'm going to be connecting with the Métis community here. I'm sure you'll be able to make some friends through the Métis Nation or Friendship Center so you won't feel so different."

Christina shrugged. It wasn't an objection, so it felt like a win—score one for Mom.

"And when we visit Moushoom, we can see if he has some other suggestions. There are probably cousins we don't even know about here. Not as many as at home—in Winnipeg—but you might be able to connect with someone."

Christina's head went up. "When are we going to go see Moushoom? That's one of the reasons you said we should move here. Well, we're here, so when are we going to go see him?"

Margie didn't even have all of their boxes unpacked. But she was glad that Christina wanted to see her great-grandfather. Other kids might roll their eyes and say they didn't want to visit some old person in a nursing home. Though it wasn't a nursing home. It was an independent living facility. Margie and some of the cousins had been worried about his still living on his own. It was hard to tell from so far away whether he still had all of his faculties or whether he should have more care and supervision. Someone looking after him and making sure he took his pills and ate what he should.

"I was going to suggest that we go out for burgers to celebrate your first day of school and my first homicide. Or… commiserate. I don't suppose 'celebrate' is the right word."

"Yeah? And then go see Moushoom? Maybe we could take him a burger; I bet he would like that."

Margie hesitated. "I don't know if he is on a special diet. We'd better find that out before we take him any food. But we could get some supper and then go see him afterwards."

Christina nodded her approval at this. "Where are we going to go?"

"I don't really know what's good. There are a ton of ethnic restaurants on Seventeenth Avenue. They call it International Avenue. But if we're going to go see Moushoom, maybe we should just get something quick, so we're not stuck waiting for an hour for our food. There's an A&W. You like their burgers."

"Do they have a veggie burger?"

Margie frowned at her. "A veggie burger? Maybe, I don't know."

"I decided I want to be vegetarian."

That was a bit of a shock. Christina had always enjoyed her meat. And even hunting. Margie hadn't seen that one coming. Her brain immediately spun into high gear. Was Christina flirting with an eating disorder? Looking for ways to cut her food intake or calories? Would she be able to get the protein she needed on a vegetarian diet? Teen girls needed plenty of iron if they didn't want to be anemic.

But she answered as calmly as she could. It was probably just a passing phase. This week, Christina would be vegetarian, and next week, she would be ordering a rack of ribs.

"I'm sure they must have a veggie burger." Stella barked from outside the back door, and Margie took a couple of steps toward it to let her in. "Why don't you look it up on your phone and make sure they have what you want? Then we can head over."

She opened the door and let Stella in. She scratched her floppy ears and cuddled her black and brown face, asking, 'Who's a good girl?' Then Stella noticed that Christina was home and launched herself at her. Christina squealed and laughed and wrestled with Stella. Margie smiled at the two of them. Stella was good therapy at the end of a rough day.

A&W did have a veggie burger, and it was pretty good. Christina gave Margie a bite and, despite her hesitation, Margie found that it tasted pretty much just like a regular beef burger. This made her wonder how much beef was in a regular beef burger and how much was fillers of some kind. You wanted breadcrumbs or something to help give it a good texture and moisture, but not too much.

"That's great," Margie observed. "Maybe I'll get one next time." She nearly patted her stomach and commented on getting too thick around the middle, but stopped herself. She didn't want Christina to start worrying about her weight or to model her own thoughts about her body after negative comments her mother made.

Christina finished her burger in a few more bites and dabbled some remaining fries in the puddle of ketchup. "Where does Moushoom live? Is it far away?"

Calgary was the big city. Not like the population of New York, of course, but it was bigger than Winnipeg, and it sprawled over hundreds of square kilometers. It could take an hour to drive across the city. Margie smiled. "He's very close. We'll drive over today, but you can walk there from the house. You can go see him any time you want."

Christina smiled broadly at that. "Really? That's awesome."

She loved her Moushoom. They cleared away their garbage and went back to the car. Margie used the GPS even though she knew it was close. She didn't want to head in the wrong direction. Once she had been there a few times, she would be able to get there without instructions. For a descendant of Cree women and explorers, Margie had a terrible sense of direction.

MARGIE SCANNED the signs on the door to the building. They were, of course, required to wear masks while visiting. There was a hand sanitizing station to wash before going up to the living quarters and upon leaving, to protect both their loved ones and themselves. There was a long list of symptoms. *If you have experienced a new cough, fever, upset stomach, trouble breathing…*

But no unexpected rules. Nothing about having to quarantine for fourteen days if they had come from out of the province. That was a relief. She had been secretly worried about it, even though she had told Christina that she could visit whenever she wanted to. They already had their masks on, so they rubbed gel into their hands and continued on to the elevators.

Moushoom was sitting in an easy chair, watching the TV when they arrived. He hollered for them to come in rather than getting up to answer the door. When he saw they were visitors rather than staff, he sat up straighter.

"Who's there?"

"It's Margie and Christina, Moushoom," Margie informed him. Christina stepped forward to hug him, but Margie touched her to prevent her. "We have to be careful of infection," she reminded.

Christina shook her head. "I'm going to hug him! I'll hold my breath, and I just washed my hands. I'm not going to infect him!"

Moushoom eagerly accepted a hug from Christina. "Is it really little Christina? But you were just a little girl the last time I saw you!"

"That was two summers ago. I… grew up."

"Yes, you did." Moushoom released his hold on her and looked her over. "You are turning into a lovely young lady. Your mother must be very proud."

"Isn't she?" Margie agreed. She drew a couple of chairs over so they could sit close—but not too close—to him. "We have a surprise for you."

"A bigger surprise than this? I didn't think they would even let people travel right now. Everything has been so crazy with the pandemic."

"A bigger surprise than this."

Margie looked at the old man with great affection. He still looked just the same as she remembered him. He wore his buckskins, beadwork, and sash proudly. He was always reminding them of their heritage. Telling them not to forget their history and where they had come from. It was all important. It wasn't just where they had come from; it was a piece of who they were. Maybe he was a little shrunken, a little more gray than she remembered him, but otherwise, he looked exactly the same. Her own Moushoom.

"What could it be? What is it?"

"We bought a house just a few blocks from here," Christina burst out. "So we can come and visit you all the time."

His eyes widened in surprise and delight. "Are you pulling my leg? How could that be? You lived in…" It took him a minute to dredge it up, "in Winnipeg."

"We did," Margie agreed. "But I got a job with Calgary homicide. And now we live here."

"That's great!" Moushoom enthused. "It will be so great to have you close by!"

CHAPTER FIVE

Margie wasn't thinking that it was so great when she was driving downtown before dawn the next morning to get a head start on her investigation. She felt guilty about having gone home so early the day before, leaving the rest of the team to handle the investigation while she went home to be with her family. No one had complained, but of course they would be watching her to see whether it was a regular thing and whether she was going to take advantage of them. They probably figured that she would have some special privileges, being female and Métis, because if they complained about her, they could be accused of being sexist and racist, of not understanding how difficult things were for her as a single mom and a minority.

She didn't want to reinforce those stereotypes. She had always been a hard worker. She hated to be classified as a 'lazy Indian' and did everything she could to avoid being seen that way, even if it meant putting in more hours and effort than anyone else on the team. Even when it meant driving to work while it was still pitch black outside, with not even a sliver of light on the horizon.

Calgary's cold and changeable weather destroyed the roads, the water seeping into cracks and then expanding when it froze there, widening the gaps even more. It was too difficult to do roadwork when it was thirty below. As the joke went, there were two seasons in Calgary: winter and construction. So Margie avoided the potholes, lost her lanes due to construction pylons and tape, and followed detour signs until she finally made it downtown and pulled into the underground parking. The lighting was dim, but what could be safer than a police parkade? There wouldn't be anyone lurking around there looking to cause trouble.

She sat down at her desk and checked her physical and electronic inboxes to see what had come in the afternoon before or overnight that she could start working on. She saw that videos had been loaded onto the server space for the new case. Lots of video. That was great, possibly giving them a way to narrow down the time of the murder and who had been in the area at that point. And it was also bad because it meant that she would be staring at the screen for a long time, processing hours of videos from various camera feeds.

Detective Siever had sent her an email outlining what video had been uploaded. She tried to remember his face. Middle-aged, round face, buzz cut. He had seemed like a nice guy when they had been introduced.

Camera feed 8302 is the camera closest to the crime scene. Start with that.

Bless you, Detective Siever. Margie started with the video prefaced with 8302. It ran from midday until about the time that Margie had reached the scene. That was what, eighteen hours of video? Margie breathed out slowly, trying to figure out how to approach it. She wasn't going to start at the beginning. Midday was way too early. There would have been a lot of people and dogs through the park at that time. Since the body had not been discovered until early the next morning, she had to assume that Robinson had been killed either shortly before or sometime after the park had closed. Referring to the park's website, she found that to be ten o'clock.

She started at the end of the video and began scrubbing backwards. She watched as all of the emergency responders backed out of the scene and the frame was empty except for a man and a dog. They reversed off the screen. Margie could not see Robinson's body with the distance and angle of the camera location, but she could see approximately where it was. Not right on the pathway, but a ways into the woods. She scrubbed backwards some more, watching for anyone else walking along the pathway or through the camera frame. There was one passerby in the wee hours of the morning, and she stopped and played the video at normal speed to watch a homeless man push a shopping cart loaded high with garbage bags past the camera. He didn't leave the pathway or deviate from his course. Margie made a notation of the time and a short explanation and continued to scrub backwards.

No golf carts. No other homeless people. No sign of Robinson himself. Back, and back, and back, until she crossed the time stamp for ten o'clock. Margie hesitated, wondering if she had missed something. But it was possible that the homicide had occurred before ten o'clock, so she kept going. She started to see the last few stragglers before the park had closed. She froze the video and took screenshots, getting the best pictures she could of the people leaving the park, walking toward the camera. She made notes of the timestamps and quick descriptions of the people. Woman with dog. Couple walking hand-in-hand. Man in hoodie. Cyclist. Skateboarding kid. Then she reached a point in the tape where there were people both coming and going, which made it more complicated. The last few people who had taken their late-evening walks on that pathway. Some of them she recognized because she had already seen them leave. The couple walking hand-in-hand. Skateboarding kid.

Then the victim. Margie watched him walk by the camera. His back was to it so that she couldn't see his face, but he had been wearing a coat. It was getting chilly in the evenings. Down to six degrees lately. She paused the video and searched for the photos taken at the scene to compare the man's attire to Robinson's. It was him, or someone dressed exactly the same way. She noted the time. She now had a much better idea of the time of death. Sometime after eight-thirty. Probably between eight-thirty and ten. Unless the killer was the homeless guy she had seen after ten. There hadn't been anyone else around. Not visible on that camera.

She watched Robinson walk down the path and wander off into the woods. Not taking pictures. Not, as far as she could tell, meeting someone else. Sneaking off to relieve himself? Just enjoying the green trees and lengthening shadows? Going to a favorite clearing to meditate or walking to the edge of the river she had seen when scouting the area earlier?

He didn't come back into sight after disappearing off of the screen. He had been killed out of view of the camera. Margie let the video play forwards, watching each of the people who arrived and left the park after Robinson. Was one of them the killer, or had he managed to avoid cameras? Was it a planned attack? Had the killer scoped out all of the cameras first and then avoided them? She thought about the injury. A single stab in the middle of the body. Not multiple wounds. Not someone who had gone for the throat or had been aiming for the heart. What did that signify? A professional hit? An accident? A lucky shot? It didn't strike her as a crime of passion. Not that a death in the middle of the park sounded like a crime of passion anyway, but she hadn't ruled it out completely.

As the video rolled forward, she made sure that she had noted the arrivals and departures in her list and hadn't missed anyone. She scrutinized the faces she could see. Anyone who was upset? Angry? Overwrought?

She didn't like the people whose faces she could not see. People with masks, baseball caps, the guy with the dark hoodie. She wanted to be able to see their expressions, to be able to identify them if she saw them again. She wanted to compare the faces to those she'd had taken of the bystanders in the morning. Had one of them stuck around to watch what happened once the body was discovered?

"Patenaude. Detective Patenaude. Pat. Hey. Patenaude!"

Margie pulled her focus from the video to the room. People had arrived without her taking any notice of the fact. Cruz was leaning close, trying to get her attention. When she finally heard him and saw him, Cruz chuckled and shook his head at the rest of the team.

"Now that's focus!"

"Sorry, I was lost in my own little world," Margie apologized.

"We have a morning briefing. You ready?"

"Uh… yeah. Give me just a minute." Margie looked at her watch and then at the papers and notes scattered around her. Morning briefing, and it wouldn't just be MacDonald briefing the team, but Margie briefing him on what they had accomplished so far, sharing progress with the rest of the team, and making assignments. It was one reason she had wanted to get there as early as she could to get a head start on the work she had left incomplete the afternoon before.

"Five minutes," Cruz advised. "And Mac doesn't like people to be late."

"I'll be there."

Margie tried to gather her notes together in some semblance of order. She looked at herself in her phone camera to make sure that she looked presentable.

"Funny time to take a selfie," Jones commented. "You should be getting a move on it."

"Not a selfie. Just making sure I look okay."

"Look fine to me. Let's go." Jones motioned toward the conference room. Margie took a deep breath and preceded Jones into the room. She was momentarily disconcerted by the fact that everyone was standing around the table, no one sitting down. Was this some kind of chivalrous behavior? The men waiting until the women were seated, or showing Margie respect because it was her case or her first briefing? She reached to pull one of the chairs out, and Jones put her hand on Margie's arm.

"No, it's a stand-up meeting."

"A stand-up meeting?" Margie repeated stupidly, trying to process it.

"MacDonald says we think better on our feet. It keeps anyone from falling asleep and ensures that meetings are as quick as they can be."

"Okay, then." Margie put her papers down on the table in front of her and waited, like everyone else, standing around the table.

Staff Sergeant MacDonald entered the room. A tall man with short-cropped gray hair, thin-rimmed glasses, and a deeply lined face. He looked around at the team and nodded briskly. "Let's get to it, then. How are we doing on the Fish Creek Park case?" He consulted his notes. "Jerry Robinson."

Everyone's eyes turned to Margie. She cleared her throat. "We are still waiting for the full postmortem results, but apparent cause of death was a single stab wound to the abdomen. Robbery does not appear to be a motive. No missing person report had been filed and there was no answer when Cruz knocked on his door, so we suspect that he lived alone; no partner or children. I have been going through video. I'm still just beginning my review of the video, but I believe I have identified Robinson entering the area at 8:23 p.m."

There were murmurs from the team.

"If it's him, that helps quite a bit with the time of death."

"Yes. We'll get confirmation from the medical examiner, but I don't think she'll be able to narrow it down any more than that. I've been making notes of everyone else that I can see entering or leaving after Robinson's arrival—looking for any aberrant behaviors, emotion, someone who is running or appears distressed. Nothing so far. I don't see anyone who seems to be out of place or behaving strangely."

"No one covered in blood?" Cruz joked.

Margie shook her head. "Sorry, no. No one covered in blood. No one who seems to be in too much of a hurry. There are not a lot of park-goers there after Robinson, so it isn't a huge pool of suspects, but of course, it's going to take some work to identify them all."

"They're probably mostly regulars," Jones suggested. "If we were to go back there around the same time tonight, we could probably get ID's on a good number on them, and maybe some suggestions on how to find the others from the regulars. These are probably people who are local who use the park all the time."

Margie nodded. "Good idea. You're probably right. We might be able to narrow down the suspects that way—if it was me, and I had killed someone in the park, I probably wouldn't go back there. Not for a while, anyway."

MacDonald gave a nod. "You may be right there. Let's get some people canvassing there tonight. Who is available?"

Margie indicated she was. Christina would be home from school. There would be time for supper and for Christina to get settled in on her homework. She was old enough to be left alone while Margie went back out to canvass the park for a couple of hours looking for witnesses and trying to match faces to names. Most of the rest of the team indicated that they would be able to help. A dedicated bunch. No one complained about not being able to spend the evening with their families or watching the NHL playoffs.

They had a lot of work ahead of them if they were going to crack the case.

CHAPTER SIX

Christina was less angry when she arrived home than she had been the first day of school, but she was still sullen about having to move there and obviously not enjoying the new school yet. Margie had been hoping that she would have made at least one friend, which would help her to get through the first few weeks of school until she started to feel more at home. But apparently, that was not in the cards. Maybe in another day or two, Christina and another new girl would gravitate toward each other, or she would be admitted into one of the already-established circles of friends.

These things took time.

They had a quick meal of tacos made with microwaved beans.

"I'm going to take Stella for a quick walk out on the pathway," Margie told Christina. "Do you want to come with us?"

Christina hesitated. Margie didn't push it. The last thing she needed to do was make Christina think that Margie wanted her to go with her. That would just convince her to shut herself in her room and refuse to go out. Margie stayed casual about it, going to the door to put on her shoes and calling Stella for walkies.

"I guess I can come," Christina said eventually. "I don't have that much homework tonight. It's too early for them to be assigning anything big. They have to figure out where everyone is first. Since people are coming from all different schools," she pointed out.

Margie nodded. "That makes sense," she agreed. "They'll need to do some remedial stuff and to get everyone on the same level first, won't they? At least with some basics."

Christina petted Stella and scratched her soft brown ears before picking up her own shoes. "We should get some moccasins like Moushoom's."

"I don't know how they would fare on the pathways. You wouldn't want them to be ruined."

"They're meant to be worn outside."

Margie nodded. She was glad to see Christina showing some interest in the traditional clothing. She didn't expect Christina to start wearing a sash to school, but she liked that Christina was aware of her culture and felt positive about what she saw Moushoom doing. A lot of kids might have just thought him a funny old man.

Margie clipped on Stella's leash, and they headed out the door. It was only a couple of blocks to the pathway. Most of the houses in the area were older, built in the late fifties or early sixties. The little bungalows all looked pretty similar. But with a view of the city skyline in the distance, and the Rocky Mountains beyond that, the lots along Twenty-Sixth Street were only fifteen minutes from downtown. Professionals were beginning to buy the little post-war houses, razing them to the ground and replacing them with designer mini-mansions. And why not? As the city council forced people to build up instead of out, people had to find a way to build their dream homes within the city limits.

"Look at that one!" Christina pointed to one of the big houses fronted with lots of tinted glass. She whistled and shook her head. "I can't believe anyone would spend the money to build something like that in the middle of the hood."

"I told you, it is not a hood."

Christina rolled her eyes.

Stella was enjoying herself, sniffing at the grass and weeds beside the pathway, wandering out as far as Margie would let her.

"It's an off-leash area," Christina told her, watching another dog playing chase with a ball. "You should let her run."

"Maybe when I know the area better. Right now… I'm not sure how responsible other people are with their dogs. You wouldn't want her to get hurt because someone else lets their dog off-leash when they shouldn't."

"Nothing would happen."

"That's what everyone always thinks. But some people are not responsible, and animals can turn in an instant, do something completely out of character because they felt threatened or excited by something."

They walked for a while in silence. There was a little viewing platform up ahead—a sort of a look-out point. Margie decided to check it out.

They stood looking down at Deerfoot and the Bow River and out at the city skyline glowing orange from the setting sun and, in the distance, the shadowy mountains.

"Isn't it gorgeous?" a man said. "No two sunsets are alike. I've heard that Calgary has some of the best in the world. I'm no world traveler, so I don't have much to compare it to, but this..." he gazed out at the city. "I never get tired of it."

Margie nodded. She studied his profile as he looked at the sunset. He wasn't wearing a mask. Mid-thirties or early forties. Good looking. Friendly and outgoing, apparently. A guy who probably would have shaken her hand before the pandemic. At his side was a large dog—a mutt like Stella, not something that Margie could classify.

"It is beautiful," she agreed. She looked at her watch. She should be heading back to Fish Creek Park to help canvass for witnesses and identify the faces caught on the tape.

"Oscar," the man said. "And this is Milo." He indicated the dog.

"I'm Margie. And this is my daughter, Christina, and Stella."

"You're not old enough to have a teenage daughter," Oscar challenged in a teasing tone.

"Well, that's a nice compliment. But believe me, I'm old enough and I feel it!"

Christina rolled her eyes as if she were being disparaged. "She was really young when she had me." In an *it's not my fault* tone.

"I don't remember seeing either of you here before. Do you live around here?"

"Just moved into the neighborhood," Margie agreed, making a motion back the way they had come. "Christina's been complaining about it, but I really like this." She looked out at the sky and the river. "And Fish Creek Park. I was just there this morning, and it's beautiful. Amazing to have such a big park right in the middle of the city."

"We're lucky to have these green spaces," Oscar agreed. He turned and pointed behind them, across Twenty-Sixth Street. "I'm just over there. If you cross here, there is a little park. There's a pond, a little waterpark for the kids, and volleyball courts with sand. A little gem hardly anybody knows about."

"Can we go over there?" Christina asked, moving away from them toward the crosswalk.

"I need to get home," Margie told her apologetically. "We can check it out tomorrow. But I have some work I need to do tonight."

Christina gave a heavy sigh. Life was hard for the kids of cops and working mothers.

CHAPTER SEVEN

Fish Creek Park had a different feeling as darkness started to fall and closing time approached. It was quiet. Voices carried, so people whispered or spoke in lowered tones as they walked. It was a slower pace, and the tang of wood smoke hung in the air from the campfires of earlier in the day.

Margie watched the shadows, thinking, drinking in the atmosphere. The weather conditions were almost the same as they had been the night Robinson was killed. She arrived at the same time as he had. She looked for the faces she had seen on the video surveillance, which she had carefully studied before arriving.

How easy would it have been for Robinson to be followed there by someone who intended to do him harm? He had left the pathway. She didn't know if he had still been visible from the path before he was killed. Maybe they should try a scene reconstruction just to test it out. Had his attacker gone there with the sole purpose of killing him? Had it been a drug deal or blackmail gone wrong? A quarrel between friends or lovers?

It wasn't robbery, that was about all Margie knew for sure. That, and it didn't look like a crime of passion.

She stopped a couple walking toward her, keeping the prescribed two meters away since they were not wearing masks. "Excuse me. You were here two nights ago?"

They looked at each other, nodding automatically but then not sure if they should talk to her.

"I'm a homicide detective," Margie explained, pulling out her ID and showing it to them. "There was someone killed here, did you hear about it?"

"Yeah, we did." The woman, blond, a little shorter than Margie, nodded again. "I couldn't believe it. That happened in our park, where we walk, around the time that we were here." She said it with a tone of disbelief, as if it couldn't possibly be true.

Margie murmured confirmation at this.

"We didn't see anything suspicious." The woman looked at the man, getting a nod from him. "It was a night just like any other. Nothing… There wasn't anything that alarmed us."

"Anything out of the ordinary that night?" Margie asked. "Sounds, smells? Someone you don't normally see walking around here? Someone who seemed out of place or lost? Sick or afraid?"

The man put his arm around the woman and tightened his grip, pulling her to him protectively. "No," his voice was strong, slightly challenging. "Don't you have any leads? How could something like this happen here? I assumed that… it was drugs. A gang. Something where they knew each other. You always hear that in police reports. 'The victim was known to the killer.' They knew each other, right?"

"We are still very early in the investigation. We're hoping that you can help us with some background. Identify the people who normally walk around this time, help us to narrow the scope."

"Like what?" the woman asked. "What do you need us to do?"

"First of all, if I could get your information. Name, address, phone number, in case I need to contact you with further questions later."

They were a little reluctant. People were brought up not to share their personal information with strangers. They grew up watching cop shows on TV where people were suspects or were framed by the police. It was scary for them to be part of an investigation.

But also exciting. She could see their excitement at the novelty of being part of the investigation. A homicide investigation. Something most people had only ever seen on TV or read about in books.

Margie took down their information. Elise and Roger Erickson. Married ten years and still walking hand in hand every night in the park.

"I have some pictures on my tablet. I wonder if you could look at them, tell me who are regulars. What you know about them."

"Sure." This was the good part. The part where they could help her to break the case. They looked intently at the tablet as Margie moved a bit closer and brought up the first of the pictures. "Oh, that's Bob," Elise said confidently. "He doesn't like bicycles."

"Bicycles?" Margie repeated, not understanding.

"Bob is the dog," Roger laughed. "I think the detective wants the name of Bob's owner."

Margie chuckled. "Yes. That would be helpful."

"I don't know his owner's name… I just know Bob's name, because I hear him calling him, especially when Bob wants to chase after a bike."

Margie wrote down the information she had. "They walk here often?"

"Most nights. Most of the people who walk at this time of night are regulars. Day-trippers come during the day. Family reunions and parties in the late afternoon and evening. The people who walk late at night or early in the morning, they're all pretty regular."

Margie swiped to the next person on the tablet. Elise and Roger studied it.

"I've seen him," Roger said, "but I don't know anything about him."

"You said you thought maybe it was something to do with drugs or gangs," Margie said. "Is that because you've seen drugs or gang activity in the park? Graffiti? People congregating? Something that makes you think that is going on?"

"No, I've never seen anything," Roger admitted. "I'm sure it goes on… it goes on everywhere, doesn't it? But I've never seen any drug deals going down or gangs. Or anything that I thought was. I just hoped… it isn't some crazy person, attacking at random…"

"I don't think that was the case here," Margie assured him. Very few homicides were random attacks. Maybe a robbery, someone with jewelry or a coat that made them look like they had a lot of money, but not random murders. "And if it is a serial killer, nobody has identified any pattern. Nothing that they had seen across a number of homicides."

They looked slightly reassured at this. Though Margie was kicking herself for using the words serial killer. That was only going to make them more worried, and they might use it when talking to other people, spreading the rumor that it was, in fact, a serial killer, when there was absolutely nothing to indicate that it was.

"If you could look at a few more people here…" She showed them the tablet again, swiping through the various people, most of whom they recognized. But they didn't have names to attach to a lot of them. At any rate, if they were frequent walkers in the park at that time of day, Margie would talk to them sooner or later.

She displayed the picture of the hooded figure. Elise shuddered. "Black hoodies always make me think of… Darth Vader or the Sith. Creepy, you know?"

"Do you recognize this person? We didn't get a very good picture of the face." Really, they hadn't captured anything of the face, just the hood and the shadows beneath it, as the hooded figure walked with head bowed past the camera. Margie didn't like it either. Not because it reminded her of the Sith, just because she didn't like anyone who appeared to have a reason to hide his face.

Who needed to hide his face in a park? Especially at night, when the shadows were already falling?

Maybe someone with a disfigurement. Otherwise, Margie couldn't think of a good reason, other than to avoid cameras and hide his identity.

"I've… I'm sure I've probably seen them here," Elise said slowly. "Not a lot, but a few times over the last week or two? Not every day. Or maybe he comes other times of the day, and not at the same time every night."

"Man or woman?" The figure was slim and could be either.

"A boy," Elise offered. "Not an adult. Maybe, sixteen? Umm… black. Not just brown, but very dark skin. I don't know…" She looked at her husband. "Maybe that's what made you think of drugs or gangs? Young Black man in a hoodie… if you watch much TV, it's sort of a trope." She shrugged, embarrassed. "I'm not racist; I'm not saying every kid in a hoodie is a drug dealer."

"I don't think it was anything like that," Roger protested, raising his hands in a 'stop' or 'surrender' motion. "I just wondered about drugs or gangs because it seems like that's where a lot of the violence stems from. Not because I saw him." He jerked his chin toward the hooded figure on the tablet and scratched the back of his neck. "I'm not judging anyone."

"We'll follow up on every possible lead. So you don't know his name or what area he lives in? Was he ever here with someone else?"

"No." They both looked at each other for confirmation and shook their heads at the same time. "No, we never talked to him or left at the same time. And he's always alone."

Margie thanked them for their time when they were finished looking through all of the pictures. Even though she didn't have many names or details, she felt like she was making progress. Lots of the people whose pictures she had clipped would be walking through the park just then. Margie would find them and talk with them, slowly gathering identities and alibis and sorting out who she felt was suspicious and warranted further attention.

※

THE CANVASS SLOWED TO A TRICKLE, and then a stop. There was no one left on the pathways but the detectives themselves. They converged and began comparing notes as they walked back to their vehicles.

"Some nice folks out here," Jones commented. She seemed to be walking a little gingerly, and Margie watched her, trying to figure out whether she had turned her ankle or had blisters or something else. "Reminds me that I don't take advantage of the parks around here often enough. We complain about being stuck in the city, but there is all of this… wilderness right here in the middle of it."

"I was really excited about that when I started to look at Calgary," Margie agreed. "I like walking and hiking and biking, and I'm looking forward to being able to check out the different parks and pathways in Calgary. There are so many places to go."

"I *think* that I like walking until I'm actually on my feet for a few hours like this," Jones said. "And then my feet start to hurt, and I start to chafe, and then I realize that I really *don't* like it very much at all."

Margie laughed. "Don't go right from being sedentary to walking for a few hours. Do it gradually; your body will adjust."

Jones smoothed her hands over her broad hips and grimaced. "Yeah. One step at a time," she agreed.

"Who on your list do you want to follow up on?" Siever asked. "We still have lots more video that we can check. Spy on people the whole time they were at the park."

"There are a few I'd like to look into further," Margie admitted. "Of course, everyone who wasn't here tonight, but the man with the pit bull and the young man in the hoodie in particular."

"Don't tell me you have a thing about pitties," Siever challenged, "sweetest disposition you ever saw..."

"I didn't say anything in particular about the dog or the breed," Margie said. "Everybody has their own opinion about that. I just mean I'd like to take a closer look at the owner. He rubbed me the wrong way. I want to explore the possibility that he might have gotten into an argument with Mr. Robinson."

"Could have," Siever agreed, nodding. "He didn't look like the most laid-back guy."

"But why would he come to walk in the park if he was that irritable?" Jones asked. "If you're spoiling to pick a fight, why go to a park? Why not a bar or somewhere else he could have blown off some steam?"

Siever shrugged. "Maybe he didn't want to get in a fight. Maybe he was trying to work off whatever stress he was feeling so that he could relax and *not* get in a fight."

"I suppose."

"Walking somewhere like this is peaceful. Get in touch with your serenity. Put all of the stress of the day behind you."

Jones nodded. "Okay. Maybe."

"I'd still like to look into him further," Margie repeated.

"Of course. We'll see if we can spot him on some of the other video, follow him back, see where he came from and went to and the times. Everyone we have pictures of was here at roughly the right time. We can't eliminate anyone just by having one conversation with them."

No, there would be a lot of footwork and further discussions to eliminate people from their lists. Like all police work, it was long hours of tedium, followed by moments of intense action or terror. It would take a long time to look through the videos to find everybody and identify their movements, and then try to find any connections with Robinson other than that they had just happened to be in the park at the same time.

Could anyone put them together? Did they walk together? Have a business? Were they friends? Lovers? Enemies? In a club? Share a vice? Lots of questions to be asked.

CHAPTER EIGHT

Margie was watching videos again the next morning. The camera locations had been plotted on a map, which was helpful, so that she could try to find people again after they walked off of one camera. Follow the trail until it came to another camera, and then watch for them to appear there. If they didn't appear, then look at some of the places it might branch off to a different location. Or had they gone off trail completely, and wouldn't reconnect with it again for several hours?

It was tedious work, but she created a profile for each person who had been at the park at the same time as Robinson, included their picture and, if they had it, the person's name and any other details they had. She ignored, for the time being, anyone who they had gathered identification and contact details from. It was more important to track down the people who hadn't come forward or returned to the park as usual. Those were the people who were more likely to have had something to do with Robinson's death. Someone who hoped that by staying away for a few days, or permanently, that he would be able to distance himself from the investigation and maybe stay below the radar.

She had identified the man with the pit bull by following his images on the videos back to the parking lot and getting the license plate from his car. That was a lucky break. With the name on the car's registration, she was able to look up his driver's license and confirm that it matched the face on the video. They would gather his contact information and pay him a visit.

Margie was having a more difficult time with the boy in the hoodie. She peered at the screen, trying to track him as he moved from one camera to another like a ghost. His dark outfit blended in with the shadows, and he drifted rather than walked along the pathway.

"Any luck?" Cruz's voice at Margie's shoulder made her startle. She looked around at him, blowing out her breath.

"You mind not sneaking up on me? Next time I might go for my gun."

He raised his brows, knowing full well that her gun was locked away while she was at her desk, the same as everyone else's. It wasn't really much of a threat. Margie shook her head.

"Working on it. Fitting together one piece of the puzzle at a time."

"You think this kid had anything to do with it?" He indicated the screen.

Margie took a deep breath, studying the young man on the monitor as if it were the first time she had seen him. "I really don't. What reason would he have to be involved with someone like Robinson? An adult. A welder. Not the kind of person he would have hung out with. No sign that it was robbery or drugs. A random attack? It's possible, but I don't think so."

"But you're still going to track him down."

"Of course."

Cruz nodded. "Have fun."

"You're welcome to take a video any time you like. I don't mean to hog all of the fun stuff."

He grinned. "No, no, you're the new one here. You should have the opportunity for as much investigative work as you want." He straightened his shirt, a bold pink color that apparently was no threat to his manhood.

"There's plenty to go around. I promise."

"I've got other files to work. This is your first, so you can put your full attention into it," he told her sagely, smiling but no longer joking. "See what you can dig up."

Margie went back to work trying to track the hoodie boy.

*

AFTER TRACKING the boy's walk through the park, they needed more. He had not taken a vehicle into the park, but had walked in. Video from traffic cams, security surveillance, private householders, whatever they could get. That meant Margie and the other detectives getting out on the street to spot all of the cameras they could and to track him half a block at a time as they backtracked his arrival and then requesting the video from the owner. The footage taken in the daylight hours when he had arrived was much easier to see than the nighttime footage after he had left.

More than once, she asked herself why she was doing it. They had a lot of people they hadn't yet eliminated. She was working on them too. But the boy who had arrived on foot with his face hidden was suspicious. He wasn't there with friends, wasn't there to work out, and appeared to be intentionally hiding his face from the cameras or the other patrons of the park. What was he doing there?

"Got him!" Jones said, banging her keyboard and sitting back in her chair.

Margie looked over at her. "Got him?"

"The boy. I have him coming out of a house." Jones smiled like the cat who caught the canary, then gave Margie the address.

"Shall we go check it out?" Margie suggested.

"You want me to come?"

"You're the one who got the address. I think you should. Unless you don't want to…"

"Oh, I want to!" Jones pushed back from her desk. "Let's do it."

MARGIE LOOKED at her watch as they arrived at the house. It was afternoon and, if they were lucky, the boy would be home from school. Back in Forest Lawn, Christina would be getting on the bus. It would be half an hour before she was home. Hopefully, this boy's school was within walking distance of his home. From what she had seen, though, the newer areas were farther away from schools. Or the boy might be one of the kids accessing online schooling during the pandemic and was therefore home during the day.

She raised her hand and knocked loudly on the door. A good, authoritative knock. The kind that made people take notice instead of deciding that since they weren't expecting any friends or deliveries, they would just ignore the door and hope that the salesperson or missionaries went on to the next house.

In about half a minute, she could hear footsteps from within, and a man came to the door. Tall and skinny. Taller than the boy on the footage. Not a teenager. His skin was very dark, just as the boy's had been reported to be. Margie decided to go with it.

"We're here looking for your son, is he home?" she asked.

He looked confused. "My son?" Then he gave his head a little shake. "Oh. Yes. Abdul."

Abdul. Margie made a mental note of it. The man had a thick accent. She wasn't sure where he was from. "Is Abdul home?"

"No. He's not back from school yet." The man looked to the side as if studying something. "He is not working today, so he will probably be home in… about half an hour?"

"Could we come in, please? We should probably talk to you before he gets home."

He looked down, frowning. Searching for a way to tell them no. He didn't want the police in his house. He didn't seem curious to know what they wanted with his son; he just wanted them to leave. Wanted a way to tell them to go. But after standing there silently for a few uncomfortable seconds, he stepped back and opened the door farther to allow them entrance.

Margie and Jones stepped in. The living room was plainly furnished. An older couch and some easy chairs. A TV on a stand. A colorful tapestry hung on the wall, and another draped over the couch, but there were no paintings or prints. The man made a motion toward the couch. Margie looked around once more. She didn't hear anyone else in the house. She didn't see any sign of drugs, weapons, or anything else that raised red flags. She met Jones's eyes to make sure she felt the same way and didn't see any concerns there. They sat down.

"What's your last name?" Margie asked, pulling out her notepad and writing *Abdul* on a fresh page.

"Paul."

"Paul is your last name?" she checked. "Not your first?"

He nodded. "Sadiq is my first name."

"Sadiq Paul?" Margie spelled it out as she wrote it, and he nodded his agreement. But the way that his eyes stayed on her face, she wondered if she had spelled too fast and he was still trying to catch up with her. English was not his first language.

"And is that Abdul's last name too?"

"No." He shook his head. "Abdul's last name is James."

"Got it." Margie wrote it down. "Did he take his mother's name, then?"

The man gave a shrug that Margie wasn't sure how to interpret. Yes, it was his mother's name? Or there was some other reason he had a different last name?

"Can you tell me where Abdul was three nights ago?"

"Three nights. He was here. He is always here. This is his home."

"Before bed," Margie clarified. "Say, between school and bedtime. He wasn't here the whole time."

"No. It takes time for him to get home from school. And some nights he works." This time, Margie saw the schedule on the whiteboard he had been looking at previously. Her eyes went to the night of Robinson's death. No shift was noted for Abdul. He should have been home.

"Where would he have gone if he wasn't working? He doesn't come straight home."

"He comes home for supper. Always home for supper, if he's not working."

"And then he goes out again after that?"

"Sometimes," Sadiq agreed.

"Where does he go when he goes out again in the evening and he doesn't have work?"

"I don't ask him. Sometimes, just walking around the neighborhood. Maybe to a friend's house. Sometimes to the park."

"Fish Creek Park?"

"Yes." His head turned in the direction of the park. "It's a good place to walk. To… reconnect with yourself after a long day."

"Do you go with him?"

"No." Sadiq shook his head firmly. "I don't get in his way. He wants to walk alone."

"I see. So you don't supervise him and you don't ask him to account for where he has been."

Sadiq shook his head and didn't offer any explanation. Maybe that was normal in the culture and background he came from. Many Indigenous parents let their children explore on their own and take care of themselves much more than their white counterparts. It taught interdependence with the land. Learning to live in harmony with others and the environment. Perhaps it was the same where this man came from. Margie wrote a few notes.

"Maybe while we are waiting for Abdul to get home, we could see his room."

Sadiq didn't move. Margie waited. He didn't offer any objection or give permission. Margie cut her eyes toward Jones. Did his silence indicate consent? Could they go ahead and look for Abdul's room, and if Sadiq didn't object, take that as his consent to a search? Or at least to a look around at what was in plain sight? Jones grimaced, not offering her opinion one way or the other.

Margie didn't feel right about it. There was, if nothing more, a communication gap. She didn't want to get herself in trouble for an illegal search and risk having important evidence thrown out.

"Could we look at Abdul's room?" she asked more plainly.

Sadiq looked at her. At first, she thought he was going to shrug, still not understanding exactly what she wanted from him, and that shrug might be able to be taken as consent. But he didn't shrug. He shook his head.

"We can't see Abdul's room?" Jones pressed. "What are you trying to hide?"

"It is not my place to give permission for you to see his room. That is his space. He can decide when he is here."

So they waited. Margie thought of more questions about Abdul and asked them here and there, but was no closer to understanding the situation of the father and son than she had been when he answered the door. Was there a wife and mother around? There didn't seem to be. Had Abdul always been with Sadiq, or was it a recent development?

"Where did you come here from?"

Sadiq considered, not answering immediately. Was he worried they would judge him? Eventually, he decided to answer.

"We are from the Sudan."

And then Abdul was there. Margie hadn't even heard the door open and close, and Abdul was standing just a few feet away from her, the black hood pulled up over his head just as it had been when he had walked through the park. Maybe the permanent state of affairs. He had on a black bandana mask, pulled up high, so that when she looked into the depths of the hood, all she could see was the glitter of his eyes.

"Abdul." Margie got to her feet, and the boy took a couple of quick steps back. "No, it's okay. We just wanted to talk to you."

He looked at his father and then back at Margie again. He pulled the bandana down to his neck, revealing fine features, midway between child and adult. Vulnerable and not yet the man's face he would grow into. But no longer quite a child, either.

"You are po-lice?" he asked in a soft voice, still high in pitch.

Margie tried to make her nod as reassuring as possible. She didn't want him running away. Kids tended to be anxious around the police even if they hadn't done anything against the law. It was part of the mindset at that age.

"Yes, we are both police detectives." She was glad she had brought Jones instead of one of the male detectives. They would not be as threatening to Abdul. "My name is Detective Patenaude and this is Detective Jones. We wanted to ask you about your walk in the park the other day."

He studied Jones and then looked back at Margie. "What day? I walk in park many days."

"Three days ago. In the evening. You were there almost until closing time. Ten o'clock."

He nodded.

"Do you remember?"

A small shrug. A look around at his surroundings for confirmation that he was still safe in his own home. He sat down on the arm of Sadiq's chair. He pulled back his hood, revealing short-cropped curly black hair. There were scars on his face. Not abuse, she didn't think. Maybe a childhood accident. "I remember."

"I want you to think about whether you saw or heard anything unusual that night. Maybe… shouting or an argument? Somebody that you hadn't seen at the park before or who scared you. Anything… that we might be interested in."

"What is this about?" Sadiq asked, his pronunciation overly precise. She was surprised that he hadn't asked before. The police showed up at the door asking for his son and he didn't even ask why?

Margie didn't answer him, but pulled out her tablet and selected a picture of Robinson. Not a picture of his body, but the one from his driver's license. She held it up for Abdul. "Did you see this man?"

Abdul looked at it. He reached out tentatively and Margie handed it to him. He brought it close to his eyes, studying it. Was he supposed to wear glasses? When had he last had his vision checked? Maybe never. They were immigrants; maybe they hadn't availed themselves of the province's health services.

After a while, Abdul handed the tablet back. "I have seen this man before. Other days."

"But not three days ago?"

His shoulders lifted and fell. "I do not remember. That day?" He shook his head. "Maybe and maybe not. I know the face."

"Do you know his name? Have you ever stopped to talk to him?"

Abdul's eyes skittered away. "No," he said in a low voice. "Why would I talk to him? What reason would he have to talk to me?"

"The other day, when I was out in a park near my house walking my dog, another man who was walking his dog commented to me what a beautiful sunset it was. We talked for a few minutes, just about the sky and the park and what it was like to live in the neighborhood." She let him think about that for a minute. "Maybe you had a conversation like that with Mr. Robinson."

"No. He never stops me to tell me it is a beautiful day."

Put like that, it did seem a little silly. A man and a woman of similar age might stop to chat, but a white man and a Black teenager?

"You have a dog?" Abdul asked, showing interest in something for the first time.

"Yes." Margie smiled at him. "Would you like to see a picture?" She pulled out her phone, selected the photos app, and found one of Stella, mouth wide in a panting doggie grin as if she had been posing for the picture. She handed it over to Abdul.

A little smile formed on his face. He touched the screen lightly as if he could introduce himself to Stella that way or reach through the screen to pet her. He swiped, looking at other photos. "Is this your daughter?"

"Yes. She must be about your age. Are you fifteen? Sixteen?"

"Fourteen," he corrected. "I am very tall."

"Yes. You are tall for fourteen. Christina is fifteen." Margie reached over and took the phone out of his hands. He didn't need to be looking through the rest of her pictures. It wasn't like she had taken pictures of anything private or inappropriate. Or had crime scene photos on it. She just didn't think he needed to be looking at pictures of her life. They were there to talk about him. His life, and how Jerry Robinson's life had ended.

Abdul's hands fell to his lap and stayed there. He didn't fidget. He just watched them. Margie couldn't imagine this frail-looking fourteen-year-old having a fight with Robinson. Physical or verbal. He was shy and uncertain. He wouldn't have a reason to approach Robinson. He said they had never talked.

He didn't appear to have any concern about talking about being in the park that night. He probably hadn't even heard that there had been a death. If Sadiq had read about it in the paper or online, maybe he had hidden it from Abdul, deciding that he didn't need to be upset by it. But Margie suspected Sadiq didn't even read the news. It wouldn't be relaxing for him to read it in a language other than his native tongue.

"The reason that we're asking questions is that man I showed you died that night."

Abdul's eyes got wide. "He died?"

"Yes. He was killed."

Abdul looked at her for a moment as if trying to translate what she had said. Maybe he was. Perhaps the shades of meaning between *he died* and *he was killed* hadn't occurred to him before and needed some thought.

"Somebody killed him?" Abdul asked. "He not just…" He clutched at his chest, miming before he found the words. "Heart attack?"

"That's right. Somebody killed him."

"Was he shot?" Sadiq asked.

Margie shook her head. She looked at Abdul, waiting for his reaction. Watching for any recollection in his eyes of something that had happened that day. He looked at his father, considering his words, and then back at Margie again.

"That is very bad," he said. "But I do not know who hurt him."

He looked directly at her with his wide, brown eyes, and Margie did not sense any deception.

CHAPTER NINE

Back at the office, Margie and Jones huddled with the other detectives who were there.

"I don't think it's the kid," Margie said. She looked at Jones. "Do you concur?"

Jones nodded slowly. "He didn't strike me as being guilty or evasive. Shy, yes, and feeling his way through things. He's clearly a recent immigrant, still learning the language and the culture."

"Is he in a gang?" Cruz asked. "That black hoodie has me wondering. Just what is he trying to hide? You know that one of the reasons bangers wear loose clothing is to hide weapons. And the hoods hide people's faces, make it harder for them to identify. You're sure that's not what's going on here? Sometimes immigrants band together for safety."

"He's probably cold," Jones said. "If he came here from an African country, then he's probably freezing, even when we would consider it warm. And at nightfall, it gets quite chilly. Under ten. I don't like to go out without a hoodie at that time."

"He was wearing a face mask," Margie said. "And that could indicate that he's trying to hide his identity… or just that he's following the rules for when he is at school or on the bus. He did take it off when we introduced ourselves."

"No suspicious behavior?" Cruz challenged. "You know that these kids can be pretty glib. They've always got a story, a disarming smile. They don't necessarily act like the hoods you see on TV."

"Not my first rodeo," Margie sighed. "I've dealt with plenty of gang kids in Manitoba. I don't think they're that different here. I didn't see any sign that he was affiliated with a gang or might have any sort of freelance drug business."

"And the father? It could be the parents. They need something to stay solvent. They get the kids to traffic, but it's really the parents who are the problem."

"No. Nothing that gave me any clue that there were illegal drugs. Or fencing or any other kind of illegal or quasi-legal side hustle I can think of. They appear to be new immigrants, just trying to start a new life for themselves."

Cruz nodded slowly. "Okay. So you're pretty sure that the kid didn't have anything to do with it. Too bad, I liked the dark hooded suspect. So it's back to the drawing board. We still have a few people we haven't been able to identify. A couple of cyclists. They would be able to get away from the scene more quickly. They could have gotten there from another part of the city, farther afield. Who else is on your suspicious persons list?"

"We have more people still on it than have been eliminated," Margie admitted. "I'll spend some time tomorrow trying to establish any connections between them and Robinson."

"Sounds like a plan," Mac contributed. He had remained silent up until that point. "I think we have as much from the video as we are going to get right now. We might have to review some footage down the line, but we only have a limited number of suspects. Like one of those closed-room mysteries. It shouldn't be too hard to figure out who had a grudge against Robinson."

"In those mysteries, everyone has a grudge," Margie said. "There is always a secret lover, an illegitimate baby, an angry business partner, a spy…"

"Then we'd better get to it," MacDonald said. "Or Inspector Poirot will beat us to it." He looked at his watch. "Tomorrow. Get a good sleep tonight and start fresh."

"Can we check out that park today?" Christina asked as Margie slid on her shoes to take Stella out for a walk. "You know, the one with the pond," Christina reminded her, when Margie just looked at her blankly, trying to figure out if Christina meant she wanted to go to Fish Creek Park. "The one that Grouch guy told us about?"

"Oh!" Recollection started to return. "You mean… Oscar. The one with the dog, Milo."

"Yeah, Oscar." Christina giggled at her mistake. "That's what I meant. He said there was a park over there, by the viewing platform. Across the street."

"Okay. Sure. We can check it out. We don't have a lot of time before it gets dark, though, so we won't be able to stay and explore for long."

"Yay!" Christina slid on a pair of sandals. "I didn't know there was a waterpark so close. That will be nice when it's hot out."

Margie nodded her agreement and snapped the leash onto Stella's collar. "Okay, girl! Let's go! Let's go walkie."

Margie was cautiously optimistic. Christina seemed to be in better spirits today. Margie didn't ask whether Christina had had a good day at school or whether she'd made some new friends. Questions like that just seemed to irritate the girl and remind her that she was supposed to be sullen and angry about the move. So they just walked, laughed at Stella's antics, looked at the houses and the other people enjoying the pathway, and talked about other things. When Christina was ready to talk about her classes or her friends, she would.

At the viewing platform, they turned and used the crosswalk across to the other side, to what a chiseled-rock sign declared to be Valleyview Park. They walked to the top of a little hill, looked down at the pond, at the playground enclosed in a fence, and the field and sand courts beyond it.

"I was expecting… like, waterslides." Christina's disappointment was evident. "Not just a little kids' splash park."

"I'm sorry. I had no idea what it would be like. I guess this is what passes for a waterpark in the hood," Margie said, hoping to raise a smile.

Christina rolled her eyes. "Well… let's at least walk around the pond."

There were soccer goals in the open field next to the pond. "This would be a good place to throw the ball around," Margie observed. "I don't want to do it over by the ditch, for fear Stella would run right off of the edge and hurt herself. But lots of space over there and away from any traffic."

"It would be good for balls or Frisbee," Christina agreed. She scratched Stella's ears. "Next time, we'll play here for a while."

They nodded and smiled at other people walking around the pond or sitting on the benches nearby. There were walkers, kids on tiny bikes, and an old man on an electric scooter who smiled and talked to everyone who approached him. Margie was enjoying the friendliness of Calgary. She was glad that she had taken the job there.

As they walked back home, Margie talked about Abdul. Not by name, of course, and not in connection with the Fish Creek Park murder. Just casually as a boy that she had talked to that day. She folded her arms, cuddling her sweatshirt closer, remembering how Jones had suggested Abdul was probably always cold after coming from a warmer climate.

"It would be a lot worse coming from Sudan than from Winnipeg," Christina admitted, staring off at the city skyline as they walked the path along Twenty-sixth Street toward home. "I mean… I'm looking forward to the Chinooks. To the winters being a lot easier than in Manitoba. And it would be like… a totally different culture. I might not have any friends here yet, but at least I know how things work, and what to expect at school and all that. Could he even read when he came here?"

"I have no idea. They didn't say he was in any special program at school, but I didn't ask, either. It was clear that English was not his native language."

"Ugh. I can't imagine having to learn a whole new language. Thanks for not moving to… Germany or something like that. Or Norway. It's cold there, right?"

"Yes, it gets cold there."

"I'm glad we stayed in Canada. Having to deal with all of that other stuff… that would be a lot harder."

Margie was glad to see that Christina could see she hadn't had it as bad as some people did. She really was a good girl. It was just hard to stay focused on everything she had to be grateful for.

They walked along in silence for a few minutes.

"Hey, there's the guy again. Milo and…?"

"Oscar." Margie waved as they got closer. "Hi, Oscar."

The dogs sniffed each other and pranced around. "Enjoying the weather?" Oscar asked.

"May as well enjoy it while we can. It's not going to last forever." Even though Margie was a little chilly in just a hoodie, she knew better than to complain about it. A few more weeks, and there would be snow on the ground and much lower temperatures.

"Yeah, you're right," Oscar agreed. "There's no keeping winter from coming."

And would business slow down with the cold weather? Margie knew that it wouldn't. Cold weather didn't stop people from killing each other. It might help with hiding bodies until the next melt, but people who were forced to live inside at close quarters tended to get on each other's nerves. And when they got into the pre-Christmas season, then not only would the murder rate go up due to the stress and other crazy stuff that happened around the holidays, but so would the suicide rate. And suicides were investigated by the homicide department. It would be a busy time—Christmas, New Year, and then the long, cold, interminable nights of February. Margie couldn't suppress a little shudder. Christina looked at her but didn't say anything.

They talked for a few more minutes with Oscar and Milo before returning home.

CHAPTER TEN

Margie would be glad to get home after a long day in front of her computer. Her time had been broken up with various phone calls and emails to follow up on possible leads, ask some more questions, and to establish either alibis for Robinson's murder or connections with him. Computer databases, web searches, talking to neighbors, Robinson's coworkers, and anyone who might be identified as friends. He seemed to have lived a pretty solitary life, and finding even tentative connections was a slog.

By the end of it, she felt like her brain had been wrung out. Her nerves and her emotions were raw. She needed to get home to her daughter and Stella, to spend some time outside in the fresh air and to move around and get some exercise. She had known that there would be a lot of desk work associated with homicide work. That just went with the territory.

As she put her office tools away into the drawers, she tried to mentally do the same with the day's stresses and worries. A ceremonial laying aside of her work life. She would try not to take any burdens home with her, but to go home lighter and happier.

She plugged her phone into the car stereo and tapped a few times to bring up her de-stress playlist. A broadly-ranging combination of Métis fiddlers, classic rock, and rap to help exorcise the demons of the office.

The rest of the week, she had managed to get home before Christina, but this time the front door was unlocked and she knew she had worked too late. She glanced at her watch before entering.

"Hi, honey. Sorry to be so long today. How was school?"

There was no answer. Christina wasn't in the living room or kitchen. Margie went down the hallway to peek in Christina's door to see if she was doing her homework with her headphones on.

Christina wasn't in her bedroom. Margie's stomach clenched. She looked back toward the front door. She was sure she had locked it that morning. Christina was home. She wouldn't still be at school or on the bus that late. Christina had arrived home and had unlocked the door.

Margie continued down the hall to the bathroom, but the door stood ajar and it was clear that Christina was not there either.

"Christina? Are you here?"

Margie exited the hall into the kitchen.

"Christina?"

She heard a volley of barks from Stella in the backyard and blew out her breath in a sigh of relief. Of course, Christina had just taken Stella outside.

Then there was a shrill shriek of fear or alarm. Margie ran to the back door and out into the yard.

"Christina? What is it?"

Christina ran to her, colliding on the step and putting her arms around Margie.

"What is it? What's wrong?"

Christina made a sobbing, choking noise. Margie looked for Stella, worried that she had run out of the yard and been hit by a car in the back lane. But Stella was standing in the middle of the back yard, looking happy and relaxed, not understanding why her young master was upset. Margie didn't get it either. She pushed Christina away from her to look at her face.

"Christina! Talk to me!"

Christina shook her head. "No, it's okay," she said, even though her expression was still distressed. She seemed unable to say anything else to explain herself.

Margie hugged her, pulling her close again and holding Christina firmly to try to convey strength and calm to her. Christina sniffled a few times and then pulled back.

"It's fine. I'm okay. Everything is fine," she again reassured Margie.

"Okay. Take a deep breath and then tell me what happened."

"Come." Christina stepped back and gave Margie's arm a little tug to encourage her to follow. She walked across the yard toward Stella. Stella started to bound around excitedly, wanting to play or show off about something. Christina pointed to a clump of leaves on the grass.

Margie took a closer look and saw that it wasn't a clump of sod and dead brown grass, but the body of a dead squirrel.

"Oh." Margie sighed. "It's okay. I'll just get rid of it."

Christina made a face. "I thought it was just some twigs. I was going to pick up a stick to throw for Stella, and then I realized…" She gagged. "Ugh. I almost picked it up!"

And that had given her quite a start.

"Try not to keep visualizing it," Margie advised. "If you can distract yourself with other things, it won't be saved as such a vivid memory. The less you think about it, the faster it will fade."

Christina ran her hands over her face as if trying to wipe it away. "Will you…?" She made a motion toward the squirrel.

"I'll take care of it. Why don't you get started on some dinner? Just let me grab some paper towel first so that I won't be in your way."

They went back into the house. Margie called Stella in. She didn't want the dog to get in the way while she was trying to deal with the squirrel. Especially if Stella thought it was some new game for her and tried to take the squirrel back away from her.

"You stay in here," she told Stella sternly. "Go lie down. I'll get you a treat when I come back in."

"Mom?"

Margie looked at Christina.

"You don't think… Stella didn't kill it, did she?"

"No, I'm sure she didn't," Margie assured her. "She likes to chase squirrels, but she's never caught one. I don't think she'd have any idea what to do with it if she did."

"Yeah." Christina's face relaxed, her relief clear. "Yeah, you're right."

She turned to the cupboard to look for something to make for supper. Margie went back outside with her handful of paper towels. She approached the squirrel's corpse with trepidation.

Which was pretty funny, considering what she did for a living. Why should she be anxious about a dead squirrel? She, who dealt with dead people all day long? A dead squirrel wasn't even going to hold a candle to the horrors of murdered men, women, and children that she had seen and would yet see in the future.

She picked it up in the paper towel. She had planned to just throw it straight into the green bin without looking at it, but she heard Christina's question in her mind and had to make sure that Stella could not have killed it. If she had, they would have to make sure that she was not allowed outside on her own. She would always have to be supervised until they were sure that she wasn't a squirrel-killer.

The body was stiff. Not a fresh kill. Margie squinted at it, looking for bite marks. Looking for the injury that had killed it. There were many ways a squirrel could die. It could have eaten poisoned mouse bait. It could have been electrocuted running on one of the power lines. It could have been hit by a car, killed by a cat or another dog. How it got into her yard was another story. But an animal could have dragged it there. A person walking down the back lane could have picked it up and thrown it over the fence. Why, she didn't quite know, but it was possible. People were highly unpredictable.

There was dried blood on the torso. It looked like a clean edge, not a bite mark. Not any of the accidents that she had thought might befall an unwary squirrel. But there could be other things. Something sharp... on the ground... or a barbed -wire fence... maybe a tin can that the squirrel had crawled into, looking for nuts or something that had smelled good. What looked like a knife edge could have been a dozen other things. She wasn't a medical examiner. She wasn't performing a necropsy and trying to analyze who or what had killed the squirrel. She just wanted to make sure that it hadn't been Stella, and it hadn't been.

Margie walked briskly to the back gate and out into the alley to toss the body into the green bin. She made sure it was well-wrapped and then threw more paper towels down on top of it, so that she would never have to see it again.

Rest in peace, little squirrel.

Margie went back into the house to help Christina prepare supper.

CHAPTER ELEVEN

The next morning as they prepared for the day ahead, Christina asked, "Mom, could we go see Moushoom again? Maybe after school today?"

Margie considered her workload and schedule for the day and nodded. "I'll try to get home around the same time as you do, and we'll go over. The staff said he could eat what he wanted, so we could take him food this time."

"Burgers?" Christina suggested.

"If that's what you want, sure. I'm sure he would like that."

"Do you think he would like something else better? Could we make him something traditional? Something he hasn't had for a long time and that you can't buy in the restaurants?"

Margie blinked. "What a great idea. I'm sure he would just love that. I don't have a lot of time and energy after work, though, I don't think we can make anything too ambitious."

"Maybe we could just make bannock this time, but we could plan something else next time. When we have more time to shop and prepare."

"Perfect. Great idea. You don't need many ingredients for bannock, so I think I can manage that without a shopping trip. Somebody said it's harder to bake in Calgary because of the altitude, so it might not turn out quite the way we expect. We might have to try a few different times before we get it just right. It's just a matter of learning how to cook in a new environment."

"How does the altitude affect baking?"

"I'm not sure. I'll have to look it up. I know that water doesn't boil at the same temperature."

Christina looked at her like she was crazy. "Water always boils at the same temperature. One hundred degrees."

"One hundred degrees at sea level."

Christina shook her head, still not believing it. She wedged more books into her bag and looked across the room out to the street.

"There's the bus! I gotta run!"

Margie wasn't even sure if Christina heard her 'goodbye' as she belted out of the house. There was certainly not going to be any hug and kiss and sage motherly advice that morning. It would have to wait until their visit with Moushoom.

※

SHE WAS glad after work that they were going to visit Moushoom. She needed something to help take her head out of her work, and her de-stress playlist had not done it. She and Christina put their heads together in the kitchen to make a batch of bannock, which had turned out fine despite Margie's misgivings. Maybe bannock was just one of those recipes that was impossible to screw up. They wrapped it up so it would still be warm from the stove when they got to Moushoom's apartment.

When they reached Moushoom's room, they again found him parked in front of the TV. Moushoom beamed at them and waved his hand at the TV. "You can shut that off. The nurses are always turning on the TV's to keep people quiet. And after trying to ignore it for a while... you kind of get dragged into it. But I don't want it on while my granddaughters are here to see me!"

Margie moved a TV table over Moushoom's knees and put down her bundle. "Wait until you see what we brought for you. This was Christina's idea."

Christina ducked her head and looked shy, but also excited and proud. "We made it together."

"Bannock!" Moushoom exclaimed in delight. "I don't remember when the last time I had bannock was!" He immediately broke off a piece and popped it into his mouth. "This is the best thing you could have brought me. It takes me right back to my childhood; sitting in my mother's kitchen, eating the bannock hot from the stove. Even in hard times, there was still bannock to fill hungry tummies."

He closed his eyes, savoring it. He opened them again.

"Come on, come on. Bring chairs over. You come have some too. We'll have a proper little feast here. Like we were away at school, sneaking food after lights out."

Margie and Christina did as he instructed. Margie laid out the butter and jam that she had brought along. She thought about what it had been like for Moushoom, back in the days of residential school, when the white man was so intent on beating the Indian out of the children. Anything that reminded them of their own culture had been banned. The Indigenous languages, spiritual beliefs, clothing, food, and ceremonies. They cut off their hair like the Philistines in the Christian Bible, trying to take away Samson's strength.

"Eat, eat," Moushoom encouraged, bringing Margie back to the present. She smiled at him and broke a piece off, eating while smiling at him. The white man had failed. They had not been able to steal Moushoom's culture away from him. They had not been able to stamp out all of the Indigenous cultures, though they had tried their best.

They sat down, lowering their masks to eat. Margie hoped that they were far enough apart to prevent an infection. She didn't want Moushoom getting sick. Sharing food and the knife for the butter was not a good idea, but they had both sanitized their hands before taking the elevator up.

"It must have been awful for you, going away to school," Margie said.

Moushoom's smile dimmed. He closed his eyes for a moment against the unwelcome memories, then shook it off and looked at her with a confident smile. "We learned far more than the brothers ever intended to teach us. They thought that they could crush us. Could squash the Métis out of us. We were like prisoners of war. But we were warriors. They could not overcome us."

He nibbled at some more bannock.

"Not all of us," he admitted. "Many of my brothers and sisters never came home." He looked at Christina and shook his head. "You seem so young to me now, but you are as old as I was when I left that place, a full-grown man, expected to fend for myself. A fully-educated man, looking and acting like a white man. You wouldn't believe it if you saw pictures of me then. But I went back to my people, grew my hair out, put on my sash, and I never let my culture go. Even when I came west and settled here, I didn't pretend to be white. I am Métis. I will always be Métis."

Christina nodded. She lifted her chin a little. "I am too. I'm still going to school. I want to get my education, but not so that I can be like them."

"There is nothing wrong with being educated. As long as you don't let them write their stories on your heart."

"I won't."

"Good girl."

Margie let her eyes drift around the room as she buttered and ate small pieces of the bannock, making it last as long as she could. Like Abdul's house, it was starkly furnished. Moushoom had not been able to bring many of his possessions there. But there were still decorations intended to remind him of his heritage. And he wore as much traditional clothing as he could.

There were certain parallels between Moushoom and the immigrants. Even though they represented opposite ends of the spectrum, one preserving his old traditions and the immigrants trying to adapt to an entirely new culture, they were similar to each other, out-of-step with the mainstream. Outsiders.

At least Abdul did not have to experience what Moushoom had. He went to public school with other children of all different races and traditions, and there was no one telling him that he could not keep his own name, no one shaving his head or beating him if he spoke his own language or didn't answer a question the way that they wanted him to. There were still rules, but they were not brutal and were not designed to erase who he was.

"What are you thinking of?" Moushoom asked.

"A boy I interviewed recently. He is from the Sudan, in Africa. Very far away and very different from the children here. I was talking to Christina the other day about how hard it must be for him to adjust to a new language and culture. Like you did."

Moushoom nodded his understanding. His dark eyes shone with interest and intelligence. There had been stories before Margie had moved to Calgary, suggesting that he was growing senile, that he didn't understand what was going on around him and easily forgot things. But so far, she had not seen it.

There was a crash out in the hallway or one of the nearby apartments, followed by shouting and swearing.

Despite his advanced years, Moushoom was immediately on his feet, his eyes wild, looking toward the disturbance. In his hand was the knife that only moments before had been on the TV table for them to spread butter and jam on the bannock.

"Moushoom!" Christina looked frightened by his reaction and rose as well, crashing into the TV table and nearly knocking it over.

Moushoom turned toward her, the knife held up in a defensive stance. Margie steadied the table.

"Sit down, Christina," she said quietly.

"But—" Christina looked at her Moushoom and then toward the noise in the hall. She looked terrified.

"Just sit down. You're safe. But you're frightening him more."

Christina looked at her mother for a minute, black brows drawn down in confusion. Then she obeyed, lowering herself slowly to her seat.

Moushoom wavered. He looked at Christina, then at Margie. His eyes, though still quick, were different from the way they had been. He was separated from them by time. How far in the past he was, she didn't know, but she would give him however long he needed to calm down and make his way back to them.

"You are safe," she told Moushoom. "I don't know what is going on out there, but I don't think it is any danger to you."

Moushoom's stance gradually relaxed. He put the knife back down with the bannock with a self-deprecating laugh. "Who wants some jam?" He sat down again in his chair with a deep sigh, as if at the end of a long, physically arduous day.

"Did it scare you?" Christina said tentatively.

Margie wouldn't have tried to question Moushoom about his reaction, but she didn't stop Christina. If Moushoom didn't want to talk about it, he could say so; Margie didn't want to stop Christina and imply that it was a forbidden topic or that Moushoom was not free to share whatever he pleased.

"I am an old man. Old men scare easily."

"Why did it scare you?" Christina's eyes were on the knife. Old men might scare easily but, in Christina's experience, they didn't take up weapons to defend themselves.

"You do not know all the things that happened when I was a boy," Moushoom said slowly. "We don't talk about it." He looked at Margie. "Not all of it. We don't want to relive those years." He was silent for a few moments. "But make no mistake… we were at war with our captors. It was a silent war. But we were still warriors."

CHAPTER TWELVE

Margie's sleep was restless, interrupted by dreams that were fleeting, sliding away from her as soon as she tried to remember and analyze them. She tossed and turned, got up and had a drink of milk in the hopes that it would help her to settle down, and lay down to sleep again.

The alarm rang too early in the morning. Margie forced herself to swing her feet over the edge of the bed and to get up and get moving. Once she had been up for a little while, once she had showered and had a cup of coffee, it would be easier. Even if she were short on sleep, she would still be able to function and make it through the day.

She listened to make sure that Christina got up when her alarm rang. She let Christina choose her own wake-up time and routine, as long as it got her to school on time. Christina was old enough to be responsible for those details herself. And she had shown herself to be responsible. Most of the time. They had both found it difficult to settle down after the long visit with Moushoom. Margie's brain had been busy with all of the things they had talked about.

"I'm up," Christina croaked from her room. She knew that Margie would be close by, checking in.

"Do you want me to put bread in the toaster for you?"

"Um… yeah," Christina agreed. They both knew that food was one of the things that was sure to get her out of bed.

Their morning preparations were slow and involved their bumping into each other and into other things a lot that day. But despite their fatigue, neither was grumpy and irritable. It was just kind of a slow-motion morning. Margie saw Christina off to the bus and hopped in her car.

※

A LOT of the high schools only had a half day on Friday. Christina would be arriving home by one o'clock, and Margie wasn't sure what she would be doing in the time until Margie returned home. Doing her homework early so that she wouldn't have to worry about it all weekend? Margie suppressed a smile. Doubtful.

She wondered if Abdul, too, would only have a half day. His father had been home when they had visited before. Margie wasn't sure what kind of a job he had, whether it required him to work on shift, or whether he could work remotely from home. Would Sadiq be watching for Abdul to come home? He didn't seem like the kind of father who supervised his son closely. He came from a culture where the children were probably allowed to run around the village barefoot all day, as long as they didn't have to be at school, work, or doing chores. Of course, that was just what Margie thought after seeing commercials about giving aid to emergency relief in the African countries. Or the occasional telethon or news report on happenings around the world from them. She didn't really know anything about the Sudan personally.

She took a break from the mind-numbing work of eliminating or prioritizing each suspect to do a quick Google search of the Sudan to learn what she should probably already know about their culture and history.

CHAPTER THIRTEEN

Margie sat with her eyes closed for a long time.

She didn't want to believe it.

She sat there, thinking things through, going through all of the variables in her mind, putting the pieces together. The picture they formed was complete, but it wasn't what she wanted to see.

She looked around the squad room to see who else was there. She'd been working with her head down for so long that she had missed the comings and goings of the other detectives. Cruz was leaning back in his chair, rubbing the back of his neck. Clearly, he had been working too long at his computer as well.

"Detective Cruz, do you want to go for a ride?"

He nodded, rolling his shoulders and continuing to rub his neck. "Yeah. Anything to get away from this desk. What do you need?"

"I think… I need to talk to Abdul James again."

He studied her face. "Abdul. I thought you had decided he wasn't a suspect. Too young and shy. Wouldn't have any motive."

"I know. I had decided that. He didn't seem like a danger. And yet…" She thought about Moushoom the night before, grabbing the table knife. Nobody would expect a frail old man to be a danger either. But he had reacted in an instant, ready to defend himself.

"You think he might be the doer, or you think he knows something?"

She wasn't ready to float her theory yet. It was too soon. She wanted some verification first. She needed more information. "Let's go over there. See if we can find anything else."

He nodded his acceptance of this plan and didn't insist that she tell him all of her thoughts. Margie agreed to go in Cruz's car. He knew his way around the city better and she wouldn't have to demonstrate her complete lack of a sense of direction. They put on their masks before sliding into the enclosed space. Cruz didn't even use his GPS when she gave him the address, but pulled out into traffic and headed toward the community.

Margie watched out the windshield, trying to memorize everything she could about the layout of the city. "Have you lived in Calgary long?"

"Fifteen years now. Four with homicide."

She was not surprised he had been there so long. He seemed to be comfortable with the culture in Calgary. He didn't sound or act like a new immigrant. And he obviously had to have the years behind him in a Canadian police force to have earned the position of detective. He couldn't do that straight off the plane.

"Do you like it?"

"Calgary or homicide?"

"I meant Calgary, but either."

"It suits me. Other than the weather. I still find it cold. The summers are nice, but they are short."

"Yes. Same with Winnipeg."

"How long did you live in Winnipeg?"

"I've been in Manitoba my whole life. Winnipeg… since high school."

"And before that?"

"A Métis community you've probably never heard of. But I wanted to get an education. There wasn't much available if I stayed home. I always figured I would go back after I finished school, but then… there's the problem of finding a suitable job. And I wouldn't have been able to find something there. Not in law enforcement."

"Have you always wanted to be in law enforcement?"

"No, not really. I kind of gravitated toward it during college. I thought I might have an aptitude for it."

He nodded and didn't express his opinion one way or the other. She hadn't worked with him long enough for him to have an opinion anyway. As long as she didn't think she was a bad detective, that was fine.

"What made you take another look at the kid?"

"Something that happened last night... and then... I couldn't stop thinking about it. I did a bit more research and thought that... I really didn't take a hard enough look the first time. I didn't get the full picture."

"You think he had motive?"

"Not exactly."

"We're going to need motive."

"Maybe."

Cruz found the street without directions. Margie wondered if he had looked it up before. Maybe he had suspected the kid and had wanted to know where he lived. How feasible it was that he had walked to the park regularly. Maybe looking for gang associations in the area.

Margie led the way to the door. She again rapped hard, demanding attention. Sadiq might not be so happy to see her again. He might want to just ignore the knock at the door and pretend he didn't hear it. Margie was impatient. "Mr. Paul!" She hammered on the door again. "I want to talk with you."

Sadiq opened the door. His dark eyes took her in, then went to Cruz, standing casually behind her, one hand in his pocket.

"What is it? I thought we were finished."

"I need to talk to you and Abdul again. Is he home?"

"No."

"Will he be home soon?"

He looked around, frowning. "Yes. It is Friday. He will be home very soon."

"We'd like to come in to talk to you."

He reluctantly opened the door and ushered them in again. Margie looked around, experiencing again the starkness of the room, the warmth of the traditional objects that made it a home, however bare it was.

"You said that you and Abdul are from the Sudan."

"Yes."

"Are you his father? His biological father?"

"No."

Margie looked at Cruz. It meant nothing to him yet, but it would.

"How did you come to be Abdul's guardian?"

Sadiq sat down on one of the chairs. "Things in my country are very bad. Terrible things happen there."

"There is a lot of war and unrest."

"Yes."

"And Abdul was orphaned?"

There was another hesitation. "Yes. Perhaps. It is hard to be sure. People disappear or are relocated. Families are broken up. They don't always know what happened to each other. Abdul lost his parents."

"How did he lose them?"

"Families get separated. His mother and sister were killed. His father… I don't know. He fought. He could not stay in his village."

Cruz turned his head suddenly and Margie realized that, once again, Abdul had slipped into the room and was standing there silently, without her even being aware of his entrance.

"Abdul. Come in. Sit down with your… guardian. We were just talking about you. About what happened in the Sudan."

He pulled down his bandana but not his hood, looking at each of them anxiously. He moved around them to sit down with Sadiq, looking only slightly comforted by being close to someone familiar.

"When your mother was killed and your father was fighting, what did you do? Who took care of you?"

Abdul didn't answer immediately. He stared straight ahead, unmoving. He didn't fidget. He just sat there like a statue.

"I had no one," he said finally. "Many children die. They sleep in the streets. Forage. No one takes care of them."

Margie nodded encouragingly. "Is that what you did?"

"At first. I didn't know where to go or what to do. But then I found out about the battalion. The Children's Battalion."

Margie's heart beat harder. It was awful to think of what had happened to Abdul. Even though she didn't know the whole story yet, her heart went out to him. She imagined Christina or another of the many children in her extended family orphaned in a war zone.

"In the Children's Battalion, they would feed you," Abdul explained. "Three times a day! As much food as you needed. We had bunks in the barracks while they were training us. We had clothing."

"How old were you when you joined them?"

"I was ten. Not old enough to fight yet. I carried messages, acted as a spy. We had a network passing the information back to our commanders."

Margie looked at Sadiq. He had made no attempt to stop Abdul from talking about what had happened.

"How did you come to be Abdul's guardian?"

"Abdul was rescued by UNICEF and the UN. They put him through reeducation. Counseling. And they brought him and some of the other… refugees here. I wanted to help. I said I would take a child."

"Were you a child soldier as well?"

Sadiq shook his head slowly. "My mother was. She was abducted and became one of their wives. She was fifteen when I was born, and escaped. She tried to return to her village, but she was shunned as a spy and a used woman. I grew up on the streets and in orphanages until someone sponsored me to come here."

Margie swallowed. The story was told without emotion. Not something Sadiq was outraged about. Just the story of his life. How he had come to be there.

It was a fact of life in the Sudan. He and Abdul had both suffered loss and privation at an early age. It had affected them, caused changes to their brains. Maybe long-lasting. Maybe permanent.

She looked back at Abdul.

"You said that at ten, you were too young to fight. Did you become a fighter before you were rescued?"

Abdul stared down at his hands. "Yes."

"You were forced to fight?" She thought of the pictures she had seen on the internet. Children cradling submachine guns. Empty eyes. Blank faces.

"They did not force me," Abdul disagreed. "It was… what we were there to do. We had to defend our country. Our honor. It was our duty. We were glad to do it."

"You killed people."

"In a war, people die," he said flatly.

"I know… but in most wars, children are not recruited to do the killing."

He shrugged. "That is the way it was where I come from."

Margie moved on. Abdul was not responsible for what he had done in the Sudan. They put a gun in his hands and trained him to use it. Even if he had joined the battalion voluntarily, he was not the one who was responsible for those deaths. The adults who recruited and trained him were the ones at fault.

"Do you like it here in Canada?"

He smiled, showing teeth. "Oh, yes. It is a beautiful country. And no war."

"You like school?"

"Yes."

Margie looked at Sadiq. She wondered if he would stop her. It didn't seem like he would. He didn't know what the laws were in Canada or how to react like a typical Canadian parent.

"Do you get scared?" she asked Abdul.

Abdul considered the question. He nodded slowly, looking down at his hands. "Sometimes."

"I was with my grandfather yesterday. When there was a big bang and people yelling, he grabbed a knife from the table. When he was a child, he was often beaten. I don't know what else happened to him. But he was afraid. He grabbed the closest thing he could use as a weapon to protect himself."

"That is good," Abdul said with a nod. "You must protect yourself. Even an old man."

"Or a child?"

"Yes."

"Do you carry a knife to protect yourself?"

"Yes."

He turned his head, looking at her with those guileless, open eyes. Why would he feel guilty for carrying a knife? Why would he think it was wrong? He had been trained. He knew he had to protect himself. For most of his life, no one else had protected him.

"Can I see it, please?"

Abdul reached into the large pocket of his hoodie and drew it out. Not just a jackknife like she might find at a department store or Scout shop. It caught the light as he held it out to her.

A folding combat knife.

Just like a soldier would carry.

CHAPTER FOURTEEN

Margie quickly pulled a glove on over her hand and took the knife from Abdul. She didn't open it. She already knew everything she needed to. It fit the description of the kind of blade that had killed Robinson. Even if he had cleaned it well, it might still have microscopic spots of blood left on it, perhaps in the hinge. Cruz provided an evidence bag and Margie slid the knife into it.

"How did Mr. Robinson scare you?" she asked Abdul softly.

"I was walking in the trees. It helps me, walking where there are lots of trees. Alone, away from all of the people. I like Calgary, where I can live close to the park."

Margie made an encouraging noise.

"He grabbed me and yelled at me. I didn't know what he was going to do, why he was attacking me. I was just walking in the trees." Abdul blinked a few times, thinking back. Replaying it in his mind. "I don't know what happened. He did not have a weapon. I thought he would have a gun." He shook his head, trying to make sense of it. "But he died. He fell on the ground."

"Did you try to help him? To stop the bleeding?"

"No."

"Did you try to talk to anyone else? To get the police or ambulance here to help him?"

"No."

"You should have."

"I didn't want them to find me. I didn't know if there were others—soldiers who had guns. I went back home. No one followed me. I went to bed."

"Did you tell Sadiq what had happened?"

"No."

Sadiq shook his head to confirm the point. "I did not know."

"Did you know he carried a knife?"

"No."

"Abdul, you're going to need to come with us."

Abdul looked down at the floor, sighing. "Am I going to prison?"

Margie's eyes were hot, and there was a lump in her throat as she helped Abdul to his feet and closed cuffs over his stick-thin wrists. "I don't know what's going to happen, Abdul. We're going to tell the authorities what happened. If it was up to me…" Margie trailed off.

What would she do if it were up to her?

What was the appropriate consequence for what Abdul had done?

How could they do him justice and still protect others from him?

CHAPTER FIFTEEN

Margie and Cruz relayed the developments to the rest of the team, gathered together in the briefing room.

"Robinson was probably telling him to stay on the pathway or to follow some other real or assumed park rule," Margie suggested. "Abdul doesn't even know what he said. Just that Robinson grabbed him and was yelling at him for something. I guess… he had a flashback or reacted instinctively, and before he knew what he had done, Robinson was dead on the ground."

"He's got to be a psychopath," Jones said, shaking her head. "I was there when you talked to him the first time. I heard him say that nothing out of the ordinary happened at the park that night. I saw his eyes… there were no tells. Nothing to indicate that he was lying or avoiding anything."

"I think… he didn't act guilty because he doesn't feel guilty about it," Margie said uncomfortably. "Not because he's a psychopath, but because that's how he's been trained and conditioned. He lived in an environment where he had to kill or be killed. Sadiq said he went through retraining, but clearly he hasn't made the transition. Whether he ever can or not, I don't know, but he doesn't live in our world. A world where you expect to get through the day without any violence, without someone attacking or trying to kill you. Robinson attacked, he defended himself, and he survived. That makes it a good day."

"He's not going to get off of murder charges because he has a troubled past," Cruz said. "He's going to go away, and they're not going to let him out for a long time."

Margie knew Canada's laws, though. At fourteen, it was highly unlikely Abdul would be sentenced as an adult. Especially not without any kind of connection to Robinson or evidence of premeditation. For a young person, the maximum sentence for first-degree murder was ten years, and for manslaughter was likely to be far less. The judge would recommend a rehabilitation program before he would be reintegrated into his community.

That was humane and wasn't designed to punish him, but to help him. But he had already been through a rehabilitation program when he had been rescued from the Children's Battalion. Would Canada's efforts be any more effective in helping him to become a normal, contributing member of society and no longer a threat to others?

All too soon, he would be back at school with other children, walking free on the streets and trails again. Was there hope that he would understand the seriousness of taking a life in Canadian society and no longer be a threat to anyone else?

She closed her eyes and said a prayer in her head for Abdul. And for those he would touch in the future.

EPILOGUE

Over coffee, he read the article in the online paper one more time, studying Detective Marguerite Patenaude's picture in the paper and rereading the few sentences that described the homicide Detective Pat was credited with solving. There were few details because of the involvement of a young offender who, of course, could not be named or identified. But there was enough there for him to understand what had happened.

Within days of moving into Calgary, Detective Pat had already solved her first murder. She thought she was so smart. She thought that she, as an affirmative action hire, could just waltz in and show everybody up.

He put his mug in the sink and filled it with water. Then he got into his car and drove to the house where Detective Pat lived with her teenage daughter. He parked across the street and gazed at the house. She had no idea what it was like to be him. She thought she lived in his world now, but she didn't. She could turn around and go right back where she had come from.

He had plans for their Detective Pat.

He would see how she handled the next case.

FISH CREEK PROVINCIAL PARK

Fish Creek Provincial Park was established in the Fish Creek valley in southern Calgary in 1975 and is the second largest urban park in Canada, featuring over 100 km of trails for walking, running, and biking.

It offers Sikome lake, a man-made lake, for swimming. Boating and fishing is permitted on the Bow River and Fish Creek. There is an environmental learning center, a visitor center, aquatic center, and day use picnicking areas.

Most of the park remains in its natural forested state.

The Friends of Fish Creek Provincial Park Society is a non-profit, volunteer-run organization which helps to provide visitor services and many essential functions around the park.

AUTHOR NOTE

The last residential school in Canada closed its doors in 1996. The effects of the abuses perpetrated in these prisons impacted thousands and continues to affect the Indigenous community today.

On May 27, 2021, the Tk'emlups te Secwepemc First Nation announced the discovery of unmarked graves containing 215 children who had been residents of the Kamloops Indian Residential School using ground-penetrating radar. This was not an isolated incident, but part of a larger genocide that took place all across Canada. Other discoveries have been made and the tragic histories of the 139 residential schools that operated in Canada need to be exposed.

The Truth and Reconciliation Commission's final report in 2012 made specific calls to action with regard to missing children and burial information which have not been honored.

How the government of Canada responds to this discovery and makes good on their many promises made to Indigenous peoples remains to be seen.

I have been concerned for a number of years about the intergenerational trauma caused by residential schools, living conditions on reservations, and

AUTHOR NOTE

discrimination faced by the Indigenous peoples in this land, and have written about some of these issues previously in *Questing for a Dream*. It is my hope that my writing can raise awareness and educate readers on both the history and the current conditions of those who have lived these experiences.

If you are also concerned about these harms, I would encourage you to write to your MP (if you are Canadian), encouraging the federal government to follow through on the calls to action made by the Truth and Reconciliation Commission and the promises they have previously made with regard to such things as clean water, medical care, and keeping Indigenous families together.

You can also make a donation to a charity that benefits residential school survivors, such as the Indian Residential School Survivors Society.

In the Sudan and many other countries in the world, children are recruited to fight in wars and rebellions. UNICEF, United Nations, and others are working hard to put an end to these practices and to rescue and re-educate children who have been harmed by this practice. Many children have been rehabilitated and live happy, productive lives away from the wars.

For a first-person account of what it is like to be a child soldier, I recommend reading *A Long Way Gone,* the account of Ishmael Beah's experience in Sierra Leone.

LONG CLIMB TO THE TOP

PARKS PAT MYSTERIES #2

*To those who are
leaving legacies*

CHAPTER ONE

Margie Patenaude didn't need to be a detective to know who had left the dirty dishes in the sink.

"Christina!"

"Gotta go, Mom," Christina said, rushing into the room. She swept her long black hair out of the way as she shouldered her backpack so that it would not get caught under the strap. "The bus will be here any second. I'll see you after school." She headed toward the front door. "Oh, and you remember what I told you, right, about the Métis Club meeting after school today? So I'll be late. Don't expect me right after school."

"You left dishes in the sink—"

"I have to go. If I stop and do them now, I'll miss the bus, and then you'll need to drive me to school." Christina had the door open and was halfway out. "Sorry. I'll load the dishwasher tonight. Okay? Bye!"

Margie watched her fifteen-year-old race across the street to the bus stop. And she was right, of course; the bus was making its way down the street, and if she had taken an extra ten seconds to have a conversation or rinse off the dishes, she would have missed it. But that was no excuse for Christina to leave them in the sink in the first place, when she knew she was supposed to rinse them and put them directly into the dishwasher.

She sighed and did it herself. She had to drive into work, and the other homicide detectives and Sergeant MacDonald wouldn't know whether she had left five minutes later because of her daughter or if she had just hit the lights wrong or run into a traffic snarl on Blackfoot Trail. She checked the table and counter for any other orphaned dishes and didn't find any. In another minute, she had the dishwasher running, Stella was settled for the day, and Margie was walking at a quick clip out to her car. It was a cool, crisp morning.

"Oh, Detective Pat!" called Mrs. Rose, a sweet little old lady who was the first and only owner of the 1960s bungalow next to Margie's.

Margie stopped, anxious to get on her way but not willing to be rude or pretend that she hadn't heard Mrs. Rose's call. She took a couple of steps toward her neighbor, but stopped the prescribed two meters away. "Yes, Mrs. Rose? What can I do for you?"

"I just wanted to make sure that you had heard that the 55+ Society is open again."

Margie's expression must have betrayed her consternation at this announcement. Mrs. Rose smiled her sweet, pink-lipstick smile. "The 55+ Society. It's over there on Twenty-Sixth Avenue, where your grandfather lives."

"Oh, yes…?"

"And it's been closed since the whole pandemic thing. But they've opened up again. And they have lots of programs for the seniors in the area. You should take a look at the activities and clubs that they run, see if there is anything that your grandfather would like to go to."

"Oh! Okay, I will," Margie agreed. She would see if there were anything that might interest Moushoom. "Thank you for letting me know."

"They probably have flyers in the lobby of the building he lives in. But if they don't, the 55+ Society is just about a block away. You can stop in there any time they are open and get their program guide. And they can give you a tour. They're very helpful over there."

"That's great. I'm glad you let me know." Margie gave Mrs. Rose a firm nod, then turned back toward her car. "Have a wonderful day."

"I will, dear. You too."

※

THE WORKDAY PASSED QUICKLY. The homicide team was working on a number of open cases, but none of them was burning hot. It was a matter of chasing down leads one at a time. Doing background checks on persons of interest, interviewing them, looking for connections or alibis. The day-to-day work of a homicide department.

She found it easier to move from one case to another than to stay focused on one all day, so she gathered shorter tasks from the primary investigator on each of the cases, read the file to bring herself up to speed, and worked on her assignment. Then she would jump to the next case.

No one on the team seemed to mind her ADHD approach. They were happy to have some of the less-desirable tasks taken off of their hands. Margie was eyeing the clock, trying to decide whether she would have time to review one more case before leaving for the day when Sergeant MacDonald—Mac—walked up to her desk. He was a tall man, towering over her when she was sitting down. His hair was almost entirely silver and he had lines of 'experience' around his mouth. He readjusted his thin-rimmed glasses.

"Yes, sir?" Margie immediately tried to think of what she might have done to attract his attention. Good or bad, she didn't want to be under the sergeant's scrutiny too often. Too much praise from him and the rest of the team would resent her, and too much criticism… well, any criticism was likely to keep Margie up half the night with anxiety over her mistake and how to avoid making it again in the future. No one liked being criticized, and Margie felt that she was particularly thin-skinned about it. She criticized herself for not accepting criticism well. How was that for a fault?

"I've got a case for you. I know you like to be home when your daughter gets home from school, but this one is going to need your immediate attention."

The duty room was still as everyone else listened in. Margie had just solved the Fish Creek Park murder case. The next case should have gone to someone else. Although everyone else already had active files and Margie did not, so maybe that was why he had picked her.

"Uh, yes sir. She's going to be later today and, of course, when it's urgent, I can take the time I need to get started on it. She's old enough to be on her own for a few hours if I'm needed elsewhere."

She didn't ask him what he had for her but, of course, that was the question on the minds of everyone in the room.

Mac nodded his appreciation. He ran his fingers through his short gray hair and leaned on her desk. "Here's the thing. It's the same MO as the Fish Creek Park murder."

Margie's eyes went wide. She stared at him in surprise. "The same MO?"

Robinson had been killed with a single stab wound. Margie had caught the killer. So they knew that it wasn't the same killer. Just because another person was killed by a stab wound, that didn't make it the same killer or the same case.

"The same MO," MacDonald agreed. "It's another provincial park. Male victim. Single stab wound with a single-edged blade. Bled out. No apparent provocation, no one heard yelling or was aware that anything was wrong. Body discovered by a family walking the trail with a toddler in a stroller."

Not a dog-walker this time. But Margie was sure there were probably a number of dog-walkers close by. That one difference didn't make the case different from the Fish Creek murder.

She hoped that the toddler hadn't seen anything and wasn't old enough to remember it later. Hopefully, she had been sleeping peacefully in the stroller at the time. It was a good time for an afternoon nap.

"Okay. I'll look up this park and go see," Margie agreed. "Is it near Fish Creek Park?"

"No. Halfway to Cochrane. It's actually outside of Calgary city limits, but we are heading it up because of the connection to the Fish Creek case. Since it looks like the same killer."

"It's not, though," Margie pointed out.

"There's always the possibility that we got the wrong person for the Fish Creek murder."

"But he admitted to it. We didn't get the wrong person."

"I don't think so either. But innocent people do confess. It's also possible that he was released on bail or under his foster father's supervision and is no longer in custody."

"But if this other park isn't close to his home… how would he get there? He couldn't walk there like he did to Fish Creek. Is there a bus that goes all the way out there?"

"No, I don't think there's any bus service out there. Tours maybe. I'm sure it's not related. But because of the similarity in the cases and the sites of the homicide, it's your case."

"Okay. Give me the details." Margie looked at her watch. If she remembered correctly, Cochrane was west, toward the mountains. Margie's home was in the east, on the opposite side of the city. She was going to be more than an hour or two late getting home for Christina. Just the travel time would add an extra hour, forget any investigative work and waiting for someone from the medical examiner's office.

"Glenbow Ranch Provincial Park," Sergeant MacDonald told her. He spelled it out for her. "Do you want directions?"

"Will it be on my GPS? If it's outside of the city, it might not be…"

"Should be. It opened in 2011, so it's been there long enough".

CHAPTER TWO

Margie hit the road, driving west down Crowchild Trail. Rush hour appeared to have already hit and both Memorial Drive and Crowchild Trail were heavy with traffic. Progress was slow, which meant she would be all that much later getting home to Christina. She couldn't rush things at the murder scene. It would take time to process the scene. That was just the way it was. She used her Bluetooth to send a message to Christina, giving her an update and asking her to let Margie know when she was home.

There were several C-Train stations down the middle of Crowchild, and the trains ran past her every few minutes. They were packed with people. Despite the pandemic and all of the new protocols to follow, a lot of people were back to working downtown, and they all needed to get home to the outlying areas. She glanced as another train went by. Most people were masked, in compliance with the by-law recently put into place mandating masks in public places and the transit system in particular. Infection numbers were down, and she hoped that they stayed low despite the reopening of the schools.

Over to her right, there was a big white temple spire with a gold figure on top. The speed of the traffic was picking up, so she couldn't gawk at it for long, but it was pretty. A surprise to see something like that at the edge of the city. In another minute, she had reached city limits and Crowchild Trail had turned into Highway 1A.

There were rolling hills, but not a lot of trees like she had expected to see. She remembered how thickly Fish Creek Park had been treed and had expected the same type of scenery. There were fields and farmyards and small stands of trees here and there.

After a while, the GPS warned her to get into the left lane, and Margie obeyed, though she couldn't see any sign of the park. It seemed strange to have a park all the way out there. They wouldn't get foot traffic like Fish Creek Park did. A road sign announced that Glenbow Park was three kilometers away, but the GPS urged her to turn immediately. She watched for a break in the oncoming traffic and turned left onto a gravel road. Once on the gravel road, there were a few houses off to the left and thick trees to the right. The gravel road was on an incline, down into a valley. Margie slowed down and took the gravel and the curves in the road carefully.

Zipping down them like it was an emergency wouldn't do her any good. She couldn't save the man who was already dead, and if she ended up with her car in the ditch, it was just going to take that much longer to get done. Not to mention the reputation she would get. Detectives often ended up with nicknames within the department, and she did not want to be "Ditch" Patenaude.

It was farther than she would have expected. There was a public parking area, but Margie saw a gray-shirted officer standing up by a locked gate, watching the incoming traffic. She drove up to him. He bent down to talk through her window. He wasn't wearing a mask, and Margie pulled back, a little irritated that he would get so close to her.

"Are you the detective?" he asked. "Uh, Detective Pat?"

"Patenaude," Margie agreed. "That's me."

"Come on through, and drive down to the parking area beside the house." He pointed in the direction of a big ranch house. "I'll walk down to you after I lock up here."

Margie waited while he swung the big gate open, then drove down to the lot he had pointed to. The house had perhaps been someone's home before the creation of the park. It had the feel of a family home rather than a conference or education center built by the government.

Margie put on her mask and got out and stretched, looking around. After the golden brown grass on the fields and hills up above, she had expected a stark setting. But down in the valley, there was lush green growth—lots of trees, long grass, and wildflowers. Bees buzzed around her and orange butterflies fluttered here and there. Despite being the site of a murder, everything seemed peaceful and pleasant.

The Conservation Officer who had let her in the gate walked down to her. "Is this your first time in the park?"

"Yes. I'm just new to Calgary. So I've seen Fish Creek Park, but that's about it. I guess you heard about that."

"Yeah. It was in the news and as soon as we came across the body here... well, it was just too similar to ignore. We called the RCMP; it's their jurisdiction, but they looped your department in right away. You're the one with the deep knowledge on the Fish Creek case, so you get control."

"Is the RCMP already here?"

"They sent a couple of guys out. Our Conservation Officers controlled the scene. Just waiting on you."

"How about the forensic team and the medical examiner? Have they been notified?"

"Notified, but not here yet. It takes a while to get out here, as I'm sure you found." He looked at his watch. "An hour since we called you. And it's rush hour."

Margie nodded. "Okay, thanks. So, where is your body? I gather it's not in the house?" She tilted her head toward it.

"No. We all manage to get along pretty well in the Park Office." He gave her a roguish grin. "No murders there yet."

Margie smiled.

"I'm CO Richardson." He put out his hand to shake.

Margie shook her head. "Sorry, no unnecessary contact," she apologized. He should have known that. The police force, by the nature of their contact with the public at large, were already at higher risk of infection. She didn't want to be out of work due to a virus or quarantine, or to inadvertently pass something on to Moushoom, who was vulnerable due to his age.

Richardson rolled his eyes and lowered his hand. "If you'll come with me, I will take you to the scene."

Margie nodded. She got out of the car. "How far is it? I can walk a ways..."

At Fish Creek Park, the murder site had been too far from the parking lot for her to comfortably walk there to investigate. She hoped that the distance would be shorter at Glenbow.

"We have almost forty kilometers of trails. The body is only a couple of clicks away, but if you want to get home to your family tonight..." He looked at his watch. Margie was sure he wanted to get back to his regular duties as well, or to sign off at the end of his day. A murder scene might be an exciting novelty, but preserving the scene and dealing with curious visitors would be a pain. And it got dark early this late in the year. Everyone would want to have the scene cleared before it was too dark to see.

"Lead the way," Margie sighed. "One of these days, I'm going to have to come explore some of these parks for recreation instead of a murder investigation."

"You like to walk?"

"Yes, I do. I'd like to do more. There are some multi-use trails near my house, but so far, all I've been able to do is walk the dog on the closest ones."

"Where do you live?"

"In the southeast." Margie knew enough now not to mention that it was close to Forest Lawn or part of Greater Forest Lawn. She didn't think that the area warranted the reputation it seemed to have all over the city. "Near Pearce Estate Park, if you know where that one is?"

"Oh, sure. Harvie Passage is over there. Where the weir used to be."

Margie shrugged, not sure of any of this. Richardson correctly interpreted her reaction.

"The weir was there for a lot of years. People would go boating or fishing over there, or swim or fall in, and they would get killed in the weir, because of the way that the water going over the weir would create a circular flow." He twirled a finger horizontally to demonstrate. "Getting caught in it would just keep spinning you over and over, like being stuck in a washing machine."

"Oh."

"So eventually, they built out a series of rapids to replace the weir. They take rafters down the river in a series of steps so it is not so dangerous. It took a few tries to get it right, but it's all in place now, much better than it was. It's named the Harvie Passage, after the same family as used to live here," he pointed to the ranch house as he led her to the garage, "the same family as donated the lands for the park."

"Wow. A pretty philanthropic family."

"They are," he agreed. "There are a lot of things named after them and after Glenbow in and around Calgary. You'll come across a lot of them. The Glenbow Museum. The Dorothy Harvie Gardens. The Glenbow Park Ranch Foundation was set up by the family and shares this building with Alberta Parks. The foundation runs the Visitor Center, other park education and programming, and various other projects."

He used a keypad to let himself into the garage and directed Margie to one of the golf carts waiting there. "We'll drive over in this."

In a few minutes, they were driving slowly down the pathway, working their way past the walkers, runners, and cyclists enjoying an afternoon at the park. It was a more open area with little shade, and she could see the rolling vistas. She could see mountains on the horizon, under bright blue sky and washboard clouds. She turned her head to look back toward the city. She could see the downtown skyline in the other direction.

"Do you like the water?" Richardson asked.

"Water?"

"Just wondered if you would be interested in rafting down the Harvie Passage. Since you live close to it. People often don't take advantage of the facilities that are closest to them."

"Me... no, I'm not really interested in boating or watersports. I know the Canoe Club is close too, just off of the trails where I walk Stella. But I don't think I'll be taking any lessons."

He gave her a look, then nodded and continued to navigate around the many park walkers. It had been a cool day, and Margie was surprised that there were so many people out in the park. But apparently, they knew enough to dress in layers and be prepared for changes in the weather. Calgary was notorious for its changeable weather. Margie thought she had seen flakes of snow that morning when she took Stella out. It seemed awfully early in the year for snow, and she hoped that winter would hold off for another month or two.

She could see the pale blue river off to her left as they drove through the hills. Margie thought they were traveling roughly west.

"That's the Bow," Richardson said, nodding to the river. "Same river as goes past Pearce Estate Park. And Fish Creek Park, for that matter."

Margie imagined boating all the way from Glenbow Ranch Park, though the city, out to Fish Creek Park. It made her a little queasy thinking about it. All of that water rushing downstream. The picture that Richardson had put into her mind of a body tumbling over and over at the old weir. Her throat felt like it would close up just thinking of all of that water over her head.

"You don't think this murder is related to the body out at Fish Creek Park, do you?" Richardson inquired.

"No. We caught the killer in that case. I don't think it's related in any way, other than the fact that the body was discovered in a park."

"And he was stabbed."

"Right. But that's not particularly unique. Lots of people get stabbed."

He nodded in agreement. "True."

They started going uphill again, into an area more heavily treed. The pathway was narrower and gravel rather than paved. "This is part of Tiger Lily Loop. A short loop. Nice for families. You avoid the steep hill that you need to use to get to the rest of the park."

It was still pretty hilly. Margie studied the landforms and vegetation with interest and looked up to the sky to watch birds wheeling around them.

"If you're lucky, you could see our osprey. It's quite something to see them diving into the water for fish."

"Wow, yes. What other kinds of animals do you have out here?"

She was glad that the dead body was, as far as anyone had said, a fresh kill, and had not been subject to predation. There must be some large predators in the park, considering its size.

"Plenty of different birds and insects. There are bee and bird counting programs. Ground squirrels—you know, gophers. Badgers. Coyotes. Porcupines. Mule deer. You'll see the cattle; they still graze the park lands as part of the vegetation management program. There is an occasional bear sighting and we are on the lookout for cougar. But there haven't ever been any attacks on humans. The animals will do their best to avoid people and dogs."

Margie hung on as the cart climbed a steeper part of the trail. They were into the shadows of the trees and there were fewer hikers around.

Then they reached the yellow tape. Richardson hit the brakes and parked the cart. "Here we go."

Margie climbed out. There were a couple of conservation officers and RCMP uniforms. Margie nodded at the nearest RCMP officer. He was wearing a gray shirt similar to the conservation officers', with a tactical vest.

"Detective Pat?"

"Yes."

"Good to see you. I'm Sergeant Shack. You've been briefed?"

"I don't know much, other than the fact that there was a stabbing victim, similar to the Fish Creek murder that we just put away."

He nodded. "Not many details to give you at this point. You want to come have a look?"

"That's what I'm here for."

She stopped to put on protective gear to keep her from contaminating the crime scene, and they worked their way around the perimeter of the tape rather than through the middle. Margie took each step carefully, eyes alert for anything that might be evidence, even outside the tape. Then they ducked under the tape and moved toward the center of the cordoned-off area.

"Male, mid to late thirties," Shack said. "Doesn't appear to be robbery. No sign of a fight, no one has come forward who witnessed an argument or violence between the victim and someone else."

Margie nodded. Similar to the Fish Creek murder. She studied the body. The man was on his back so she could see the location of the stab wound. "I might be wrong, but I think the point of entry is a bit higher than the one in Fish Creek," she said. She leaned closer to get a better look at the body without touching it or compromising anything else at the scene. "Hard to judge his height and the angle of entry from this position."

"Your suspect in the Fish Creek case..."

She raised her brows at Shack. "Yes?"

"It was a juvenile offender?"

"Yeah. Tall for a fourteen-year-old, but still not an adult. How long ago, do you think?" Margie had nitrile gloves on. She touched the man's wrist to gauge his temperature. She couldn't feel any warmth through the thin layer of protection. It hadn't just happened. But she knew it had been over an hour since the Calgary police had been called in. Presumably, it had taken some time to sort out who should be involved in the investigation, and the family with the toddler had not reported seeing or hearing any violence, so the body had probably been lying there for some time before they saw him.

"Medical examiner will give us a better idea," Shack said. "I'm not sure yet. There's no predation or significant insect activity, so probably not long. It's close enough to the trail that you would think someone would have noticed him within a couple of hours."

"Definitely today."

"Oh yeah. Maybe early morning, but I'd be more inclined to think that it happened while the park was open. The conservation officers are pretty good at keeping people off of the park until it opens. You can't catch everybody, of course, but there's only one public lot, and not many people hike in."

Margie looked back in the direction of Calgary. "That would be quite a hike."

"Pretty impossible to come in from Calgary, actually. You need to take the highway, because there's no trail access through Haskayne Park yet. Eventually, there will be, but for the moment, Glenbow is cut off from the Calgary trail system." He pointed the other direction. "Cochrane, on the other hand, is only a couple of clicks away, and there are some pathways into the park from there."

Margie pulled out her notebook and made a couple of notes. "And those pathways would not be patrolled."

"Not likely. Checked now and then, but the CO's are going to be focusing on the public parking area."

Margie looked around. "How many people come through this trail during the day?" It seemed unlikely that a murder had been committed while people walked by on the trail. It would take a pretty bold murderer.

"You'll have to get those details from the CO's. They might have some video footage too. But it's not busy. You can often walk this area and only see a few other visitors. It's relatively remote."

"The family that found him, are they still around?"

"They had a kid. Couldn't stay around for long, but they left their information. You can call or go see them."

Shack pulled out his notebook and relayed the contact information he had taken down from the witnesses. Margie wrote it in her own book.

"Did the child see…?"

"No. I don't think so. Didn't seem to be upset about anything except having to sit around while the grown-ups talked instead of exploring."

"Good. You always worry about trauma."

"If she saw him, she probably didn't understand what was going on. Just that someone was sleeping in the grass." Shack looked at the body. "I mean, it's not horrific."

"No. You're right." Margie could make out the hole that the knife had made and the darker areas of the shirt where blood had soaked into it. No pools of red blood or gore.

They could hear a vehicle approaching and all turned to look for it. In a few moments, a white van came into view.

"Medical Examiner's office," Margie observed. "Hopefully, they'll have a few answers for us."

CHAPTER THREE

Suited up and masked, Dr. Kahn from the Medical Examiner's office took a cursory look at the body, then looked at Sergeant Shack and Margie.

"Whose scene is it?"

"Calgary's," Margie said. "That's me."

"Okay. Nobody's touched the body?"

"I touched his wrist. Gloves on. Conservation officers and RCMP were here before me."

Shack took a few minutes to run through the steps since the body had been discovered with Dr. Kahn to establish the integrity of the scene. Kahn went through the motions of checking the body for any vital signs.

"Body is in rigor," he observed. "No pulse or respiration. Cool to the touch. I'll take ambient and liver temps. Looks like he's been here for a few hours."

Margie nodded. They would narrow it down more once the medical examiner had run through all of the usual protocols. And perhaps there would be video, like there had been at Fish Creek Park, to establish the time that the victim had arrived on the trail.

"Is there any identification on the body?"

Dr. Kahn took a brief look at the stab wound before moving the man's clothing and feeling for a wallet. It was there in a zipped jacket pocket.

Kahn passed it across to Margie. She examined it closely before opening it, looking for any trace that they needed to preserve. Then she opened it, keeping her gloved fingers on the very edges.

"David Smith."

"Well, great," Shack grumbled. "There are only a few hundred of those in Alberta."

"He's got a driver's license, so we have his address and date of birth." Viewing the card through the display window, Margie calculated the date in her head. "Age thirty-eight." She looked at the edges of the cards that peeked above the card slots. "Looks like Visa, Air Miles, Bank of Montreal access card, and AMA."

She displayed them to Shack, and he nodded his agreement. Margie didn't pull any of them out, and didn't pull out the plastic card accordion file she could see tucked into the next section. The forensic team would want to handle those, check for fingerprints and any other trace evidence.

Margie thumbed the cash section open to see a couple of bills. Blue and purple. "Fifteen dollars in cash."

She took an evidence bag from her shoulder bag and put the wallet into it. "Anything else in his pockets? Keys? Business cards? A list of people who might want to kill him?"

Shack snorted in amusement. Dr. Kahn didn't crack a smile. "Keys. Water bottle. Phone."

"Is there phone service coverage out here?"

"From my experience, yes, most of the park has coverage," Shack advised. "The exception being a blind spot as you get to the top of Glenbow Road. That's the gravel road you drove in on. Right at the top where you'd expect the coverage to be the strongest, it completely cuts out."

"Weird. Just today, or all the time?"

"As long as I've been coming here."

"Do you come here a lot?"

"Yeah. A couple of times a month, usually. I like to walk, take pictures."

"That's nice. You must live close."

He didn't answer at first, but when Margie kept looking at him, eyebrows raised, he realized that she expected an answer and it hadn't just been rhetorical. "Uh, yes. I'm just over in Tuscany."

"I'm new to Alberta. Is that in Cochrane or Calgary?"

"Calgary. West side. Did you see the Mormon temple as you drove out? White spire with an angel on top."

"Yes."

"When that's on your right, Tuscany is on your left."

"Oh, okay. That is nice and close. I'm not sure, but I'm thinking it's going to take me an hour to get home from here."

"I probably wouldn't be coming every week or two if I was that far away. Especially city driving." He gave a shudder. "I'm a country boy at heart. Southern Alberta farmland."

"Is that like this? Or prairie?"

"Prairie. Definitely. You can grow some crops around here. You'll see a couple of fields across the river growing canola or other crops. But it's hilly, so mostly this is ranching country—cows—rather than food crops."

"I'm from Manitoba."

"Ah, so you're used to flat. Yeah. Southern Alberta is more like that. Glenbow is mostly riparian. River and foothills."

❧

THE SUN WAS GETTING low in the sky by the time David Smith's body was loaded into the medical examiner's van and the forensic tech had finished going over the ground with a fine-toothed comb looking for any possible evidence in the case.

"There isn't a lot to find," a technician named Joe said apologetically. "Looks pretty clean. The ground hasn't been trampled. There isn't any litter. It's a stab wound rather than a gun, so there aren't any shell casings to look for. No sign of the weapon here. The killer must have taken it with him."

Margie remembered Abdul, the killer in the Fish Creek case, casually pulling a hunting knife out of his hoodie pocket when asked about it. It had been cleaned and well-maintained, but they had been able to find traces of blood in the hinges and in the hoodie itself. No matter what anyone said, she knew that Abdul could not have been David Smith's killer, and that he had been Jerry Robinson's killer. There hadn't been a DNA match on the blood evidence yet, but there was blood on the knife. Abdul had not just confessed to murder for attention. The confession had not been coerced. He reacted as he'd been trained to, killing the man who had confronted him in the park. He thought it a perfectly natural reaction and the only way to protect himself from possible violence.

Darkness started to gather, the chill in the air deepening. The medical examiner's van was gone. The forensics team was gone. She and Shack and the others who were still there removed the yellow tape perimeter, looking one last time for anything that might have been missed. None of them found anything.

"You'll check for video evidence and send it on to me?" Margie asked Richardson, continuing the conversation they'd been having while the forensic experts were combing the ground for any other evidence. "Parking lot, trail cams, wildlife cams, whatever you've got. You never know how it might be helpful."

"Sure," Richardson agreed. "We'll go through it in the morning, make sure you get a copy."

Margie kept her mouth shut and didn't tell him that he needed to get it to her that night, and not wait until morning. But what did it matter? She wasn't going to look at it until morning anyway. As long as he got it to her, she didn't have anything to complain about.

He gave her an amused look, and Margie suspected that her irritation had been clear even with her face mask. Sometimes her emotions were too transparent.

CHAPTER FOUR

Margie's estimate that it would take her an hour to get home from Glenbow Park had not been far off. She followed her GPS directions, which seemed to take her all the way around the north end of the city. But the speed limit was mostly one hundred and there was no significant traffic, so she really couldn't complain about the route it had selected.

She paused for a moment before unlocking the front door. She did her best to mentally push the homicide aside, walling off all of her questions and theories. Tomorrow would come soon enough and she didn't want to be crabby with Christina or to bring her down with her own mood. She took a couple of controlled breaths, then turned the key in the lock and opened the door.

"I'm home!"

There was a thunder of running feet, and Margie braced herself for the full weight of her dog, excited about seeing her after a long day apart.

"Who's a good girl? Were you a good girl? Were you good for Christina?" Margie scratched Stella's soft brown ears and kissed the top of her head, trying to calm the excited animal. "Such a good girl. Yes, you are."

Christina was at the kitchen table with her school books spread out around her, but she was on her phone rather than working studiously on her textbook and computer. She waved at Margie, but made no sign that she intended to break off the call.

Margie took another deep breath, reminding herself not to be impatient with her teenager. She petted and scratched Stella some more, then went to the fridge. She'd had a granola bar in the car, but otherwise had not had any supper. Not that there was very much in the fridge. She hadn't gotten into the habit of cooking. Things had been too disrupted since moving to Calgary. Getting everything unpacked and in order, registering Christina for school, visiting with Moushoom, solving the Fish Creek murder. It hadn't left much time to stock the fridge.

Christina shoved her books around on the table looking for something and came up with a half-package of fries from A&W, which she handed to Margie.

They were cold, but maybe they would give Margie the energy she needed to open a can of something. Margie smiled her thanks at Christina, pulling her mask off to make sure that Christina could see that her gift was appreciated. She squirted some ketchup on top of the fries and stood leaning against the counter. She nibbled the fries, checked her email using her phone, and waited for Christina to get off of her call. It sounded like she was talking to a school friend, but not about the homework scattered over the table.

That was okay. With the amount that Christina had complained about having to move to Calgary, and then how bad she had said things were at school, Margie would happily accept her daughter being distracted by a friendship for a bit.

After finishing the fries, she checked the fridge again, and then the freezer. There was ice cream. Fries and ice cream were not a healthy dinner, and she would never have let Christina get away with a meal like that, but she really didn't have the energy to make much else. She sliced a slightly-soft banana into a bowl—that was fruit, and fries were a vegetable serving—and then added a small scoop of ice cream. Dairy. And there was nothing wrong with a moderate amount of sugar. At least it wouldn't keep her up at night when she needed to sleep.

Christina finally got off of her call. She looked at Margie, brows raised. "Ice cream is not dinner."

"Do you want some?"

Christina laughed. "I already had some."

"I hope you at least had a burger to go with it."

"Veggie burger. Yeah."

"I'll be sure to take Stella out for a long walk. Burn off the extra calories."

"I already took her out. And it's dark; you said not to go out after dark."

Margie looked for an excuse why it was okay for her to do, but not for Christina. "Well… I don't know; it will still be dark in the morning if I take her out before work."

"Safer early in the morning than late at night."

"It's not that late yet."

Christina gazed at her.

"Fine," Margie sighed. "But I'm the one who's supposed to be parenting you, remember?"

"Grover says hi."

"Grover?"

"Whatever his name is. Oscar."

"Oh, Oscar." Oscar was a man in the neighborhood who often walked his dog Milo on the pathway when Margie and Christina walked Stella. "Well, hi back, the next time you see him."

CHAPTER FIVE

The video from the park wasn't in yet the next morning, so Margie checked the server to see what other evidence might have been processed by the medical examiner's office or forensics department. She would need to give a briefing on the Glenbow Park murder to the homicide team that morning, and so far there wasn't much to tell them. It might be a look-alike to the killing in Fish Creek, but the parallels were very general and could simply be a coincidence. How many people were normally stabbed in and around Calgary in a month?

Pictures of the contents of the wallet and the man's pockets had been posted to the workspace for the David Smith murder. She paged through them one at a time, looking at each of the cards and bits of paper in the wallet. It all seemed pretty routine. The usual bank and credit cards and customer loyalty cards. The cash that she had noted, a five and a ten. A scrap piece of paper with a woman's name and number on it. A photo of what looked like a high school, with kids in the distance. Maybe he had a kid in school. A club membership card and a rec club card. No sign of anything illegal or alarming.

The contents of his pockets were not much more enlightening. House and car keys. Loose change. Cough drops. Parking ticket stubs. The same type of stuff as she would expect anyone to have in their pockets.

She reviewed the pictures of the crime scene carefully, looking for anything that she hadn't noticed while she was there. There was no medical examiner's report yet, but she hadn't expected there to be. The body had been logged in, that was all.

Margie sighed. She went through her notes and thought through the various angles. They would need confirmation that it could not have been the same killer as the Fish Creek murder. She looked up the number for the Young Offender Center and gave them a call. Identifying herself as a law enforcement officer, she explained that she needed to know whether Abdul James was still in custody.

"Just a moment," the phone receptionist said politely. Margie could hear computer keys tapping rapidly, and then a pause while she waited for the results to display. "And the answer is… yes. Abdul James is still in custody."

"And you're sure he couldn't have been released or… wandered off. Sorry to be such a stickler about it, but sometimes these things do happen, and I need to reassure my investigative team that there is no way he could have been involved in this incident yesterday. No day release?"

The receptionist spent some more time looking through the records, tapping her keys briefly now and then. "No. I don't see anything. He's definitely still here and hasn't had any kind of day pass or work release. He hasn't even been out for court or medical care. Nothing that would have taken him out of the building."

"Good. That's very helpful, thank you."

By the time she got off the phone, she could see the others gathering in the briefing room for their morning "stand-up" meeting. Margie took her notes with her and joined them. Using the computer in the boardroom, she displayed a couple of pictures of the scene and the evidence on the big screen.

"How are things going?" asked Kaitlyn Jones, a blond, round-faced detective. "Were you very late getting home yesterday?"

"Later than I would have liked. But that's gonna happen when you have a murder. Couldn't very well leave it until today. Some coyote might have dragged off the body."

Jones's eyes widened. "Really?"

Margie laughed. "No, I think it would take several of them together, or a bear, to drag away a full-grown man. More likely they would just… eat in rather than take out."

Jones made a face. "Gross, Patenaude."

Margie knew that Jones had seen plenty of murder scenes, many of them more gruesome than an outdoor scene with animal scavenging. But she was still sensitive enough to be disgusted by Margie's suggestion. Or at least to pretend to be disgusted.

"So, anything helpful at the site?" Jones looked at the pictures on the screen.

"We'll go over that in a few minutes. But... not really. Nothing yet. And it was a pretty straightforward stabbing; I don't think they're going to find anything on the post."

Staff Sergeant MacDonald entered the room and everyone straightened up and stopped their conversations. Mac, a tall, gray-haired man with a military bearing, looked around to make sure that everyone expected was present.

"Good morning, all. Detective Patenaude, why don't you brief us on the new case?"

Margie nodded. She outlined the basics and indicated the pictures on the screen. There was little to tell them. "And I have checked with the Young Offender Center about Abdul James. He was definitely in custody all day yesterday and could not have been at Glenbow Park." She shrugged. "Not that I thought he had anything to do with this from the beginning."

"No," MacDonald agreed. "I don't think any of us did, but it is a little disconcerting to have two such similar cases so close together. Where do you plan to go next?"

"I'm waiting for video surveillance and the postmortem. Maybe those will help to narrow the investigation for us. We have his driver's license; I will start to track down his friends and family. Ask questions. See if he was dealing with someone in his life who might have done something like this."

MacDonald nodded. "I doubt that this was a random thing. It will be someone that he had regular contact with. An ex or his ex's new boyfriend. A family member. No sign of drugs or gang membership?"

"No. everything seems clean. And he has no record."

Margie looked around at the team for any other suggestions. But it was a reasonably straightforward stabbing. All she could do was go through the usual police work. Chances were, family and friends would have some idea of directions to look.

They went on to discuss other cases.

David Smith's girlfriend—actually his fiancée—was absolutely baffled by the suggestion that he might have been killed by someone he knew. She dabbed at her eyes and blew her nose repeatedly, trying to stay in control of her emotions as she answered Margie's questions. Cathy Lin was an Asian woman with delicate features, several years Smith's junior, with short hair that framed her face. Margie sat on the other side of the conference room table, as far away as she could and still feel like they were having an intimate conversation rather than shouting across the room at each other. She would have to disinfect everything before interviewing anyone else, with all of the tears and mucus…

"I don't know anyone who would want to hurt David." Cathy sniffled. "He didn't have any ongoing arguments with anyone. He didn't have an enemy or an unhappy ex. He was just… David. He was quiet, got along with people. He wasn't involved in drugs or gambling. None of that makes any sense."

"Please don't think that we're accusing him of anything," Margie said. "We're just exploring all of the possibilities. It is very rare that someone does something like this randomly. The victim is almost always known."

"But it still does happen randomly." Cathy sniffled. "There are still… mentally ill people who hear voices telling them to stab someone. It doesn't have to make sense."

"Of course it is possible, but most killers do not have diagnosed mental illness. Hallucinations commanding people to hurt others are very rare. That's why you hear so much about them when they do occur. Because they are novel. Something that doesn't happen every day. Of course we will be looking into the possibility. But it is more productive for us to look at David's life and figure out if someone targeted him. I know it's a shock, and I'm sorry that we have to talk to you about it right now, when your grief is so fresh."

"It's okay. I don't mind. It's just that… I can't think of anything that would help you. I can give you the names or numbers of his friends and family, but there is no way any of them had anything to do with this."

"Did David walk in the park a lot?"

"Yes, he liked the outdoors. He likes to walk and be in nature. Liked. It's calming. He would relax at the end of the day or get out there in the early morning."

"Did you ever go with him? Did he have any walking partners?"

"Sometimes I would go with him on a Sunday, when I had more time, but not usually during the week. I couldn't get out of bed that early, and I don't like walking while it is dark."

"Did he have other people he went with?"

"No. Sometimes when I would go with him, he would see people that he knew. You know, he would wave and say 'that's Ken' or whatever. They were regulars that he saw other times. Some people were in the park all the time, walking or volunteering, and they got to know each other by name. But they were just acquaintances. Not anyone that he brought home for dinner or went out for a beer with."

Margie nodded. She took a minute to make some random notes before pursuing her next question so that it wouldn't sound like an accusation. "He drank?"

"No. Not a lot. He would go out for a beer now and then. He wasn't an alcoholic. He never got drunk."

"And he never said anything to you about getting into a fight at the bar. An argument. Losing a darts game and someone got upset. Something that seemed overblown or that he was worried about."

Cathy took longer to think about it, really considering the question. Maybe she hoped to find an explanation that was simple and wouldn't point to anyone she knew. Something that made sense.

But she shook her head and dabbed at her eyes. "No. I don't remember him ever saying anything like that."

"Okay. If you think of anything, please let me know." Margie pressed one of her business cards into Cathy's thin, moist hand. "I'm so sorry for your loss."

CHAPTER SIX

Margie had dealt with enough grieving family members and friends for one day. She needed a break. Everyone had said the same thing anyway; they couldn't think of anyone that David Smith ever had a problem with. He was shy and kept to himself and was a genuinely nice guy. He enjoyed walking in the park and was recognized by many of the regular walkers there. No one knew of anyone he'd had an argument with, cut off in traffic, or beat out for a promotion at work. He hadn't stolen or slept with anyone's girlfriend. He didn't have a load of money put away that his next of kin would like to get their hands on.

They were all just grief-stricken and Margie really couldn't deal with it anymore.

She decided to learn more about the setting. Maybe what had happened to David Smith had to do with something that had occurred in the park. Perhaps Smith and his killer preferred their own company but had the same favorite place to sit and reflect. Maybe Smith had a memorial there for a family member and someone had disrespected it, or vice versa. People sometimes became possessive about places or about a certain set of rules being followed, even if it didn't make sense to an outsider.

She pulled up the Alberta Parks website and read through the details about how the park had been established by the Harvie family, following through on the legacy their father left, protecting his favorite place from encroachment by the city. There were facts on the names of the trails, the elevations, the hours of the Visitor Center.

Margie switched to a broader internet search to see what other information was available and found the Glenbow Ranch Park Foundation's site. There were a number of educational programs and opportunities being run. A review of the social media sites and image searches showed a wide variety of flora, fauna, landforms, and old buildings and equipment that could be found in the park. There was a book on the history of the land, *Grass, Hills, and History*. Margie thought it might be a good idea to get a copy for herself to see what the history of the place was.

There was always the possibility of a land dispute. Someone who thought that the land should belong to him. Or maybe Siksiká lands or sacred sites that had been taken away from them.

She looked through the pictures of the old houses, school, and other buildings that had once graced Glenbow in its glory days. There had been a thriving village, a sandstone quarry, and many other services at one time. Now it was all gone.

Margie read it all with interest. She saved some of the files to the case workspace to refer back to later. While there was the possibility of a land dispute, why would someone kill David Smith over it? He didn't have any claim over the park or the land. He wasn't misusing it, just taking walks out there. If someone had a dispute, it would be more logical to aim it at the provincial government or the Foundation, or even the Harvie family members. Not a random park visitor.

Unless David himself had a bone to pick with someone about it. But from what his family and friends had said, she didn't think that was very likely.

She came across a treasure hunters site which claimed there were Indigenous artifacts still in the park, that there was something of value from the old quarry, or that one of the old residents of "Millionaire Hill" had buried money somewhere on the grounds to keep it safe. Margie read the remainder of the page. Maybe somebody had thought that there was something of value there. It wasn't very likely, but people loved to believe unlikely stories. Especially when finding treasure was a possibility.

Had David Smith found something? Or said that he knew where some priceless artifact was? If he was always walking the park, then who was more likely to have an idea of the location of a treasure or artifact?

She jotted down some notes. It probably wasn't anything, but it was a nice diversion from talking to the grieving family and friends.

After consideration, she called the number of the Visitor Center. It was answered by a cheerful female voice offering to help.

"I don't know if you can help me." Margie identified herself. "I am working on the investigation of the... death out your direction. I was just reading some information online about the possibility of artifacts or treasures in the park. I don't suppose you would have any information on that, do you?"

"Well..." the voice on the other end of the phone was hesitant. "We consider the natural features of the park to be its treasures. The plants and animals, the landforms and viewscapes... it's all very important to us and brings joy to our visitors. You can't put a price on that."

"Of course." Margie couldn't help smiling. "But you know that's not what I'm talking about. Nobody killed David Smith over a viewpoint. Are there other artifacts in the park? Things of monetary value?"

She didn't suppose there was any point in asking. If there were something known to be of value, then it would have been removed, not left in place.

"I suppose there are," the receptionist said. "We don't make public any of the archaeological sites where there may still be artifacts present, but we are aware of several sites with archaeological importance. There was a study done before the park was even formed, and there have been a number of follow-up studies since then by various organizations or students."

"What kind of sites?"

"I really can't discuss them. They are not disclosed to the public so that they won't be overrun. People wouldn't leave them alone if they knew where they were. We have taken our lessons from other parks."

"Indigenous artifacts?" Margie questioned. "Money or treasures from the old ranchers or townspeople? Something still in the quarry?"

"The only thing that was ever in the quarry was sandstone," the woman replied with a laugh. "And not even the highest quality sandstone, at that. It was used to build several of the buildings in downtown Calgary and the Legislature in Edmonton, but they found better quality sandstone elsewhere, and the quarry was turned to a brickworks. But then it too went under. There wasn't any way for Glenbow Village to survive without industry, and gradually people moved out until it was a ghost town."

Margie made a couple of notes in her notepad. The helpful visitor information lady had not answered whether there were any Indigenous artifacts or treasures from the old ranchers. What had they discovered on archaeological digs in the past? It was frustrating that they wouldn't release the information to her. She didn't have enough evidence that it was relevant to get a subpoena to demand copies of the archaeological studies. There might be some of the information she needed in the Glenbow history book, but she suspected that if it was not fit for public consumption when someone called the information line, it would have been kept out of the book too. Still… it might be worth looking and finding out some more information about the park's history. Then she would have a better idea of whether there were anything worth pursuing.

"So is Glenbow considered a ghost town?" Margie asked. "I didn't realize that any of it was still standing. Do you have people exploring there?"

"The ruins of Glenbow are out of bounds. Visitors are not supposed to be on or in those ruins. We don't want anyone stepping on a rusty nail or having some other accident out there. It isn't safe. It's in our best interests to just keep people away from the townsite."

"How much of it can you still see?" Margie was still tapping in computer searches and paging through the various image results. On typing in 'Glenbow Village ruins,' she was presented with pictures of a house with a sagging roof and several chimneys or other brick or sandstone structures that remained of houses long since gone. "Hmm. Not very much, I guess."

"No. We only have one house still standing, and no one is allowed to go inside. That would be very dangerous. And we don't want any vandalism." Her voice lowered to a serious tone. "People have very little respect for historical sites."

"I'm not surprised to hear that." Margie remembered being a patrol officer, and the amount of graffiti and destruction they'd had to deal with in Winnipeg. It was sickening how little people cared about historical sites or even just the spaces they lived in. A lot of hard work went into building communities, and their appearance and reputation could be destroyed in a few minutes with a can of spray paint or a few bullets or kicks.

"Do you get a lot of vandals in the park?"

"Luckily, not a lot. We are far enough away from the city that people don't happen onto the park by accident. They have to plan to come out here and have transportation. And we have Conservation Officers patrolling the park and trying to keep any… unwelcome parties out of the park."

"Yes, I've met a few of your CO's. They seem to be very diligent and dedicated to the parks they patrol."

"Our CO's are some of our greatest fans. We have some of them out here even on their days off, just because they want more time to walk the park and just relax and recharge."

Margie felt a sense of longing to be home with her daughter and to take Stella out to the park for a walk. Even just that little strip of green space along the ridge of the irrigation canal meant something to her. She could see how the Conservation Officers would fall in love with the parks they spent so much time protecting.

"Do your CO's use the golf carts all the time, or do they do foot patrols?"

"They walk, use carts or trucks, or ride horses. Whatever is the best way to get to where they want to go."

"They ride horses?"

"Yes, we have a few horses in the park that they can take out as needed."

"That's awesome." Margie had only ridden horseback a couple of times, and she had loved it. She didn't know if it was in her blood, because of her ancestry, or if she just happened to enjoy it, but she wished that she lived somewhere she could ride occasionally. When she had some spare time. But so far, spare time was just about as rare in Margie's life as a horse to ride.

"If I was to come to the park tomorrow, do you think someone could give me a short tour?" she suggested. "I'd like to get a better sense of the scope of the park, and whether these archaeological sites might have anything to do with David Smith."

"Of course, someone would be glad to help you out. Let me just look at the schedule for tomorrow and make sure that we will have someone available with a cart." There was silence for a few minutes, then the woman was back. "Yes. I'll make a note of it here. If you will come by the Visitor Center in the morning, we can have someone help you out."

What were the chances that Margie was going to find anything related to David Smith's death on her little guided tour? Margie put them at slim to none. But she would at least get a ride around a beautiful park, and that was almost like taking a holiday.

CHAPTER SEVEN

Margie had not planned on just vegging out in front of the TV when she got home. She had lots of plans. After taking Stella for a walk, she and Christina would take some time to unpack the few boxes that were left. They would wash the windows, vacuum, and maybe she would make some of the phone calls that were way down on her list that she just hadn't been able to summon up the energy to make.

But she was wiped out at the end of the day, and a person had to take a break now and then to just rest and regenerate, didn't they?

"Mom? Mom!" It took several calls before Margie was roused from her deep meditation in front of the silver screen.

"Christina! I'm awake. What was that?"

"Mom, did you see the way Stella is acting? I think there might be someone in the back yard."

"What?" Margie blinked herself awake, shaking away the cobwebs with a quick twitch of her head. She looked across the kitchen to where Stella slunk at the back door, sniffing the crack on the bottom edge with great concentration. "Stella? What is it? Is there someone there?"

Stella looked up for a moment, regarded her, and then put her nose to the floor again to sniff the air coming in under the door.

"Can you see anyone out there?" Margie went into Christina's bedroom, which looked into the back yard. She held her face against the window, staring out into the darkness. She could see little more than darkness. But looking out the window with the light of the kitchen and living room glowing behind her, she was probably very visible to anyone who happened to be in the yard.

"Is there anyone there?" Christina asked in a hushed voice.

"Not that I can see. She might have just smelled a skunk. There are a lot of them around."

"Yeah." Christina giggled. "Every time I look at the community page, somebody is complaining about their dog getting sprayed by a skunk. So probably *not* the best time to let Stella out into the yard."

"Probably not," Margie agreed.

As she pulled back from the window, she thought she saw a movement. Just her own reflected image in the glass? Or had there been something else out there? Something or someone who waited until she had pulled back from the window and couldn't see out anymore?

Margie shook her head. She was tired, and if she let her imagination get away from her, she wouldn't be able to get any sleep. Every noise the house made would sound like someone breaking in.

They were in a safe place. Nothing was going to happen to them there. Stella would be barking if there were some sort of threat outside the door. She would go nuts if there were an intruder and she thought she needed to protect her pack.

"I don't think it's anything to be concerned about, hon," she told Christina in a calm voice.

Christina nodded and took it in stride, not doubting Margie's words. Margie went to the freezer, wondering if there were any ice cream left.

***

Maybe because she had been worrying about not being able to sleep, Margie ended up tossing and turning. It seemed impossible to find a comfortable position in her bed. She usually slept well. She worked hard, and she had a walk with Stella after she got home, and after unwinding for a while in front of the TV, she was able to get to sleep quickly after tucking herself in.

But it was different this time. She closed her eyes and then, a few minutes later, opened them, wondering why she had bothered to close them in the first place if she was not tired. She had so much to do. It was going to be a busy day the next day if she were going to make her way all the way back out to Glenbow Park for another look around and a golf cart tour.

Margie was wide awake. It wasn't like those super frustrating nights when she was so overtired that she couldn't find sleep. She felt perfectly awake. She had no desire to sleep or sense of sleepiness at all.

She got up quietly and checked to make sure that Christina was in bed with the light off and all of her devices tucked away for the night. She walked around and checked the locks on the door, even though she had done that as part of her regular get-ready-for-bed routine. Stella noticed that she was up and padded after her, sniffing at each of the doors studiously, gathering whatever information her prodigious nose could sniff out. Stella looked up at Margie and whined.

"I know," Margie said. "There's nothing to worry about. I just couldn't get to sleep. I know there isn't anything out there. I just needed... to be sure."

Stella made a noise halfway between a huff and a sneeze. Margie wiped off her wet ankle. "Gee, thanks. Do you think you could slobber on your own feet?"

Stella pushed her nose into Margie's hand, demanding pets and scratches. Margie scratched her ears. "Yes, you're a good girl. You're a good dog. Even if you do sneeze and drool on me."

Margie warmed up a glass of milk in the microwave. Not the way her grandmother would have made it but, hopefully, it would still do the trick. She and Stella took one last circuit around the house, looking out each window and making sure that everything was secure.

˙˙˙

SHE WAS sure that would be the end of it. Just one of those nights when things seemed disrupted. When she woke up in the morning, everything would be just like normal and all of the unease of the previous night would have disappeared. But instead, Margie felt worse than ever when she forced herself to slide out of bed and get started on her day. There was a tension in her belly, a tightness like a knot. Margie looked in on Christina and was relieved to see her in her bed sleeping peacefully. She'd dealt with too many parents in the past who had put their children to bed at night, and when they got up in the morning, they were gone. Teenagers, usually, but sometimes younger schoolchildren or even toddlers. They wandered off sleepwalking or were abducted by spouses. They ran away or left to go to a party and never returned. The parents had to live with the guilt that went along with letting their child wander off in those few hours they were blissfully unconsciousness.

A person couldn't be vigilant all day. Margie couldn't protect her child from all evil influences. There were things she could never protect Christina from, no matter how hard she tried.

Margie started the coffee brewing. While she was trying to cut back and not have coffee every morning before breakfast—or *for* breakfast—she knew that she couldn't do without it after a night like that. She was going to need the caffeine to get her motor running.

Of course, caffeine didn't help with anxiety. In fact, it amplified it. She reminded herself as she breathed in the smell of the coffee as it brewed that she would probably feel worse in the afternoon. She would get an initial kick from the coffee, but she would have a mid-afternoon crash. Being so tired and anxious, it would probably be a doozy, and she needed to keep in mind that it was just because of the caffeine. It didn't mean that anything was really wrong with the world or that anyone was out to get her.

Stella was scratching at the back door to get out. Margie let her into the yard. She went into Christina's room, where she could see through the window that the back gate was still shut and latched.

"Hey, sleepyhead. Time to start getting up."

"Not yet," Christina groaned.

Margie was going to protest that Christina needed to get up and moving if she were going to catch the bus and get to school on time.

"You said I can choose what time to get up," Christina mumbled. "You said as long as I was getting to school, you wouldn't bother me."

She was right, of course. Margie was trying to allow her daughter the space to learn to be a responsible adult, and that meant that if she didn't choose to get up until ten minutes before the bus and ended up having to eat on the run and fly out the door in a panic, that was the natural consequence of her choice. As long as Margie didn't get reports from the school that Christina was late to or missing classes, Margie wouldn't enforce a specific bedtime or wake-up time.

"Okay. I just wanted to check the back gate. If you want to get a few more minutes sleeping, you can."

"'Night." Christina's long, even breaths resumed. Margie was impressed with Christina's ability to go back to sleep once she'd been awakened. She herself probably would have found it impossible to get back to sleep again and would have had to get up, whether she liked it or not. Margie went back to the kitchen to start on her coffee, then to the bathroom for a quick wake-up shower. If she got hers in early, she wouldn't have to fight Christina for it later when there was no longer time for both of them to use it.

By the time she got back to her coffee, she could hear Christina stirring. She got up and used the bathroom. When she came into the kitchen, she ran her fingers through her tangled hair, blinking in the sunlight.

"Hi." Her voice was rough and sleepy still.

"Morning. Did you have a good rest?"

"Yeah, it was fine." Christina helped herself to a cup of coffee.

Margie bit her tongue and didn't say anything about it. She couldn't very well criticize Christina for drinking coffee when she herself did. Allowing Christina some privileges of adulthood helped Margie enforce more important rules, such as no alcohol. At least, Margie hoped it would work that way.

Christina took a few swallows of her coffee. She went to open the door when Stella barked to be let in.

"Mom!"

Margie moved quickly at Christina's cry of alarm. She saw Stella on the back step, mouth open in a pant, her muzzle bloody.

"Is she hurt?" Margie crouched down in front of Stella for a closer look. She pushed back Stella's lips to look at her teeth and gums and examined her nose and face for any sign of an injury. She'd heard of people tossing meat spiked with sewing needles into back yards to injure pets. She couldn't see any sign of injury on Stella. She looked around, scanning the yard for the source of the blood. If it didn't come from Stella, then…?

"There's something over there," Christina motioned to a dark mound Margie could just barely see.

Margie slid on a pair of garden clogs—one day, she was going to start gardening—and strode through the cold, wet grass to see what it was.

It took a minute for her to be able to recognize the lump of fur stippled with dark blood as a rabbit. She stared, trying to process it. Stella surely hadn't killed the rabbit. She chased rabbits sometimes when they were out for a walk, and Margie knew that she was hopeless at it. The rabbits always zig-zagged away, leaving her in the dust. Maybe if one were already sick or injured…

Her stomach was tied in knots. She knew there were city by-laws about vicious animals, including animals that had killed other animals, but she didn't know all of the details. She might have to look them up.

Margie looked more closely. She was a homicide detective; it didn't bother her to look at the dead body of a rabbit. Except it did. Just as looking at a human body always stirred deep emotions despite her need to remain impassive and to compartmentalize those feelings. She tried to look past the areas where Stella had worried at the body. Stella had not been hungry, but curious. Margie tried to figure out how the animal had died. Maybe it had been hit by a car and crawled into their yard. Or another animal had killed it.

But she saw a wound with straight edges.

That didn't make any sense. She remembered the squirrel they had found in the yard. Also dead. Also cut with something with a straight edge. Margie had explained it away to herself that time. The squirrel could have caught itself on something sharp. Animals did get hurt in the wild. Maybe there was a sharp can or a piece of abandoned equipment that she wasn't aware of. A lawnmower blade someone had put aside to clean and sharpen and then never followed up on.

But two dead animals in her yard with injuries caused by a straight edge was hard to explain. The first time she had picked up the body and discarded it in her compost bin. This time it was a bigger animal. Harder to ignore. Harder to explain away how a second dead animal came to be in her yard. It would be one thing if an animal had mauled them. Everyone would assume Stella had killed them. But Stella didn't carry a switchblade in her pocket.

"Mom? What is it?"

"It's just a rabbit, Christina."

"Did Stella—kill it?"

"No. I don't think so."

Christina stood on the back step, looking at her, waiting for her to explain further. But Margie didn't want to clarify unless Christina asked for more details. It was better if she didn't know. Christina didn't ask for more. Maybe she knew better from Margie's silence or her body language.

"Are you going to clean it up?"

"I'll do it a bit later. You'd better finish getting ready for school."

Christina looked down at Stella, still by her side. "What about Stella? Will you clean her up?"

Stella would probably eventually lick everything off. But it would be better if Margie wiped her muzzle and face with a towel so they didn't have to look at it or worry about Stella getting flecks of blood inside the house.

"Yes. Would you get me a towel?"

Christina nodded and went to get one.

CHAPTER EIGHT

Once Christina was on the bus, Margie placed a call to her own department. MacDonald was in and was able to take her call.

"Detective Patenaude. How can I help you?"

"This is a personal matter, sir, but I wonder if you could help me out and tell me who to call. And to let you know that I won't be in until later today."

"What's up?"

Margie explained about the rabbit in her yard, and he wasn't too concerned about it until she described how both it and the previously discovered dead squirrel appeared to have been killed by a blade or sharp piece of metal and left dead or dying in her yard.

"You're sure they weren't killed by your dog."

"We've never had anything like this happen before. Of course she chases squirrels and rabbits, but she never catches them. I'm not a pathologist, but I don't see how a dog could leave marks like that. A clean incision. It's possible that once, it could just be some weird accident. I thought maybe a tin can or piece of sharp trash. But twice? Left dead in my yard both times? It wasn't the dog and it couldn't be a coincidence."

"Have you had any threats? Anyone been hanging around your yard? Any contact from someone you didn't want to have anything to do with?"

"No." Margie cast her thoughts back, trying to identify any threats she might have received, any anger that seemed inappropriate or weird behavior from anyone she'd arrested or had anything to do with since she got to Calgary. It wasn't very hard. She hadn't really had contact with that many people since arriving in Calgary. And the only person she had arrested was Abdul. She had talked to other people. But Abdul was the only one who she had taken into custody.

She remembered Abdul asking about her dog and looking at Stella's picture on her phone. Flipping through the pictures without asking, seeing Christina's photo too. A girl about his own age.

But Abdul was in custody. That had already been established.

"There's… Abdul's foster father. But he never made any threats or said anything inappropriate. He didn't even seem that upset, he just sort of took it in stride."

"He could have been masking deeper emotions. Sometimes it's the quiet ones who feel things the most. Do you want us to pick him up?"

Margie resisted. "No. I don't think it could be anything to do with him."

"Would he know about your dog? Where you live?"

"Well… it's a possibility. He was there when Abdul and I talked about Stella." She was embarrassed and tried to explain further. "I was trying to establish a relationship with him. To talk about how he might have come to be talking with Robinson. You know, two people out walking dogs start talking to each other about the dogs, the view, and so on. Maybe Abdul and Robinson might have struck up a casual conversation about the weather or the view or the fact that they had seen each other there a few times before."

"Are your phone number or address listed anywhere? Somewhere searchable? Do you find them if you Google search yourself?"

"I've been careful; I don't think so. I'll check."

"Did you talk about what area you live in? What it's close to?"

She tried to remember what else she might have revealed around Abdul or his foster father, Sadiq. "I don't think so, but I don't remember every word I said around them."

"It might be a good idea to check in on him, ask a few questions."

"Yeah. I'll think about that. Who should I call about this rabbit? Is there someone who will come and have a look and not just brush me off as a hysterical woman? I have a daughter. If one of us is being stalked…"

"Let me get you a name. I'll text it to you."

"Thanks. And I'll be late getting in today. Actually, I was thinking of going back to Glenbow Park today for a tour and another look around. Maybe I'll just go out there once I finish here? If I'm going to miss the stand-up meeting anyway, it's a lot faster to take Stoney Trail than to go through downtown rush hour traffic."

"Sure. I'll let everyone know that's where you are. And they can call you if they have questions or information you'll want to hear?"

"Yes. I'll be available on the phone. One of the guys I talked to at the park said there's only one place that has spotty reception; my phone should be working the rest of the time."

THANKFULLY, the officer who came out to have a look at the dead rabbit and talk to her about what had happened was serious and engaged and didn't act like Margie was crazy for thinking that someone might be trying to send her a message. Constable Evans nodded and made notes and looked at the body of the rabbit, with flies starting to buzz around it. He pulled down his mask to speak to her, standing well back.

"I'm going to take this with me, if you don't mind. I agree that it doesn't look like it was killed by an animal or an accident, so we'll want to follow up and see if this is something to be concerned about. If we have some sicko out there killing animals then, even if he isn't specifically targeting you, there is still reason to be concerned."

Margie nodded. Everyone knew that killing or torturing animals could be the beginning steps of someone who would later turn to killing or torturing his fellow human beings. If they could catch him before he moved on to people...

She squirmed, anxious and sick to her stomach. She had just arrived in Calgary. She wanted her daughter to be safe. She didn't want to have to worry about some sicko who wanted to terrorize them or was just really enjoying his brutal hobby.

"Do you think...?"

"I think you were meant to find it," Evans said slowly. "If he was just randomly killing animals and throwing them over fences, then I wouldn't expect him to throw them into your yard twice in such a short period of time. If your neighbors were all finding dead animals in their yards, I think you would hear about it pretty quickly."

"Yes. We don't know everybody, but we do… say hello, talk over the fence, stuff like that. And there is a community Facebook page. If there were a lot of animals being killed, I'm sure it would have been mentioned there. Unless it just started."

"Maybe he'll move on to another area to avoid being caught, and this is all that you'll see."

"I hope so. I have a daughter. I don't want to keep finding things like this in the yard. She's here alone sometimes after school or if I have to go out to a crime scene. I want her to be safe being here alone."

"Of course. We'll look into it and see what we can find out. See if there are any similar reports anywhere else in the city, especially in this area. Have the lab examine the rabbit and see what they can tell us about it."

"I'm sorry I already got rid of the squirrel. I expect the bins have been emptied since then. And even if they haven't, it will be buried in there under everything else. I don't imagine the lab techs would be able to tell much about it in that state."

"Maybe if this was an episode of *Bones* and I was from the Smithsonian…" he teased. "But I'm not," he added seriously. "I wish I could tell you that the body is bound to give us the answer as to who is doing this, but I can't do that. Maybe it will tell us something, maybe nothing."

They grimaced at each other. Evans pulled out a business card. "You can call me directly if anything else happens. Even if you just have an insight or a random thought about who could be doing something like this. Call, text, or email."

Margie took the card. "Thanks."

He nodded. "I'll let you get on to work now. Good luck with your case."

CHAPTER NINE

The young man who met Margie at the Visitor Center introduced himself as Ian. Margie was surprised at how young he was. She had expected that, like at a lot of the museums and conservation areas she had gone to, the docents would be retired folks. People who still wanted to keep their hand on a pet project even when they were no longer able to work there.

"Ian. Nice to meet you. How long have you been working here?"

"A couple of years. Don't worry; I know all of the important stuff. If you have any questions I can't answer, we'll look them up when we get back or I'll find out the answer from someone who knows."

He opened the garage, and Margie saw several golf carts that hadn't been there when she had last seen it. Big carts for a lot of tourists, with a canopy sunshade overhead.

"Oh, I wasn't judging, just surprised that someone so young would be working here."

"We get a lot of kids. University students who are working on their thesises, looking for a summer job, wanting to do a particular study in the park. We have older guides as well, our park stewards in particular, but today you get me."

"And I'm sure you'll do a great job. This is a fascinating place. I was doing some research on the internet about it. There's really a rich history."

"There is," Ian agreed, climbing into one of the smaller golf carts and motioning for Margie to take the seat next to him. Margie sat down. He backed up, turned around, and off they went. He didn't take the same trail as Margie had taken the day of the murder, west to Tiger Lily Loop, but went the other way and, in a few seconds, they were nosing down a long, steep hill.

Margie hung on to the side of the cart and leaned back, but she didn't need to worry that it was too steep for the golf cart. Of course, Ian was used to driving up and down it all the time, and he didn't have any trouble controlling the cart or weaving slowly between various small groups of walkers, cyclists, and mobility scooters.

He smiled at her. "Downhill is easy. The hard part is always making sure you've got enough electricity to get back up the hill again."

"What do you do if you don't?"

"Walk. Or everybody walks except for the driver and, hopefully, he has enough electricity to get it up the hill without the extra weight of passengers. Otherwise, you're going to need to get a tow or a lift in the back of the truck, and that's pretty embarrassing. They'll call you 'Juice' to the end of your days because you ran out of juice."

Margie laughed. "That's cute. Is that your nickname?"

"Not mine." He crossed his fingers and looked heavenward. "Hopefully, it won't ever be."

After the hill, they traveled over a long, level trail out in the sun. It would be a challenging walk on a thirty-degree day.

"Is there running water in the park?"

"No. The washrooms are outhouses. And there are no water fountains. If you need water, you have to carry it in with you. There is bottled water available at the Visitor Center when it is open, but it isn't always open. If you've been here once, you generally remember after that."

"I guess so!"

She was silent, looking at the brilliant azure sky with barely a cloud in it. The trees in the direction of the river were starting to change into their autumn colors, pretty yellows dappled among the green. She watched the birds, butterflies, and bees flying among the flowers and bush beside the trail.

"There was frost this morning. I wasn't expecting such a warm day."

"September in these parts is very changeable. You can have frost overnight and twenty-eight or nine during the day. I don't think we'll see any more thirty-degree days this year, but you never know. We still could. What they used to call an Indian summer, before it became politically incorrect."

"Not that anyone in your generation ever called it that."

"No."

He pointed out several different topographical features for her and talked about the bee homes and bird and bat houses built to help preserve various species in the park. The special fescue grasses that were important in the sequestration of carbon. What people had done there when the village was still populated. He mentioned the cattle kept on the property that helped to keep the long grasses cropped down so that they wouldn't be a fire hazard.

There was a growing noise behind them. Margie searched the trees for the origin of the loud rumble. Ian slowed the cart to look, and pointed out the train that Margie could just see through the trees. "You'll be able to see it better in a minute. The CPR line runs through the park and is still quite active. We are part of the shipping route between the coast and Eastern Canada. The CPR line runs from coast to coast."

Margie knew some of the stories of the building of the railway. It had been an important development for Canada, helping to build a unified country. But it had been built on the backs of migrant workers under terrible work conditions, with four Chinese workers being killed for every mile of the railway line through the Fraser Valley. Immigrant labor had just been a commodity, and the big corporations didn't particularly care how many lives were lost in building the railway, just as long as there were plenty more available. Building the railway had also meant moving Métis populations, which had led to the Red River Rebellion.

"What can you tell me about the Indigenous peoples who lived here and any artifacts left by them or the villagers?"

Ian looked at her sideways. "Are you…?"

Margie raised her eyebrows, waiting.

"Are you Native? I mean, you look a little like it…"

Margie chuckled. She patted at her bun, which kept her long, black hair coiled neatly away. Her face would rarely be mistaken for anything but Indigenous Canadian. Maybe Asian or mixed race if you squinted, but her Cree heritage showed.

"I am Métis."

"Oh, okay." He looked relieved that he hadn't put his foot in his mouth by thinking she was something she was not. "Do you come from around here?"

"Was this a Métis settlement?"

"Well, no. The people here are mostly Nakoda. There are other tribes as well, but it was the Nakoda who mostly settled along the Bow River here."

"No, I don't come from this area. I come from Manitoba."

"The Red River Rebellions and all that?"

"Yes. All that."

He nodded wisely. "Well, to answer your question, of course there were Native peoples on this land thousands of years before the white man. It is Treaty 7 land, and the Tsuut'ina Nation is just to the south. We have a good relationship with our neighbors, and they sometimes join us for special park programs and observances."

"So what kinds of things could you find around the park? Teepee rings? Arrowheads? Graveyards?"

"They can answer some of those questions at the Visitor Center. But we can't say too much about what archaeological sites there are in the park or where they are located, so that we don't have treasure hunters ripping stuff up and destroying it. We study what we can. In a very respectful way, following proper archaeological procedures."

"Do you get a lot of people who ask? Or people who wander around here on their own looking for treasures? Have you had much vandalism because of it?"

"We field questions about it pretty regularly," he agreed. "But we do what we can to discourage people from trying to find artifacts. It is destructive."

Margie watched as the vegetation and topography transformed around them again. Every few minutes, they went from one kind of tree dominating the landscape to another; the trail went out to the water and wound away from it again. The shaded areas were cool and the open areas made her break out into a sweat. It was such a varied landscape; she could see how walkers and bikers would want to see it again and again, exploring all of its different facets.

"Tell me some more about Glenbow Village."

He had pointed out the ruins that they had passed, but it was all too quick, and Margie wanted to get a better sense of it. She knew, in the back of her mind, that it really didn't have anything to do with her investigation, and she should finish up her tour of the park and get back to the office where she could continue her desk work. But it was nice just being out in nature, even if it was zipping by a little too fast.

Ian told her some more stories about the village as they continued, pointing out various pieces of their life that the former residents had left behind. Wagon wheels and the shell of a motor car. The old quarry and brickworks. He talked about the school and how it had been moved and preserved.

"This is as far as we are going to go," he told her as they approached the Narrows. "I'll just get turned around, and we'll head back."

"And the trails don't continue through to Calgary?"

"Not yet. But someday soon…"

"Is there a projected date?"

"There are plenty of projected dates. They are doing work on the Haskayne Park access right now. So hopefully *soon*…"

Margie nodded. She knew how city projects could drag on for years. Building and developments promised, infrastructure that had been projected for years and still wasn't anywhere in sight. They couldn't be prepared for all of the changes in the economy. For a downturn in development due to red tape. For the pandemic. Who could ever have predicted the way 2020 alone would unfold?

She recognized the trail as they got close to the steep access hill. "Can I get back to Tiger Lily Loop from here?"

"Yes." He looked at his watch. "But I can't take you there. I have to be back for a scheduled tour."

"That's okay. If you can just point me in the right direction, I can get there. I'd just like to take another look around and to… walk the victim's footsteps, if you know what I mean. Maybe something will occur to me that hasn't before."

"Well, of course you're welcome to walk around and have every right to be investigating up there, so have at it. Just take this trail." He pointed. "Watch for a branch to the right, take that trail, and then you'll be on Tiger Lily Loop. You can go either direction and it will get you back up to the top where the access to the parking lot is. There is a map, so you can stop and look and orient yourself if you're not sure. Or ask someone else who looks like they know where they are going. We have a lot of visitors who come back multiple times and know their way around the park very well. Okay?"

"Yes, that sounds good." Margie looked along the trail but couldn't see where it branched off. But it sounded very straightforward. "Thanks very much for the tour and all of the information. I don't know that it will help at all with the case, but it has certainly made me want to come back for another visit, and to bring my daughter with me next time. Maybe my dog too."

There had been lots of dogs amongst the walkers that she had seen. She knew that there was a leash rule, which was fine with her. Stella was happy to be on a leash, and it would ensure that she didn't chase after any of the ground squirrels or the cattle or a moose or something else that could do her harm.

Ian waved goodbye and turned up the steep pathway to the top.

Margie started out along the trail.

It was afternoon and she hadn't had lunch. She'd barely had breakfast. She had only walked about a kilometer when she realized that she should not have started out without a bottle of water. No food in her system and no water with her, the sun beating down on her on a trail that had minimal tree cover. Not a very good idea if she wanted to complete her walk quickly and still get back to the homicide department to do more work there before the end of the day. All in all, she was afraid it was going to be a wasted day, having gotten no closer to tracking down David Smith's killer.

She shook her head and kept walking, but at a reduced pace. She didn't want to overheat and overstress her body trying to get the walk finished too quickly. One step at a time at a steady, leisurely pace, and she would eventually come out on top and wouldn't be too much worse for wear.

Bicyclists whizzed by her in both directions. She saw walkers of all shapes, ages, and descriptions, from fit-looking oldsters with neatly pressed clothing and wide-brimmed hats to young people in skimpy outfits showing off brilliantly tattooed bodies. Mothers with little children, retirees and amputees on electric scooters; it seemed like everybody had chosen that day to be out enjoying one of the last hot days of the year in the park.

Margie wiped her sweaty forehead and neck and kept going. She hadn't even thought to bring a hat with her. She hardly ever needed a hat; she was never out in the sun long on her walks with Stella and, with the shortening days, the sun was usually too low in the sky both in the morning and the evening to worry about exposure.

She stopped and looked back behind her and then ahead of her. She didn't see any sign of a branching trail. Had she somehow missed it? She didn't see how she could have. She had stopped at a map and looked over it but, to her shame, Margie was terrible at the spatial planning and memory needed to read a map and keep it in her head as she walked. She tried turning on her phone and looking at Google Maps, but the paths were not well marked and were not labeled, so she couldn't be sure if she were on the correct route or not.

She reached a lookout and stood there for a few minutes, looking at the mountains in the distance, the trees beside the river, and a stone chimney jutting up toward the sky. It was not the same view as she had been able to see from Tiger Lily Loop. She was pretty sure she had missed her turn. She didn't know if the trail she was on would eventually loop around and return her to the place she had started with Ian. Even if it did, she was pretty sure she had covered about three kilometers already, and she really didn't want to guess how much farther it would be. She swore under her breath. She turned around and retraced her steps, trying to remember what the turnoff Ian had taken had looked like so she wouldn't go too far back again, but could get up the steep hill and to her car in the parking lot and not keep wandering into the middle of the park, where she might eventually have to call to have someone rescue her.

Ian had told her to watch for the branching trail to her right so, having turned around, it would be on her left. She mentally reviewed both hands and clenched the left so she wouldn't get confused as to which side the branch would be on.

CHAPTER TEN

Margie was relieved when she found the trail that broke off to her left. The tension in her shoulders and abdominal muscles relaxed, and she felt like she was in control again. She enjoyed the view, smiled and nodded at other walkers, and stepped forward with confidence. She would check out the loop, satisfy herself that she hadn't missed anything —or alternatively, gain some insight that they had not had before—and she would still have some time to go back to the office to review any other evidence or leads that had come in during her absence. She might be a little late getting home, but Christina would be fine on her own for a couple of hours.

Margie's stomach tightened again when she remembered the squirrel and the rabbit and the possibility that someone was stalking and threatening her. She didn't want to be late getting home. She didn't want Christina taking Stella out for a walk alone. A dog was good defense, and people wouldn't usually attack someone accompanied by a large dog. But it didn't always hold. There was still the possibility that someone would recognize Stella's true wuss nature and not be worried about her reaction. Or they would bring a knife or a gun and be ready to take her out. Or a piece of meat spiked with poison or sewing needles.

She picked up her pace. She shouldn't be wasting so much time walking around the park. Her tour hadn't given her any insight into whether the killer or Smith might have been some kind of treasure hunter, maybe rivals in hunting artifacts. It had been a long shot, but she had hoped that being there would provide the key piece of information that she needed to solve the case.

Nothing on the pathway looked familiar. But Margie had come onto it a different way than she had previously. Or was it the same route as she had taken when Richardson brought her in on the golf cart, and it was just her perspective or speed that made it seem foreign? Margie scanned the scenery, not seeing the beauty anymore, just desperately looking for something that resonated with her. Something familiar that would reassure her that she was on the right path. She had taken her first left, so it should have been the Tiger Lily Loop. She'd missed it the first time but, when she had reversed, coming back from the tall, ominous-looking chimney, she had taken the correct turn. She was sure of it. Ian had said to take the right, and she had reversed direction and taken the left.

For a long time, she didn't see anyone else. The trail dipped down when she had expected it to continue to rise. The trees didn't look right. Nothing looked right. A couple of cyclists whizzed by her, too fast for her to flag them down or ask any questions. Finally, she saw a woman neatly dressed in khakis and a white hat coming toward her, a trekking pole in each hand.

"Excuse me…" Margie stopped her.

"Yes?"

"Is this Tiger Lily Loop?"

"Oh, no, dear. This is the Badger Bowl. Tiger Lily Loop is that way." She gestured back behind Margie.

"Are you sure? I was following the directions that the young man from the Visitor Center gave me…"

"Yes, I'm sure. The trail heads are quite close together; it's easy to mistake them."

Margie turned and looked back the direction she had come, heart sinking. She kept taking the wrong turns. She was going to have walked a half-marathon by the time she got back to the parking lot. On an empty stomach and no water.

"Are you okay, dear? The Badger Bowl is still a nice walk. I'm sure you'll enjoy it."

"I need to be on the Tiger Lily Loop. That's where… I'm a police detective, and that's the one I'm supposed to be checking out."

"Oh, I thought the police were finished with all of that. Didn't you get everything you needed earlier?"

"We gathered all of the evidence. I'm just looking for... inspiration, I guess."

The woman smiled, her wrinkles curving gently upward. "Well... you'll get out of the Bowl faster if you go back the way you came than if you continue around the loop. If you don't mind walking with me, I can show you which way."

"That would be really helpful, actually. I'm so turned around. I don't know the park, and I thought it would be simple to get from one place to another, but I'm not good with directions."

"Not everyone is," she agreed placidly. "My name is Joanne. I'm not fast, but I know my way around. So if you just stick with me, I'll get you to where you need to go."

"I really appreciate that."

They started walking, Margie turning around to go back the way she had come. She sighed. "It really is a beautiful place. I wish I was here for a reason other than the investigation, so I could enjoy it."

"You'll have to come back sometime when you can just relax and take it all in. Or take one of the cart tours. The park is pretty big, but the cart tours can get you from one end to the other so you can get a better idea of the scope."

"I took a quick tour today. It is pretty impressive."

"There's a lot to see."

"Do you know of any artifacts or anything valuable in the park?"

Joanne considered. "Its value is its history and all of the diverse species in the park. Not in anything of monetary value. The park land itself is worth millions. But you can't put it in your pocket and sell it on the street."

"No." Margie made a face that Joanne couldn't see behind her mask. She was puffing a little as she went up the hill again. Joanne seemed to be breathing just fine, keeping a steady rhythm with her trekking poles. Margie was probably just breathing hard because of her anxiety and the feeling that she had to get to the Tiger Lily Loop quickly, even though she didn't expect to find anything there.

"I was so sad to hear about David Smith," Joanne said. "You're investigating the stabbing?"

"Yes. Did you know him?"

"Not well. Just to say hello when we passed each other in the park. He seemed like a nice man. He cared about the park and his health. Like most of us here. We are all doing what we can to stay active, to take care of ourselves and the environment. Getting time in nature is very important. You can't sit in front of electronic screens all day without negative effects. I like my Netflix as well as the next person, but you need to take a break regularly to get your dose of nature and fresh air."

Margie nodded. She felt guilty that she hadn't been able to exercise very much lately, but she was just settling in with a new job. She would find more time. She was walking Stella every day or twice a day. Not long walks, maybe, but it was something.

"I guess I don't need to tell you about the benefits of nature," Joanne said, giving a little laugh. Margie looked at her.

"What do you mean? I mean—I do try to get out, but I'm not sure why…"

"Because you're Indian, I mean. Or whatever the politically correct term is these days. You are, aren't you? I'm glad to see that someone like you is able to get onto the police force. You always hear about racism and how people like you can't get into anything but physical labor."

"Oh. Yes, thank you. And you're right; I was raised to love and respect nature. I don't spend as much time as I should, but I love to be out here." Margie made a motion to include all of the plant and animal life around her.

She thought of Moushoom. She needed to go see him too. Maybe she could take him from his little apartment over to the pathway along Twenty-Sixth Street where she walked Stella. He would probably really like that. She was sure he needed the exposure to nature too. Probably more so than she did. He had grown up in a much more traditional lifestyle, where he had been much more in touch with nature than she had. Maybe that was why he had a much better sense of direction than she did.

Or maybe that was just something about the brain she was born with. While her Cree progenitors probably had an excellent sense of direction, who knew about the early explorers? How many of them had just happened to stumble upon their discoveries because they had no idea where they were going?

She realized that she and Joanne had stopped talking and were just walking in silence. She felt suddenly awkward. "Sorry. Did you ask something?"

"No. Just enjoying the quiet."

"Oh. Okay. Me too. I don't do this very often."

She relaxed as they walked, listening to the rhythm of their feet. They would get there when they got there; there was no point in her getting all wound up about getting back to the office at a specific time. If there were anything urgent, someone on the team would call her. She pulled out her phone to make sure that she still had power and coverage. Both appeared to be strong. They could get her if they needed her.

Eventually, they reached the trailhead.

Joanne pointed. "This is the one you need to follow," she said, indicating the gravel pathway and tracing its directions in the air in front of them. "You can go either way, it's a loop and they will both get you to the parking lot eventually. You're about halfway, so you can take the one you want."

Margie tried to remember which she had taken with the conservation officer to get to the murder scene. She thought it was the left.

"Thank you so much for your help. Who knows how long I would have been wandering if it wasn't for you."

"Oh, someone else would have helped you. You only have to ask. Chances are, the person you ask will know the way. If they don't, just ask the next one. Most of the visitors come regularly."

"I appreciate it. Thanks."

Margie started up the left leg of the trail. "And I can't get lost from here, right? There's no way I'm going to end up in the Badger Bowl again?"

"No. You'll either end up in the parking lot or back here again. Those are the two connection points. And it's pretty hard to miss the parking lot. There's a big sign." Her eyes crinkled as she smiled. "A whole bunch of parked cars."

Margie laughed. "Thank you. Have a great day."

"I will. You too."

Margie breathed a sigh of relief as she started up the trail again. She was going to be just fine. A short walk through the loop. Richardson had told her it was only a few kilometers, and she could walk that far. Then she could stop somewhere in Calgary for a couple of bottles of water and something to eat, and she'd be back at the office again.

CHAPTER ELEVEN

Margie was dragging her feet, but she started to recognize some of the landmarks that showed she was at or near the murder scene. She couldn't remember enough to locate it precisely. It was a lot steeper than she remembered. She wandered off of the path, looking down at the ground for some sign of where Smith's body had been. The vegetation should be crushed—if not by his body, then by the various law enforcement officers and techs gathering forensic evidence and the vehicles that had been parked nearby. There would be some sign that they had been there.

Margie walked back to the trail, went a little farther, and veered off again. It felt closer. But she still wasn't sure.

As she looked around for some sign of where the vehicles had been parked and the yellow tape tied, she suddenly felt as if she were being watched. She stopped and listened. There was no sound of anything but the birds singing and the wind in the trees.

A twig snapped off in the distance somewhere.

An animal? Someone watching her? Someone exploring on their own?

Was someone else looking for the murder scene? Maybe the killer realized he had dropped something? Or was there a treasure he had been afraid David Smith was going to discover first?

She looked around, trying to pick out a figure in the trees. She couldn't see anyone, but couldn't shake the feeling that she was not alone. Why had

Smith been killed there? Was there any significance to the place? Or was it just by chance? A random stranger? As much as she had emphasized to Cathy Lin that most murderers were not random crazies, there were a few. Every now and then, it did happen.

Another twig snapped, from a different direction this time. Margie turned slowly, aware of her peripheral vision, paying attention to whether someone was trailing or flanking her, trying to avoid being seen.

"Excuse me! You're supposed to stay on the pathways!"

The loud male voice made her jump, and Margie whirled around to confront the speaker. For a split-second, she was afraid. The man was closer than she had expected. Big, well-built, not someone whom she was going to be able to beat easily in a physical confrontation, if it came to that. But within a couple of seconds, she recognized him as the RCMP officer who was involved in the investigation.

"Constable Shack."

"Detective Pat." He rolled his eyes and blew out his breath. "It's you. I'm sorry, I didn't recognize you when your back was to me. Figured you were some curiosity-seeker, or maybe our doer, returned to the scene of the crime."

Margie wasn't sure whether she should be insulted that he had identified her as a potential suspect. But there was nothing to say that the killer hadn't been a woman. A sharp blade skillfully handled didn't require the upper body strength of a man to be effective. She wondered whether there was anything in her mailbox from the medical examiner's office yet. They should have had the time to do the postmortem—at least the preliminary results.

"You startled me."

"Sorry about that," he apologized again. "Force of habit. And I have a naturally loud voice. My wife is always getting after me for shouting when as far as I know, I was just using a conversational tone."

"Am I in the right place? Is this where he was?"

"Just a little farther up the trail." He pointed the way and then led her on. "Are you looking for anything in particular?"

It was strange that he had been drawn back there too. Was it because they had so little to go on? They had both returned, hoping to find a little something more to make sense of the situation?

"No. I just needed to see it again. Get it firmly in my mind. See if I could connect up anything… anything that might have been motive. I don't like the idea of a killing without a connection to the killer. There had to be some kind of motive. If it wasn't robbery or drugs or something personal like jealousy or rage, then what was it? What made him kill Smith?"

Shack nodded his agreement.

They went a little farther up the trail, and then Smith indicated the area. "Right over here."

They walked through it silently, separating and casting about on their own. Margie was becoming more and more anxious about Shack being there. She had wanted to be there alone. She had wanted to connect with the murder scene somehow, and having him there was blocking her. She felt like she had to watch him and be aware of him the whole time.

Eventually, they both stopped and looked at each other. "Nothing?" Shack asked.

"No. Nothing."

"Me neither."

She looked carefully at his hands and then his face. He had stooped down a couple of times to examine the ground; she had watched him out of the corner of her eye. But he didn't appear to have picked anything up. If he had, then he was skilled at sleight of hand.

Margie took out her phone to record the GPS coordinates. If she came back again, she would be able to find it on her own. And she might search the GPS coordinates on some treasure hunter sites, just to see if anything popped up. It was far from the village or any artifacts as far as she knew, but it would be worth checking out, just to be sure.

"Calling someone?" Shack inquired.

"No. Just making a note."

He waited, she thought, for an explanation, but she didn't give him anything more. Their departments were cooperating, but that didn't mean that she needed to float all of her ideas past him. They would share evidence and information that had been verified, but she didn't have to tell him everything she was thinking.

She remembered the medical examiner. "Do we have the post results yet?" she asked Shack. "I have been busy with other things and haven't seen it."

"Yeah, about an hour ago. Nothing unexpected. No drugs or poison or tattoos of secret societies." There was a smile in his voice at this joke. Margie didn't smile in return.

"So, nothing of interest."

"Nothing that jumped out at me. But of course, you might see something. I haven't read it in detail yet either, just skimmed through for any red flags."

"Okay. I'll look at it when I get back to the office." Even so, she wanted to make sure that she had received it, so she unlocked her phone and navigated to her mail, running her eye down the list of email subject lines. She tapped to open the email and then the attachment.

One thing she wanted to check just to confirm to herself… she found the description of the stab wound and what the medical examiner had been able to deduce about the blade used and the attacker.

"It was a downward stroke," she pointed out, demonstrating stabbing down into someone.

"Yes," Shack agreed.

"The Fish Creek murder was not. It was lower, and an upward stroke. Someone shorter than the victim. Going up under the ribs instead of trying to stab down through them." Abdul had been trained to kill. He knew a knife went in more easily under the ribs.

"What are the comparative heights of the victims?"

"They were both a shade over six feet."

"And the Fish Creek murder fits with the guy that you arrested. A kid. Someone shorter than him."

"But not this one. For a downward stroke to hit him in the chest where it did at that angle, you're looking for an attacker who is taller than Abdul. Someone closer to six feet tall himself."

"Good to know. But you already checked that it couldn't be the boy anyway, didn't you?"

"Yeah. I just want to eliminate him as a possible suspect in as many ways as possible. He didn't do it. There's no point in speculating that it could have been him."

Shack nodded. "Okay. The kid is off the table. At least there's one thing we know, in a whole lot of nothing."

Margie sighed. "Yeah."

"Can I walk you to your car? You know where it is?"

"Oh, no. I'm fine. I just follow this trail until I get to the parking lot."

He nodded. Margie went back to the pathway and started walking.

"Uh, Detective Pat?"

"What?"

"Other way. Unless you want to take the long way around."

She squinted at the sun, which was too far overhead for her to tell directions by it. She didn't think she was walking back the direction she had come. But she wasn't sure enough to argue with him.

"Oh. Right. Thanks."

She turned around and walked the other direction. She could tell that Shack was watching her all the way until she was out of sight. Even then, she couldn't relax. She couldn't shake the feeling that she was still being watched.

CHAPTER TWELVE

By the time she reached the parking lot, she was exhausted, hungry, thirsty, needed to use the washroom, and was irritated with herself and everyone else for the long hike. It was supposed to be an easy walk. Just a quick zip around the loop. It had ended up being a lot more than that, and she was still jumping out of her skin every time she heard a voice, a dog bark, or a twig snap.

Luckily, there was a washroom just off the parking lot. Only an outhouse, as Ian had told her, but it was better than nothing. That took care of one problem. She then climbed into her car, turned it on, and blasted the air conditioning. She didn't have any water in the car. Maybe she should keep it stocked if she were going to go on unplanned walks in the park.

She pulled back onto Glenbow Road and pointed her car uphill to get back to the highway. She hit her Bluetooth button and called the office. Detective Jones picked up on the third or fourth ring.

"Well, hello, stranger. Long time no see."

"Sorry I've been MIA today. I spent longer at the park than I expected to."

"I hope that means it was a productive trip and you found something."

"No, it was pretty much a bust."

"Pretty much?"

"I ran into Constable Shack out there."

"Really?" Jones's voice was curious. "What was he doing there? You're the primary. I would think that he would let you know if he was chasing anything down."

"Me too. I don't know that he had anything, though. I guess he was just doing the same thing as I was, looking for some clue as to why the killer attacked Smith. There had to be a motive for killing him."

"But you didn't find anything."

"No. Neither of us found anything. Or if he found anything, he didn't tell me about it."

"But you were there together, so he couldn't have found anything."

"I don't think so. It kind of creeped me out, Shack being there at the same time as I was. He had no way of knowing that I would be there. I didn't even know that I was going to be there at just that time."

"So, he wasn't there to meet you."

"No."

"It was just luck that you both ended up there at the same time."

"Exactly." Margie pondered on it. "I felt like I was being watched. Both before I ran into him and after."

"And you think…" Jones trailed off, waiting for Margie to jump in and complete the thought.

"I don't know. Was he watching me? Following me? He offered to walk me to my car. Why? Did he want to make sure that I was really leaving? Or was he being polite? Or did he think that I could be in danger?"

"He's an RCMP constable. I'm sure he was just being polite," Jones said firmly.

Margie wished she could believe it, but her imagination was running overtime. She hated the wired, anxious feeling. She looked in her rear-view mirror. There was a car behind her, but she couldn't see the face of the occupant through the glare on the windshield.

"I saw that the postmortem results came in. I'll have a look at them when I get back. Was there anything else?"

"Nothing that seemed to lead anywhere. An inventory of the items collected at the scene. What has been processed for prints. Pictures. It's kind of weird—"

Suddenly, Jones was gone.

CHAPTER THIRTEEN

Margie looked at her display and saw that the call had dropped. She looked in her mirror again at the car that was following her, as if it might somehow be his fault.

What did she think? That he was jamming her signal to keep her from talking to her office? That it was Shack, making sure that she couldn't get some vital piece of information on a piece of evidence that had been processed?

She pulled quickly onto the highway, spraying gravel behind her as if Shack were pursuing her, and she had to get away before he could ram her or force her off the road. The car behind her didn't pull out at such a reckless pace, but smoothly pulled into traffic and hung a few cars back from her. She watched to see if it would stay behind her. It did. But more than likely, he was going back to Calgary just as she was. There was only one way to go to get there. He stayed behind her because she had pulled out quickly and was staying just over the speed limit. He wouldn't pass her unless he broke the speed limit.

She kept an eye on the car, but started to relax. Shack or Dr. Kahn had told her there was a spot where the cell signal dropped, right at the top of the hill where she had been cut off from Jones. That was all it was. Right where you expected the signal to be the best, there was a blind spot and the call would drop. And he had been right.

Feeling silly about her panic, Margie called Jones back. "Sorry, I lost you there. Bad cell signal. What were you saying?"

She still kept an eye out for the car that had followed her off of the park, but tried to push away the anxiety.

"Just that I was hoping you would go through the items that he had on him. Something doesn't feel right."

"What?"

"I don't know. I can't put my finger on it. There's that woman's name and number…?"

"Right, I remember that. Nothing weird about someone writing down a phone number."

"Except today, who writes it on a piece of paper and puts it in his wallet. You'd put it in your phone, wouldn't you?"

"Well, I would, but some people are not big on technology. My mother wouldn't."

"And it's not a phone number."

Margie frowned. "It isn't?"

"Not unless he wrote it down wrong. It's only six digits. I think it is something else. Like a serial number."

Even though Canada had required ten-digit numbers for several years, Margie still often only wrote down the seven digits after the area code, unless it was a different area code from what she expected. Calgary had long been area code 403, and people still left it off when giving their phone numbers or writing them down. Margie hadn't even noticed that the number on the slip of paper was only six digits long.

"Hmm. I guess it could be something else. Maybe… he reported a theft?" Her mood lifted a little. Maybe it was a break in the case. "Maybe… if there was a theft, could it have been related to his murder?"

"I don't know," Jones's tone was doubtful. "That doesn't really… make much sense. How would a serial number lead the police to a burglar? How would killing Smith keep them from finding out?"

"Maybe he hadn't made the report yet, but he was going to. Maybe the killer knew, and he knew that if the report was made, it would lead him to a pawnshop claim ticket or a Kijiji ad. Maybe…?"

"Maybe. But it doesn't feel right."

"Okay. Well, I'll look at it when I get there. Maybe something will come to me. I'm a little muddled right now."

"You'll be here in half an hour or so?"

"Bit longer. I'm going to grab a bite to eat. I haven't had anything today, and I've been walking forever."

"I thought you were going on one of those golf carts?"

"I did for the first part, but then I wanted to walk the Tiger Lily Loop, and I ended up in Badger Bowl…"

Jones giggled. "Are those really the trail names? I like Badger Bowl."

"Yeah, those are really their names. I didn't see any badgers, though."

"Luckily. I understand they're pretty vicious."

"Are you going into Cochrane to eat?"

"Into Cochrane? Why would I? That's the opposite direction."

Margie automatically checked the road sign coming up to confirm that she was driving toward Calgary, not Cochrane.

"Ice cream."

"Ice cream?"

"Yeah, MacKay's. They are the best place in the region to go for ice cream. You have to go there."

"Well… not today. What makes them so good?"

"They make all kinds of cool flavors. They're an institution. They've been there since I was a kid. Since my parents were kids."

"I'll have to take Christina there one day. Make it a mother-daughter date."

"Yeah, you have to do it," Jones said, sounding envious. "I should have told you before you went out there today. I forget that you're not from around here, so you wouldn't know about MacKay's."

Her blood sugar back on an even keel and one bottle of water under her belt, Margie was feeling a lot better when she got back to the squad room. She laughed at herself for being so paranoid about somebody following her or being anxious with Shack being there at the same time as she was. She should be happy to know that he was investigating as well. She needed all of the help she could get.

She said hello to the various team members who were working away busily on their cases, staring at computers, talking on the phone, and making notes on the files. Jones greeted her cheerily. Margie sat down at her computer to look at the evidence again. Everything that had been in Smith's pockets had seemed normal at the time, but she might have overlooked something. Like the woman's phone number not being a phone number.

She brought up the photograph of the piece of paper and studied it.

Stella.

Like her dog. It was always funny to run into familiar names in other places. She didn't think she had ever met a person named Stella. That didn't mean that there weren't any, just that it wasn't a very common name anymore. People associated it with that scene in *A Streetcar Named Desire*. If she went by Jones's instinct that it might be a serial number, then Stella might be a brand name. Margie did a quick internet search.

A fashion company. A new Calgary condo development. Lager. She followed a link to the Stella condos and clicked through a few pages. Maybe Smith had been planning to move. The number could be a real estate listing. A phone number that he'd copied down wrong. Maybe some kind of land titles reference number. She would call around and see if she could find out.

While she was at it, she figured it was time to look at the other items that had been on the body again. Pictures of his phone had been posted, but none of the content. Maybe they hadn't gotten to it yet, or maybe there was nothing on it. Or they were still trying to get it unlocked. Those things could take time. There was a photo that had been in his wallet. His cards.

Margie cracked open her second bottle of water as she leaned forward to study the screen. She had a headache at the back of her head that she thought was from dehydration or the sun, so she needed to drink more. She enlarged the photo on the screen.

Having met Cathy Lin, she expected to find the young woman in the picture somewhere, but she was not there as far as Margie could see. She was too old to be a high school student, if that's what the building in the picture was, but she could be a teacher. She didn't remember asking Lin what her profession was. The picture didn't seem to focus on anyone in particular. Like it was a stock photo of a school, very generic. A day in the life. Apparently, nothing to be found there.

Cards in the wallet. Driver's license, credit cards, bank card, Canoe Club, Calgary Co-op membership, Community Natural Foods membership, Optimum points, library membership. Just a regular guy doing normal, everyday things. No firearms permit. No radical or religious groups. No cards in names other than that of David Smith.

She rubbed the back of her head and neck, hoping the pain and fatigue would go away. She had another sip of water and went back to the workspace for the case to check for further information.

CHAPTER FOURTEEN

Margie made sure to get off of work in good time. She could do some more work on the case later in the evening while Christina was working on her homework. But she didn't want Christina to be alone in the house after she got home from school. It was important to make sure she was safe.

Margie wasn't sure what to tell her about the rabbit and her suspicion that someone might be stalking or trying to scare her. Christina knew, of course, that since Margie was a police officer, she could be hurt in the line of duty. They both knew there were risks, though Margie wasn't sure whether Christina understood them as well as someone older and more experienced. Teenagers tended to have a strange relationship with mortality, not understanding how frail human life was and that they and those around them were only on the earth temporarily. They took risks. They acted as if they didn't know the consequences of the things they chose to do. Or as if the rules wouldn't apply to them.

So she didn't know whether Christina would take the news of a stalker in stride, or whether she would overreact to it, or if she would have another reaction that Margie hadn't even foreseen. She had come to accept that Christina was different from her. A separate and independent person with her own headspace. It was sometimes difficult as a parent to understand that this person who had come from her didn't think and react the same way as she did.

So she didn't say anything to start with. She would see if Christina brought it up herself. Then play it by ear.

"Shall we take Stella out for her walk?" Margie asked.

Christina had barely gotten home and might well complain that she needed some time to relax before having to go out again. But instead, Christina seemed relieved by the suggestion. "Yeah. Let's go out. Walkies, Stella!"

Stella went excitedly to the peg her leash hung on and panted happily as she waited for one of them to hook her up. "I think she's ready," Christina laughed.

"Sure looks like it. She's such a good girl!"

Stella's tail swept back and forth, appreciating the praise. Christina attached her lead and they left the house, headed for the pathway along Twenty-Sixth Street. They had to stop every couple of minutes for Stella to sniff at lamp posts and rocks and bugs crawling across the sidewalk and whatever scent signatures the other dogs in the neighborhood had left in the grass and on the trunks of trees. But it was relaxing. A nice, unhurried journey.

"How was school today?"

"It was okay." Christina's shoulders lifted and fell.

"Has it been as bad as you thought it would be?"

Margie knew what answer she wanted to hear. She wanted Christina to tell her that it was fine, that she was adjusting quickly and making friends, and it wasn't as bad as it had seemed the first day when she'd practically had a meltdown over having to go to a new school.

Christina didn't answer at first. They walked along, letting Stella set the pace, breathing the cooling air scented with car exhaust fumes, freshly-cut grass, and a hearty garlic scent from someone's supper cooking in a house they walked past.

"It's been better and worse," Christina said finally.

Margie didn't press for more details, just waited.

"The classes aren't bad, and I think the teachers are ten times better. A lot of stuff is the same wherever you go. Riding on the bus sucks, especially in the middle of a pandemic. School lunches." She rolled her eyes and shook her head. Margie wasn't sure whether she disliked taking lunch to school or buying lunch at the school cafeteria. She had a choice. Maybe she disliked both equally.

"And what's worse?" she prompted eventually, when it seemed that Christina wasn't going to explain any further.

"I didn't think it would be so hard to make friends. I didn't realize how few Métis there would be. And we had lots of racism in Manitoba, but at least there were a lot of us, so we could band together and just shrug it off. But here, it's more subtle, and I don't know who will have my back. There are kids who are not white but have white friends, and there are groups that will only hang out with other kids who are the same race. And there are others that… I just don't know. I'm kind of afraid to get to know the white kids, especially if they're popular, but I know they're not all bad." She shrugged. "I hate being in the youngest grade at the school. It's good because everyone is making new friends with kids who went to different schools than they did, but I don't like being… so vulnerable." Christina sighed and shook her head. "I just wish I didn't have to be there."

"Do you want me to look at other schools? Or do you want to do online? A lot of kids are right now because of the pandemic. No one would think you were weird."

"No," Christina used that long-suffering teenage voice that asked her why Margie was so intent on ruining her life. "I don't want to do that."

"Is there anything I can do?"

"We could go back to Winnipeg." After she said it, she looked at Margie. "I know we can't. You've got a job here…"

"Would you really want to? Go back to the way things were before? Leave Moushoom here by himself?"

Christina scowled, staring down at the pathway as they walked. "I don't know."

"I thought we should bring him out here one day. Do you think he would like that?"

Christina brightened, as she always did when they were talking about her grandfather. "He would like that," she agreed. "But could he? I don't think he can walk very far."

"We could use a wheelchair."

"I think that would be great. He's always so sad, stuck inside like that. He should be out where he can commune with Mother Earth."

"Good. We'll do it, then. Maybe this weekend."

Christina nodded, smiling at the opportunity to do something for Moushoom. They got to the block where they usually turned off to go home. Christina pointed farther down the pathway, where there was a branch off to a steep downhill road.

"What's over there?"

Margie looked for a moment, knowing she had been down that far before when she checked out the route to the bicycle overpass and downtown.

"Oh. The Canoe Club. They put their canoes into the irrigation canal down there."

Christina nodded. "We should try that sometime. Do they do lessons?"

"I don't know. We could find out."

Christina knew that Margie didn't like watersports, so Margie didn't see the need to point it out. If Christina wanted to take some canoe lessons, Margie was sure it could be arranged. She would just be watching with her feet firmly planted on the bank. She was willing to spring for anything that would help Christina to feel like she belonged there.

Or almost anything.

❧

SOMETHING HAD BEEN NIGGLING at the back of Margie's mind since she had returned from her walk with Stella and Christina. She felt uncomfortable and anxious without knowing why. She kept an eye on the windows as it started to get darker, not liking it that she couldn't see out. She turned on the outside lights so that she would know if someone were in the yard again. Christina was doing her homework at the kitchen table with her headphones on, and if she thought this was strange behavior, she didn't bother to say anything about it. Margie wondered how much money it would take to get a good alarm system installed. Or maybe just motion-detecting lights and a webcam, so that they could get a picture of whoever entered the yard.

She sat down at her computer to review the postmortem report on David Smith. She was finding it difficult to focus, but the report didn't say anything she didn't already know. She looked again at the various personal items that they had recovered. Still no more information on the contents of his phone.

Stella

Membership to the Canoe Club

A picture of a high school

Margie sucked in her breath so suddenly that it made her cough and choke. Christina pulled one of the earbuds away from her ear, looking at her. "Are you okay?"

"No!"

Christina looked startled. She got up quickly and went to the sink to run a glass of water for Margie. Margie took it with shaky hands. She took a few sips, trying to calm the racking coughs.

"What happened?" Christina asked. She patted Margie on the back. "Are you choking?"

Margie shook her head and put her hand over her mouth to try to stifle the cough. With her other hand, she pointed at her screen. Stella and a reference number. Christina peered at it and shook her head.

"Stella's license number? What about it?"

Tears running down her face, Margie patted her leg to call Stella to her. She looked at the number on the tag attached to Stella's collar. Christina was right. It was Stella's license number. She forced more of the water down.

"The Canoe Club," she choked out.

"The Canoe Club? Yeah? What about it? Mom, you're being weird. It's like we're playing charades, but I don't even know what the theme is."

Margie scratched Stella's ears and bent down to kiss her on the top of the head, trying to calm the coughing.

"Make sure—the doors—locked."

Christina didn't ask why this time. She just took a few steps to the front door, made sure that the bolt was turned, and then jogged through the kitchen to the back door and checked that one.

"They're locked," she reported back. "Now tell me. What's going on?"

"I just think… something is wrong. I have to call Constable Evans. And Sergeant MacDonald. I think…" Margie cut herself off and shook her head. She couldn't finish the thought. It was like saying what she was thinking was the last line to complete a spell, and if she said it out loud, he might materialize in front of her.

When Constable Evans had come to take her report on the dead rabbit, she had put his business card in her pocket and had not yet entered it into her phone. Margie felt her pockets and eventually came up with the card.

She cleared her throat a few times and seemed to be able to talk without more coughing, though her voice was weak and rough. She grasped Christina's hand before placing the call.

"It's going to be okay, Christina."

"What's okay? I'm scared, Mom."

"I know." Margie looked at the windows again. She still couldn't see anyone outside. Once it was dark, people didn't walk around the neighborhood anymore. Not much. They might drive to the grocery store or to do what other errands they needed to, but they wouldn't be out taking a stroll. There wouldn't be any reason for anyone to be walking down her back alley or peeking into the yard.

She tapped Evans's digits into her phone and waited for it to connect. Of course, she probably wouldn't be able to get him until the next day, when he was back on shift again. If he was even on shift. He might have the day off.

"Evans."

"I'm sorry to be calling you after hours, Constable," Margie apologized. "It's Margie Patenaude, from this morning. The rabbit."

"Yes, I remember you. I'm afraid I don't have anything back on the case yet. These things take a few days. But rest assured, we are taking it seriously."

"There's more. I'm worried… he may be dangerous."

"Has he been back? Do you know who it is?"

"I don't think so. And I'm not sure exactly, but… he may be connected to another case I'm working."

Evans knew that Margie was in Homicide. Christina did too, but she didn't seem to put it together, at least not as quickly as Evans did.

"Oh. I see." His voice was serious. "We'll put a rush on it, then. Are you in danger? You should have called 9-1-1 if it is an emergency."

"I haven't seen him, though, so I don't know that it is. I just… do you think you could send a couple of patrols by tonight? Just to be sure everything is okay?"

"Yes. I'll get on that. Do you have any evidence that ties the two cases together?"

"Can you tell me… how someone would get my dog's license number?"

Evans was silent for a moment. When he spoke, it was in a tone that suggested that Margie might be completely off her rocker. "How would someone get your dog's license number? From you, I guess. Or if they were right there to look at the number on her tag. Or maybe someone who worked in the licensing department."

"Somebody had it."

"Who?"

"Somebody had her name and the license number written down."

"Who?" Evans repeated urgently.

"The Glenbow Park victim. It was in his wallet."

"Oh." He was taken aback, but also calmer upon hearing this. "Well then… if he's dead, he isn't going to do you any harm."

"He was dead before the rabbit. He died… between the squirrel and the rabbit."

"That doesn't make much sense."

"It does… if the killer put it in his wallet."

CHAPTER FIFTEEN

"Mom... I'm freaking out," Christina said. "I don't get what you're saying here. What do you mean the killer put Stella's number in the dead guy's wallet? Why would he do that?"

"To taunt me." Margie tapped Sergeant MacDonald's number into her phone. "He copied everything he could from the Fish Creek murder so that I would be called in on the Glenbow Park murder too. And then he planted things on the body to taunt me. To tell me that he was close to me, and I didn't even see him there."

She swallowed and held tightly to Christina's hand. Christina squeezed back. Neither let go.

Margie's phone was in speaker mode so that she didn't have to pick it up and could continue to hold Christina's hand and to work her mouse at the same time.

"Patenaude?" MacDonald said sharply.

"Sir. I'm sorry to call you at home. I may have a break on the case. And... I might need some help."

"Of course. What have you got?"

"You remember the name Stella and the number on the paper in his wallet?"

"Yes."

"That's the name and license number of my dog."

She gave him a moment to process that. It didn't take him long.

"He knows you."

"He must. He couldn't get that number from anywhere else. Unless he works in the licensing department. He could only get it from me or by looking at Stella's collar tags. And I didn't give it to anyone. He wanted me to know… that he's been close to me."

"It's an assumption, but let's go with it. Was there anything else on Smith's body that was suspicious?"

"His address is close to Glenbow."

"Yes. Makes sense, that's why he's able to walk there frequently."

"But he had a membership card for the Canoe Club."

"They must canoe on the Bow over there. Put out on the water in Cochrane, maybe."

"Do you know where the Canoe Club is?"

"No."

"It's two blocks from my house."

"And you're not in the northwest."

"I'm about as far from there as you can get."

"You're in Forest Lawn, aren't you?"

"Almost. Greater Forest Lawn."

"It still might make sense. He could be a member of the Canoe Club and still canoe over by the park. It's a possibility."

"Yes."

"Anything else?"

Margie gave Christina's hand a tug, encouraging her to sit down on the couch beside her. Christina sat down and put her arm around Margie.

"Sir, you're on speaker and my daughter is here." She probably should have told him that at the beginning of the conversation.

"Christina, right? How are you, Christina? Hanging in there?"

"Yes," Christina said in a small voice.

Margie clicked through images on her computer. "Christina. Can you look at this picture?"

Christina leaned in toward the screen. She nodded.

"Where is this picture taken? Do you know?" Margie asked.

"Yeah. That's my school. Forest Lawn High."

"Are you sure?"

"Yes."

"Sir, that picture found on Smith—" Margie started to tell MacDonald.

Christina put her finger directly onto Margie's computer screen. "You see... there I am. Right there."

Margie wouldn't have recognized the back view of her daughter. The sliver of her caught in the photograph was too small. But she realized that the shirt and pants could have been Christina's, and the girl in the picture had long black hair. Margie took another swallow of her water, trying to wash down the lump that was suddenly stuck in her throat.

"Christina, are you saying you're in the picture that was found at the homicide scene?" MacDonald demanded.

"If that's where this picture is from. Yes."

"It is," Margie agreed.

"I don't like this," MacDonald said. "I want someone there with you. Especially considering—the other thing we discussed this morning."

"Christina knows about the squirrel and the rabbit," Margie told him. "And I already called Constable Evans to ask him if they would send patrols by the house."

"This guy clearly knows a lot about you, including where you live and where Christina goes to school. He's planted clues to let you know he's out there watching. You don't know who he is?"

Margie drew in a long breath and let it out slowly, trying to clear her mind. Who had been close enough to them to see Stella's dog tags? Had he been in the yard? Maybe Stella had run up to greet him when he had planted the squirrel. She was a gentle creature and would have considered a stranger who brought her a dead squirrel her new best friend.

Had he been following them? Or was it someone they knew?

"We don't have the parking lot video yet?" Margie asked.

"Not yet. I'll light a fire under someone. And I don't know if the phone will hold any clues... it is possible that he took a picture of the view and managed to catch the killer in the frame at some point. I doubt we would be so lucky, but I'll push to get that phone cracked too. I'd like someone there with you tonight, just in case... Do you have any preferences?"

"Well... two single gals here... I'd rather it was a woman, so we don't have to be worried about walking around in our PJ's."

"Jones, then?"

"Yes."

"I'll see if she's available. If I can't get her, you'll take someone else on the team?"

"Yes. Of course."

"Okay. Expect one of the team on your doorstep within a couple of hours. Don't open the door without verifying who it is first."

"I won't."

He hung up the call without saying goodbye. Christina leaned her head down onto Margie's shoulder and stayed cuddled there, like she was a little girl again, and not a couple of inches taller than Margie.

"Are you okay?" Margie asked.

"Yes."

"It's scary."

"Yeah."

"But you're okay?"

"I'm here with you."

"Is it all right with you if I get my gun out?"

Christina nodded.

While Margie's duty weapon stayed in her locker at work when she returned home at the end of the day, she did have a personal weapon at home. She left Christina sitting on the couch and went to her bedroom closet, retrieving the gun and ammunition from the gun safe on the shelf. She had never needed it for personal protection before. She kept it oiled and took it to the range every couple of months, but she had never before felt like she needed it. She returned to her seat beside Christina and lay the gun down within reach on the side table.

Christina didn't return to her homework, cuddling up to Margie once more. Margie turned on the TV to provide a distraction. Neither of them paid it as much attention as they normally would have, aware of every noise that Stella or the house made as they sat there waiting for something to happen.

CHAPTER SIXTEEN

Morning came too soon for Margie. She hadn't slept more than a couple of hours, and what little sleep she'd gotten had been restless and plagued by nightmares. She peeked in on Christina and found that she was still asleep. Detective Jones was still sitting in the living room, prowling occasionally to each of the windows to check for any intruders.

"Hi," Margie greeted softly. "No trouble?"

"No. Quiet neighborhood. Some neighbors heading out to work already, a few walkers, but nothing suspicious."

Stella whined at Margie and took a few steps toward the door, wanting to be let out. Margie ducked into Christina's room to look out the window. It was still dark but, with the outside lights on, the yard was fairly well illuminated, and she couldn't see anything suspicious.

"I'm just going to check out the yard before I let Stella out," she told Jones. "Make sure we don't have any more little surprises."

"Take your gun with you."

Margie wanted to argue that it wasn't necessary, but she didn't. She retrieved her weapon and went outside, preventing Stella from following her out until she could clear the yard. Stella barked and yipped in protest.

Margie took a quick turn around the yard, but didn't find any dead animals this time. She heard footsteps crunching down the alley and followed them with her eyes, waiting for the walker to come into view. She relaxed when she saw it was Oscar. He smiled and waved at her

"Hello, Oscar. Hi, Milo." She couldn't see Milo walking beside him, but could hear him panting and his chain jingling.

"Looks like it's going to be a nice day," Oscar observed. Margie agreed. He kept walking, disappearing from her view a few houses down. Margie went back to the door and let Stella out. She stood in the doorway with Jones, watching Stella race around the yard and then check out each of her scent posts one at a time.

"That was one of your neighbors?" Jones asked.

"Yes. And no."

Jones raised her brows in query.

"I know him from walking the dogs. He walks Milo and we walk Stella. We run into each other on the pathway. Stop and talk for a minute sometimes."

They were both silent.

"He's a nice guy," Margie said.

"Nothing suspicious there, then?"

"No."

Margie gave Stella a couple more minutes and then called her back in. She got herself a cup of coffee. Christina came out of her room, blinking owlishly.

"Hi," Margie greeted, and pulled Christina close to kiss her on the forehead. "How are you this morning?"

"I didn't think he lived over here," Christina said, and it was an instant before Margie connected that Christina was talking about Oscar. She must have heard her talking with Jones or seen her wave at Oscar. "I thought he was in Dover. Just… not here. I've never seen him in the neighborhood before. Only on the pathway."

Margie nodded.

She looked at Jones, who was standing nearby listening. "She's right."

CHAPTER SEVENTEEN

Margie was reluctant to let Christina get on the bus to go to school. Christina told her with forced cheerfulness that everything would be fine and gave her a hug and a kiss on the cheek, then ran to catch the bus just in time. Margie watched until the bus was out of sight. There didn't appear to be anyone following it, friend or stranger.

In a few minutes, Margie was on her way back to Glenbow Park. It would take her nearly an hour. She couldn't help being nervous about what the day would bring. She tried deep breathing when she got out to the ring road. She tried chanting. She tried putting her de-stress music list on the radio.

None of it helped very much. Margie was still just as anxious when she got to the Glenbow Road turnoff from the highway. She looked behind her as she slowed down to make the turn, but couldn't see anyone tailing her.

The Alberta Parks guy that MacDonald had talked to told her the gate would be unlocked for her; she just had to get out of her car to swing it open. Then she could drive down to the Park Office. There she would meet with someone who would have the various surveillance videos for her.

She had known that the gate would be a pinch point. She could feel eyes on her as she got out of her car to open it. She brushed her fingers over her gun in its holster. As she walked to the gate, another car drove down Glenbow Road and pulled to the side. A tall figure got out. Margie watched with a sense of disbelief as his dog jumped out to join him. Man and his dog. Doing everything together.

"Margie!" Oscar smiled pleasantly. "Fancy running into you here! I thought you would be at work by now."

It was, of course, no coincidence that he was there. Despite Margie not being able to see him behind her on the way over, one of the tail cars had picked him up and informed Margie of the fact.

"You're very smart, aren't you?" she asked Oscar blandly. "You had everyone fooled."

His eyes narrowed a little. "I don't know about that," he said. "The news never reported any connection between the two murders."

"No one ever thought they were the same killer. They were just similar enough to get me over here to investigate."

He nodded. "That was all I wanted."

She could tell that he was bursting with pride. Excited to tell her how smart he had been. How he had planted every clue and watched her trying to break the case, laughing at her when they would meet on their evening walks.

She could see him in her mind, making a fuss over Stella, scratching her ears and telling her what a good dog she was. Cuddling her close to his face. Close enough to see her license number.

"You took longer than I thought to figure out the clues. I thought you would get *Stella* right away."

"And when I figured that out, was I supposed to know that it was you?"

"No." He laughed. "I could tell you were suspicious this morning. But that didn't stop you from coming back here. Why did you need to come back here again when you were here so long yesterday?"

So he *had* been watching her. It hadn't just been an overactive imagination.

Oscar was walking toward her. Just inching forward every now and then, like if he did it slowly enough she wouldn't know he was within striking distance until it was too late. It was difficult for Margie not to pull her gun immediately to protect herself.

"I came for the surveillance tapes. To see if I could find you on any of them."

He nodded. "Well, you're not going to get the chance, I'm afraid."

His hand was in his pocket. Holding an open knife, if she weren't mistaken.

"Why would you do all of this? Go to all this risk? Kill a man you didn't even know just to get my attention?" Her voice was getting higher and louder, though she tried to keep it under control.

"*Detective* Patenaude," he said slowly, sounding each syllable out distinctly. "You didn't tell me you were a cop when we first met. Or any time after that."

"It didn't come up. We just talked about the dogs and the weather."

"You thought you were smarter than me, but you weren't."

He took another step toward her, closing in quickly, pulling his hand with the knife in it out of his pocket and raising it to stab downward into her chest, as he had with David Smith. But Margie had her gun clear of the holster, and there were shouts from half a dozen other police officers who had been watching and listening from their vantage points, now visible with guns raised and shouting at him to freeze.

Oscar looked around at them, stunned. "How…?" He dropped his knife and raised his hands, giving them no reason to shoot him. He blinked, baffled.

Margie secured him in handcuffs and patted him down before answering. "It was a good idea you had, using Stella's license number."

He shook his head. "What?"

"I didn't know your last name or where you lived. So we looked up Milo. There aren't very many dogs named Milo licensed in the southeast. Actually, just one in the Greater Forest Lawn area."

"But you didn't know I was coming here! You didn't know I was following you again."

"I didn't see you. You're pretty good. But the cars a kilometer back were able to spot your vehicle, when they knew what to look for. And *I* knew where I was going, even if you didn't. So that officers closer to the scene could get here ahead of us."

His usual wide, white smile was gone. His face was red with fury. She waited for him to shout at her that it was not fair, that she had cheated. And maybe she had. She hadn't let him play out the game the way he had wanted to.

But he said nothing more.

CHAPTER EIGHTEEN

"I don't get it." Margie sighed as she worked her way through the reports that had to be filed to document all the evidence that had pointed to Oscar as a suspect, and his capture and arrest in the park. "What would make a person do something like this? So random and... so bizarre. He didn't even know Smith. He did it all just so he could feed me clues and watch me work the case?"

Detective Cruz was leaning against Detective Jones's desk nearby, giving her a hand in getting everything filled out properly and offering his own commentary on the case.

"Not much in his background that explains it. No prior arrests. No restraining orders. He seems to be a law-abiding citizen, right down to properly licensing his dog."

"And picking up after him," Margie contributed. "He was always very diligent. Never 'forgot' his bags at home or pretended not to notice a mess."

"I did find one thing," Jones offered, catching a stray curl of blond hair and smoothing it away as she stared at her computer screen.

Margie waited for more information. Cruz leaned toward Jones to look at her computer screen. "What?"

"He washed out of the police academy."

Margie stopped typing. Other keyboards and discussions all went silent at the same time. The room was still, everybody listening in.

"He was a cop?" Margie demanded, flabbergasted.

"He wanted to be. Did fine at the written test and initial screening." Jones's fingers tapped the keys lightly, the key-clicks loud in the silent bullpen. "But during training… something happened. He dropped out. Resigned or was asked to leave; there aren't really any details here. You would have to talk to his trainer." A few clicks of the mouse to drill deeper for the information. "Christensen." Jones paused. "Elizabeth Christensen."

Margie's mind went back to Oscar's words. *You didn't tell me you were a cop…. You thought you were smarter than me.* The anger in his tone. Accusation.

"He had problems training under a woman," she guessed. "Doesn't think we should be cops. Much less to be successful at something. Like at being a homicide detective."

Cruz and Jones were both nodding.

"And not just a woman," Cruz pointed out, "but a Native woman. You've heard, haven't you, about how all these ethnics are pushing out the qualified white men?" His sarcastic tone dispelled any thought that he gave such an attitude any credence.

"You'd better watch out," Margie warned. "They'll be coming after your job next."

"I'm not a white ma—" Cruz caught the glimmer in Margie's eyes and cut himself off. He shook his head, letting out a puff of breath. "You almost had me there, Detective Pat. Almost."

Margie winked at Jones.

It hadn't been *almost* at all.

MARGIE HAD one more trip to make to Glenbow Ranch Provincial Park. It wasn't exactly on her way home, and it was hard for her to take that time away from her family, but she believed that community policing in Calgary meant more than just catching the bad guy and going on to the next file.

Justice and healing required more than an arrest.

After she parked her car in the staff parking area, a woman came out to meet her. Long, brown hair, fine wrinkles around her eyes, and a light step as she approached Margie and offered her hand to shake.

"Alice," she offered, as Margie squeezed her thin, dry hand. "I'm glad to meet you in person, Detective Pat."

"Thank you. You're sure this is okay? I don't want to do anything that would get you in trouble or reflect badly on the police department if someone complained."

"Oh, no," Alice proclaimed. "We acknowledge this is Treaty 7 land. Our First Nations have been allowed to perform ceremonies here. It's never been a problem."

Margie had run into many people who mouthed treaty acknowledgments as they were expected to when they clearly didn't mean or understand them, but Alice seemed to be sincere.

"Even though I'm not part of that treaty?" Margie asked, making sure there could be no misunderstanding.

"Of course not. We know you're Métis. But it isn't like you're some blond-haired thirteen-year-old making excuses for starting a grass fire."

"Okay. Thank you."

Margie had made the decision not to go all the way down to where David Smith had been murdered. She didn't want to get lost or spend that much more time away from her family. She walked instead into a stand of trees a short distance away, the closest wilderness space, and prepared herself.

Despite Alice's words, she watched Margie from a distance, eyes sharp to make sure that there were not any sparks or embers that might start the dry grasses on fire. Margie ignored her. She unfastened her braid that had been coiled into a bun and let it hang down her back.

Margie took several items out of her shoulder bag. She draped the sash that had been given to her by her band before leaving Winnipeg around her shoulders.

She unwrapped the bundle of sacred herbs and placed them in the smudge bowl. She lit them with a match and blew gently to make them smoke. Smudging was not actually a traditional part of Métis culture, but her people were open to new rituals and traditions, and many had adopted smudging as part of their spiritual practice.

Thinking about Smith, she offered the bowl in each of the four directions. The smudge smoke drifted down the hill. Margie started a low chant, praying for healing for Smith's girlfriend and family, for the family who had discovered his body and the other park users who had been troubled by it.

For the police and professionals who had all helped to gather the evidence to address the wrong that had been committed.

And for Oscar, a man whose soul had been so hurt that he had struck out in violence against someone he didn't even know, and someone he thought he did.

She prayed for peace and healing for them all.

When the herbs stopped smoking, Margie picked up a hand bell and tolled out nine chimes. The low ringing of the bell stretched out over the landscape and faded like the smoke.

Margie packed her things and left the park without looking back.

CHAPTER NINETEEN

Christina wanted a turn pushing the wheelchair, so Margie let her take over. As the sun started to set, there was a chilly wind setting in. She bent down to tuck the extra blanket around Moushoom to make sure that he was comfortable.

"How is that? Are you nice and toasty?"

"This is wonderful," he said comfortably. "It has been so long since I was able to get out."

Margie smiled, pleased that her idea had been a good one. Moushoom wrapped his hands around his Tim's hot chocolate and raised it to his mouth for a sip. "It is nice to have family around me, and to be able to get out into the fresh air and make contact with nature again."

It wasn't exactly like he was in the wilds. Maybe one day, she would take him to Glenbow Park for a cart tour. Then he could really get out somewhere that he could connect with Mother Earth. But for now, he was happy being out on the pathway, with the long, yellowing grass beside him, trees growing in little bunches putting on their autumn colors, and people out for a stroll or to walk their dogs. Stella waited patiently for them to start walking again, her tongue hanging out of her mouth.

"I'm glad we could all get out together too. I like that we live close and can come by for a visit whenever we want. I'm sorry it's been a few days, I've been tied up with work."

He nodded and had another sip of hot chocolate. "Remind me again what it is that you do."

Others in the extended family had whispered about the possibility of senility, but to Margie, Moushoom had seemed sharp and aware in the times they had seen him so far. This was the first time that he appeared to have forgotten something she had told him. But he couldn't be expected to remember every piece of information, could he?

They started walking again, Margie staying beside Moushoom, where he could still hear and see her.

"I'm a police detective," she reminded him. "I work on the homicide squad."

"Homicide." Moushoom shook his head slowly. "That must be very hard on you."

"Well, it's not easy. But our solve rate is eighty percent. We do good work."

"I didn't mean that it was hard to solve them," he said, as if that should have been obvious. "I mean, it is hard on your mind and your spirit."

"Oh. Yes, I guess so." She didn't know how long it would take her to get over the nightmares or to stop jumping at every little sound in the house, to stop herself from checking on poor Christina every fifteen minutes.

And even though she had known that they needed to take Stella out for a walk and she wanted to take Moushoom out, it had been hard to make herself put her plan into action.

She felt vulnerable walking on the pathway as the sunlight began to fade, and they were left in twilight, and then in darkness. She scrutinized every face as people walked by them, looked at every dog. She knew logically that it had only been one man; only one dog walker had been dangerous. But that didn't stop her brain from checking every single face and dog to make sure that it wasn't Oscar and Milo, or someone else who might have bad feelings toward her.

As safe as the pathway seemed, she wasn't sure she would ever feel one hundred percent safe again.

GLENBOW RANCH PROVINCIAL PARK

In 2006, the children of Alberta rancher Neil Harvie sold 3,246 acres of land to the Government of Alberta to conserve the land, fulfilling the vision of their father. At that time, the author was working as a legal assistant with Andy Crooks, the family's lawyer, and had an insider's view as plans for the park rolled out. She was involved in and present at the park opening in 2011.

Workman has worked closely with the Glenbow Ranch Park Foundation (a non-profit organization that handles many of the visitor services for the park) on a number of levels and like many of the stewards and Calgary west/Cochrane residents, considers it "her park."

As indicated in the title and storyline, the park features some challenging hills. It is a dry park, so when you visit, be sure to bring your water bottle!

DARK WATER UNDER THE BRIDGE

PARKS PAT MYSTERIES #3

*That all fears may
be overcome*

CHAPTER ONE

The sun was still low in the sky, orange light filtering into the kitchen. Margie "Detective Pat" Patenaude was sipping her morning coffee and staring into the depths of her fridge, trying to decide whether to make herself a bag lunch to take to the police station with her, or whether she would take a break and go find something over lunch. She hadn't explored many restaurants near the office, so she wasn't sure what was available. Not that she was that picky.

"The same things are in there as the last time you opened the door," Christina teased, echoing the same words Margie used when her daughter stood staring vacantly into the fridge. "Nothing new is going to materialize while you stand there with the door open."

"You're a smart aleck," Margie told her.

But Christina was right. Margie already knew what was in the fridge, and inspiration wasn't going to strike just because she was standing there with the door open, letting all of the cold air spill to the floor and raising the energy bill. She sighed and closed it.

"I don't know what I want today."

"We need to go shopping. Get something good."

"I think you're right," Margie agreed. They could go to the Co-op, or the No Frills down Seventeenth Avenue, and stock up on some easy to prepare meals. Margie never seemed to have the time or energy to make much when she got home from work.

The phone rang. Margie looked at it, hoping it would just be some telemarketer so she could ignore it. She didn't want to have to deal with a real phone call so soon. She didn't even have one cup of coffee down yet. But it was Detective Cruz, a Filipino-born cop on her team.

"Patenaude," she answered briskly.

"Is this Detective 'Parks' Pat?" There was a note of amusement in Cruz's voice.

"Parks Pat?" That was a new one. Margie understood where the nickname came from, of course. Since she had moved to Calgary, she had been primary on a murder in Fish Creek Park first, and then a similar one in Glenbow Ranch Provincial Park. They had not been related, except by circumstances, but both had been reported in the news, and it would seem that she had now earned her homicide team nickname. Parks Pat.

"That's what they're calling you," Cruz acknowledged.

"Well, okay. It could be worse. What did you need?"

"Have you ever been to Ralph Klein Park?"

Margie let out a puff of breath. "Ralph Klein Park. No, I haven't even heard about that one. Is it out there near Glenbow?"

"No, actually this one is close to you. That's why I figured you might have been there. It's new. Just opened in 2011."

Margie thought about the little park she had visited while taking Stella out on a walk with Christina. It had a little pond and a splash park for young children. She couldn't remember the name off the top of her head, but was sure it wasn't the one that Cruz was talking about. "Another provincial park?"

"City of Calgary park, this one. Though it might be out of city limits, I'm not clear on that. It's right on the eastern edge of the city, anyway. Think you could get out there?"

"Yes, of course. What… am I going to find there?"

"We've got another body. Sorry."

Well, that was to be expected when she worked homicide. "Another body in another park? But we know it isn't either of the same killers, because we already caught them both. They're locked up where they can't do any more harm. Was it the same cause of death?"

"You'll have to get more information when you get out there, but preliminary indications are that it is not. No visible stab wounds on this one."

"Good. I think if it was the same cause, I might have been a little freaked out."

"We're all a little on edge. I'm going to head out there before long too; I'll back you up."

Margie wondered why he hadn't gone to investigate first. If he was the one who had taken the call. "I'm primary on this one? Why?"

He chuckled. "Because they asked for you in particular."

"Me?"

"Parks Pat. They figured if it's in a park, you should be the one in charge."

"That's just—"

"I know. And don't worry, I'm sure that sooner or later you'll get a body that wasn't found in a park. But for now, that's your assignment. Go to the park, make nice, find out what you can about our newest victim."

CHAPTER TWO

Christina assured Margie that she would be ready to get on the bus when it arrived and wouldn't be late for school. She was grown up enough to deal with her own transportation. And Margie knew the fifteen-year-old could handle it. She had been going to the high school via bus since the first day, when the body at Fish Creek Park had been discovered. Margie had promised to drive her that day, but it had not worked out. As a teenager, Christina was as independent as Margie would let her be. Margie figured she should be thankful that she wasn't getting constant requests to be driven here and there all over the city. Calgary sprawled over a huge area, and it could be challenging to get from one end to the other. So far, Christina had been content just riding the bus between the house and the school.

So Margie left Christina to finish getting ready and climbed into her car. She put the park's name into the GPS. She quickly braided her long black hair and coiled it into a bun and waited for the GPS to start receiving coordinates from the satellite and plotting a course. She should be happy that she was being assigned to parks. She enjoyed being outside, connecting with nature. She liked to walk and hike and might even take Stella out there with her one day. For sure she was going to take the whole family out to Glenbow Ranch. When she was off and could arrange it around Christina's school schedule. She would schedule a golf cart tour so that they could take Moushoom, Margie's grandfather, with them. He would like it there. Sometimes, the Nakoda out that direction participated in ceremonies in the park. Moushoom would really love that. They didn't speak the same language or come from exactly the same culture, but Moushoom would understand the symbols and the ceremonies.

The GPS beeped and the robotic voice directed Margie what direction to drive. She put all other considerations aside and focused on following the GPS instructions. Despite her Métis heritage, she had a terrible sense of direction and, if she made a wrong turn, it could take another twenty minutes to get back on track again. Not just because it was sometimes difficult to get turned around if you ended up going the wrong way on a highway or main thoroughfare, but also because she was totally capable of then getting back on the exact same road headed the wrong direction a second time. Or getting flustered and taking another wrong turn.

So she kept an eye on the GPS screen previewing the curves and intersections ahead so that she would not miss any exits or turn the wrong direction. She was glad that Cruz had mentioned it was on the edge of or just outside the city, or she might have started to panic when she ended up driving alongside golden brown fields in an area that felt too remote to bother with a park. But she remembered how Glenbow Park was down in the valley below the highway so, even with its vast size, it had been invisible until she had driven down the last road.

There were a couple of signs, and then she could see a few people walking or cycling to the left of the highway. She turned onto the access road into a grouping of trees. The road curved toward a building that looked like it was built with children's blocks. The medical examiner's van and the forensic team were there, pulled up onto the sidewalk. Rather than parking beside them, Margie followed the road past the building to a public parking lot. It probably filled up on a weekend, but early in the morning on a weekday, it was quiet. A few scattered vehicles. Unlike at the provincial parks, there were no Conservation Officers in gray shirts waiting to drive her in an electric golf cart to the scene of the crime. She had seen a small group of people gathered past the playground, so she knew where the body was and it wasn't too far to walk.

Margie got out and strode towards the big education center. She walked through a small plot of short apple trees that declared itself The Orchard. The apples were turning from green to a rusty red. Some were scattered on the ground with two or three small bites out of them. Not the work of squirrels, by the size of the bite marks.

She stopped when she got to a railing and looked down. What Cruz had not bothered to mention to her was that Ralph Klein Park was a wetland. She stared down at water, which was nearly black and seemed bottomless. The education center jutted out over the water, walkways around it in two tiers up above the water. She swallowed and looked around to focus her mind somewhere else.

She circled the education center around the land side. There was an unusual playground like a pile of sticks, a zip line stretching away from it toward a pond or canal where the rest of the crime scene investigators were. Margie picked up her pace and strode toward them.

Bodies in the water could be ugly. Bloated up with gases, swollen and unrecognizable features, skin starting to separate from the flesh. Predator and insect activity.

But she would stay calm and keep things moving forwards. She would be strong and professional and there would be no issues.

One of the figures by the water waved at her. Margie nodded and joined them just outside the yellow tape perimeter. The group parted so that she could see the woman's body. She was wearing a white blouse and dark blue or black pants. She was face-down in the water, close enough to the shore that they would be able to pull her out without hip waders.

"You're Detective Pat?" a man in a Calgary Police Services uniform and black mask asked.

"Detective Margie Patenaude, yes," she agreed. "Who discovered the body?"

"Early morning jogger. Over there." He nodded to a young man in tights and a jacket sitting some distance away from the scene. "I've got a brief outline from him, but you can take his statement."

"And this is where she was? He didn't move her?"

"He says he didn't touch her."

"Okay, good. Do you think he did?"

The constable considered her question seriously. She took the moment of silence to read his name bar. Archambault. "I don't think he did. It's natural to reach out to someone like this, check to make sure they're really dead and that it's not just a mannequin. But his shoes were relatively dry." Archambault looked down at his own shoes. His shoes and pant cuffs were covered in mud.

Margie raised her brows. "So, you did touch her?"

"Just did what I'm supposed to. Made sure she was good and dead, then came back here and called your team. Preserved the scene."

There was a large area cordoned off with yellow tape. Margie would have made it bigger, but it was a judgment call.

"You checked for a pulse?"

"Just radial. It was obvious touching her that she was dead."

"Rigor?"

"Yes. And… sodden. She's been in there a few hours."

Margie didn't feel the need to touch the body herself to verify this. She felt sorry for Constable Archambault. But she'd had enough opportunities to check for life signs herself. It was one of the less enjoyable parts of being a law enforcement officer.

"Thank you." She nodded to him.

He nodded back his thanks. Margie looked at the body again. A sweeping glance. She was trying not to commit more to long-term memory than she could help. "Did she have a purse? Wallet? Anything to identify her? There's no missing person report?"

Everyone there shook their heads. Margie looked around. "Let's protect any nearby garbage cans or bins. Extend the perimeter up and down the stream another… twenty-five meters. Watch for footprints. She didn't fly into that water. Someone killed her here or dumped her here. We want to find out all that we can about that. Surveillance video in the parking lot?"

"We're waiting for someone from the education center to get here. Apparently, they will have access to the security video," one of the forensic guys advised.

"Okay." Margie hoped that there was good video. They wouldn't have been able to identify the killer in the Fish Creek case if they hadn't had good video footage. Multiple pathways, several cameras in the parking lot, and even wildlife cams had enabled them to establish the people who had been in and out of the area the victim was killed in. That made it a lot more practicable to find the killer.

"I'll let you guys work out the best way to get her out of the water and collect any evidence," she told the forensic team and the doctor from the medical examiner's office, whose nametag identified him as Adrian Galt.

They seemed to be happy that she wasn't telling them how to do their job. Margie was sure they would be much better at working out the best procedure than she would. And she wouldn't have to get any closer to the water herself.

CHAPTER THREE

It was a while before someone from the education center came out and met Margie a short distance from where the forensic team was erecting screens. Margie was afraid it would be a teacher or docent who didn't have any authority or in-depth knowledge of the park, but the tall, thin man who introduced himself as Arby Finkle seemed to be in charge of operations there. He wore a suit and tie, which seemed excessively formal.

He was literally wringing his hands, his expression deeply distressed. Margie was glad Finkle couldn't see the body past the screens. He might have had a complete breakdown.

"I'll need you to tell me everything you can about the security here and…" Margie tried to focus, "about the water system. Some of this is man-made." She motioned to the deep pool she had first seen adjacent to the parking lot. "I just need as much background as you can give me. Whether or not you think it would be relevant."

"Of course, of course." Finkle wrung his hands more. He looked at her with great intensity, eyes glittering with emotion. Becoming aware of his hand-wringing, he tried to hold still, but he just ended up squeezing the blood out of both hands until they were as white as the woman's corpse. "I can't believe that something like this could happen here. Why would anyone…" He shook his head, not even able to finish the sentence. Margie waited, hoping to hear whether he said 'kill someone here' or 'dump someone here.' Which did he think it was?

But he didn't finish; he just shook his head, sobbing in a low thrum Margie could barely hear.

"We will need the security video," she prompted, trying to get him started.

"Yes. Of course. I'll get you whatever I can."

"Whatever you can? Don't you have a fully operating system?"

"Well… yes, most of it is functional. What we have."

"I don't like the sound of that," Margie warned.

"Yes… well, we've had some vandalism over time, and it takes the city time to get around to fixing it. Our little park isn't exactly high on their priorities list. There are probably buildings downtown they are more interested in. City Hall. The new library. You know, they'll get *their* security fixed a lot faster than us."

"How long has it been out of service?"

"Well… a while," he admitted, unwilling to put a time estimate on it.

"Get me what you can." However much that was. She was gathering from his reluctance that there wasn't going to be very much at all. Would they at least have something showing who had been in the parking lot during the hours before the woman's body was found?

"I am sorry," Finkle apologized. "There is more coverage inside the education center. We have some very valuable displays, so we want to keep them protected…"

"Yeah. That makes sense," Margie said flatly. Not because she was feeling gracious. She could see that they had not prioritized the security of the park itself. The indoor footage was not likely to help them much unless the woman and her killer had been in the education center before she had been killed, which Margie thought was unlikely.

She pulled out her phone and thumbed through the photos, including the ones that Dr. Galt had texted to her just a few minutes earlier. The victim was wearing a semiformal blouse and slacks, not a t-shirt or other casual wear. She suspected it might be the uniform worn by the education center staff. The ones who didn't dress quite as formally as Finkle.

"I'd like you to see if you can identify the victim for me," she said slowly. "Do you think you're up to looking at a picture?"

"Yes, of course."

Margie didn't show it to him. "You need to be prepared. I am going to show you a picture of the dead woman's face."

He nodded impatiently. The two hands with the death grip on each other stayed intertwined, and he leaned forward, waiting for Margie to show him the picture.

"You need to understand what the water does to bodies," Margie warned. "There hasn't been a lot of animal or insect predation yet, but her face will seem quite swollen. It may be difficult to recognize her."

"I want to help in any way I can."

Margie waited for a few seconds longer, then finally turned the phone around to show it to Finkle. He stared at it without expression for a long few seconds. Margie expected him to shake his head and tell her that no, he didn't have a clue who it was.

Finkle turned away from her and, for a moment, Margie thought he was going to unlock one of the doors to the education center and take her inside. But that wasn't why he was turning away from her.

He staggered a couple of feet away and threw up. Margie took a couple of small, discreet steps back. It was a few minutes before Finkle regained control of himself. He wiped his mouth on his sleeve and turned back to her, looking miserable.

"I don't know who that is."

"Okay. Thank you for giving it a try." Margie hesitated. "Why don't you go on in, get yourself together and have a glass of water or cup of coffee and, when you're ready for me, let me know." She handed him one of her business cards. "Just give me a quick call or shoot me a text when you're ready."

"I'm sorry…"

Margie waved the apology away. "No. It's a shock, and you weren't prepared to see that. You're certainly not the first guy to react that way."

"It's not like it is on TV, or seeing a picture in the paper."

"No, it's not."

He nodded and wiped his mouth again. "I'll just be a few minutes, then," he said, and walked away from her, heading for the education center.

Margie didn't need to supervise the technicians as they gathered their evidence for Dr. Galt as he prepared the body for transport. She was the most senior law enforcement officer on the scene, but they had much more training than she did in handling evidence and they knew what they were doing. After the medical examiner's van drove away, Margie stood watching the forensic team searching through the garbage cans. The whole process included taking pictures of the garbage cans before they were touched and laying everything out on a plastic sheet. Harvesting one layer of trash from the can at a time as if it were an archaeological dig. They needed to be able to say exactly which layer anything suspicious had come from.

Detective Cruz arrived. Margie gave him a brief update. They stayed outside the yellow tape at the bank of the creek and around the garbage cans. As far as Margie knew, they hadn't found any footprints that would be helpful.

Of course not. That would have been too easy.

"No ID yet?" Cruz asked.

"No. Hopefully, they'll find her wallet or purse in one of the garbages, or drag this part of the stream to see if it was dumped here with her."

Cruz looked up and down the waterway at the area that had been taped off, and seemed satisfied with it.

"What have you found out about the water system?" he asked. "Was she killed here? Dumped here? Or was she dumped somewhere else and the water carried her downstream?"

Margie breathed shallowly.

"I assume she was just dumped here. The water doesn't seem to have much of a current. I guess we'll hear more from the medical examiner. I'm waiting for this guy," she motioned to the education center, "to pull himself together so he can answer some questions about how she got there, what else we need to know about all of this… water."

Looking upstream, she saw a floating dock, where several children sat examining the contents of buckets of water scooped out of the stream. Her stomach turned over queasily.

Cruz looked at her, then at the children. "What's wrong? You think they're going to dip something out of the water that's evidence in the case? The woman's wallet or fingers or something?"

"She still had her fingers," Margie protested.

"Well, the way you were looking at them…"

"I just… I'm worried about them being out there. It doesn't look safe."

Cruz looked at them again.

Margie tried to keep her tone casual. "They're kneeling on the edge. The adults are several meters away. If one of the kids went in…"

"It would probably scare them. But as you say, there isn't any noticeable current. And there is a lifesaver right there that their dad could throw to them and one of those rescue hooks to pull them in."

"Oh, is there?" Margie pretended that made it okay. "I didn't see that. Right."

He gave her a quizzical look but didn't pursue it. "So… what's with the monument on top of the hill? Is that some kind of memorial?"

"I didn't go to the top yet, but I guess it's some kind of art installation. There are actually three monoliths and some berms. I'm afraid it's a bit highbrow for me. I don't really *get* it."

"Doubt if there's anything to get. I'm not much of a modern art guy myself." Cruz looked at the garbage can the forensic techs were currently going through, and the screens still up at the water's edge. "Tell you what, why don't we go up for a look?"

Margie agreed. She didn't want to get in the way of the investigation. They wouldn't think much of her if she ended up messing with any of the evidence.

She and Cruz walked down a gravel path along the river, then up the small hill to gaze at the art installation. Tall grasses and wildflowers grew beside the trail.

"Well… I still don't get it," Cruz admitted, staring up at the monoliths.

"Me neither."

They looked down at the crime scene. Margie realized that from their elevated position, she could see over the screens. They should have used a tent. At least it had still been early morning and there hadn't been a bunch of kids or their mothers at the top of the hill, hysterical because they had seen the dead, drowned body of a woman on the other side of the screens.

CHAPTER FOUR

"Whoops," Margie murmured, looking at the screens. There was nothing to see anymore, so it was too late to do anything about it. But the next time, she would remember to look up at possible vantage points.

Cruz chuckled through his mask. "Glad we didn't end up in trouble over that. Let's go down to the dock."

The 'we' was generous, since Margie had been the one in charge of the scene and Cruz hadn't even been there when the screens were set up. Margie walked down the hill with him, and then along the path to where the children were dipping minnows out of the stream into their buckets. Cruz stepped confidently from the land onto the gray plastic cells that formed the little dock. Margie stayed back on the path. Cruz walked up to the edge where the children were and started a conversation with them. The father stood close to Margie, a tall, sandy-haired man. He looked at Margie.

"You're police?"

"Yes. Detective Patenaude. My partner there is Detective Cruz."

"What's going on here?"

Margie knew he would find out eventually anyway. And he wasn't likely to be calling any reporters.

"There's been a death."

"A murder?" he asked immediately.

"That hasn't yet been determined."

The man looked toward the screens. "I don't think too many people just come out here and die of natural causes. It isn't like it's a swimming hole or the ocean."

Margie shrugged and didn't agree or disagree. "How long ago did you and the kids get here?"

"Oh, about twenty minutes ago. We're homeschoolers," he explained, "this is a really good hands-on activity. They like the education center, but the best part is getting out here and playing in the water."

"Sounds like fun." Margie smiled, but she didn't go out on the dock. She let Cruz talk to the children. He seemed to be enjoying himself. Her queasiness returned when he leaned out over the edge to look into the dark water. "So you didn't see anything unusual when you arrived today? Anything that seems different or out of place?"

"Just you guys. Normally it's pretty quiet this early in the morning. A few people out getting exercise. Walking, running, biking. Sometimes we see other homeschoolers out here, but most families don't get out until later in the day."

Margie looked around, her eyes sharp for anything in the area that didn't belong or might have been dropped by the killer. It was pretty clean, no garbage blowing around. But the water was murky. She couldn't see down into it. It was impossible to tell how deep it might be out at the edge of the dock where the children were or what might be under the water.

"Are they safe over there? Should they be wearing life jackets?"

"No, they're here all the time," he told her with a tolerant smile. One of those parents who thought she was overprotective and nothing bad would ever happen to his kids. But he hadn't seen the things that she had. "They know what they're doing, and I'm here if anything happens. Which it won't."

But before she and Cruz had approached, he'd been looking down at his phone. Reading his email? A text from his wife? Facebook? His eyes had not been on the children, even though he should have been showing more caution than usual with his awareness of the police presence.

"You haven't had anything unusual happen around here the last few days? People around who you don't know and who don't look like they belong? Arguments? Smells or sounds that were out of place?"

"No." His brows came down in a frown. "You don't mean that a dead body has been here for a few days, do you? I would think that someone would have noticed that."

"We're still in the very preliminary stages of investigation. We can't make any assumptions."

"Well… no, I haven't seen anything unusual. It's just been normal."

"Thanks. Can I get your contact information in case I think of something else I need to ask you?"

He was hesitant. "I said I don't know anything. I don't know why you would need to ask me any other questions."

"You never know when I might need the insights of someone familiar with the park. You can't beat the knowledge and insights of someone who has boots on the ground." Margie laid it on as thickly as she dared.

The man looked pleased. "Yes, of course. I guess that makes sense. And we really know our way around here. If you have any questions about the wetlands, my kids probably know more than the teachers in the education center, they've been here so much."

CHAPTER FIVE

Margie waited until Cruz was finished talking to the children, and looked toward the education center to let him know that she wanted to go there next. He walked back over the dock, making the floats bounce up and down in the water as he moved over it. The kids laughed in delight.

"Find anything out from the dad?" he asked once they were a distance away.

"No. Got his information just in case, but I don't think he knows anything helpful. How about the kids?"

"Good kids. Really into the wetlands thing. They could tell you all kinds of things about how these different features filter stormwater naturally. But anything about how a body got in the creek? No."

"As long as it's not their mom."

"I think someone might have mentioned if they were missing her." Cruz agreed dryly.

"I want to see if the head guy here, Finkle, is ready to talk to us yet. He was a little bit… wobbly after seeing a picture of the dead woman."

"Yes, I can see how he might be. You thought it was a good idea to show it to him?"

"I thought it might be someone who worked here. Went out for lunch and never came back… something like that."

"And did he know her?"

"Didn't recognize her. But drowning victims bloat up so much…"

He nodded. "Still could have been an employee."

"Hopefully, he's settled down enough to talk now. I want to get security video from him, and any information he can provide on how things work around here. Whether she was dumped there or washed down from somewhere else…" Margie trailed off. She started walking around the building.

Cruz held out his hand to stop her. "We don't have to go all the way around the far side of the building. We can get to the front doors from this side. Just over the catwalks. They go all the way around."

Margie looked at the catwalks over the deep, dark water. "I think I'd rather go around the other way."

"This is more convenient, and we've already seen the other side. Come on." Cruz strode toward the nearest walkway. He paused to look back after a minute. "Come on, Patenaude. You afraid of heights?"

"No."

"Let's go, then."

Margie looked for a reasonable excuse. She wanted to check on the techs out by the creek again. She thought they might have missed a garbage can in the corner of the building. She wanted to check under the unusual playground equipment to make sure nothing had been dumped there. But they would all have sounded like fake excuses. Which they were.

She dragged her feet after Cruz. He made it look so easy. He was very casual as he stepped from the gravel path to a small grillwork bridge. To Margie, it was nearly as bad as the pictures she had seen of the glass lookout over the Grand Canyon. Why couldn't it at least have been concrete? Why did it have to be something with holes in it?

She forced herself to walk over the bridge and followed him onto one of the boardwalks that hugged the building. They weren't actually boards, but were fully concrete and shouldn't have been a problem for her like the grillwork. However, the railing along the side was an open mesh or grill that she could see through to the still, dark, bottomless water. She grasped the top rail, and it was all she could do to keep from gripping it like a drowning man. She just steadied herself, tried to keep vertigo from kicking in and making her stumble or fall. It was like her worst nightmare, the thought of falling into the dark water in the pool beneath her.

Cruz looked back a couple of times, but kept going, not stopping to help or harass her. They climbed a metal flight of stairs to go up to the second level. Farther from the water, but a longer distance to fall if she went over the edge. She didn't know if it was better or worse. Finally, Margie managed to make it around the walkway to the building's front entrance where Cruz was waiting. He raised his brows. Margie couldn't see his mouth under the mask, but it didn't look like he was laughing at her.

"You *are* afraid of heights."

"No." She looked down at the black glassy surface. "Water."

"You're afraid of water?"

Margie tried to shrug it off. "Everyone is afraid of something. That just happens to be mine."

"You were really struggling to get over there."

"Yes." She waited for him to laugh and tease her about it.

"Good for you. You kept going and you did it."

Margie stared at him, surprised at the response. She hadn't expected any kind of understanding. He was a tough cop. And he came from the Philippines. An island. Surrounded by water. He had probably been in the water every day of his life before immigrating to Canada. It was as natural for him as breathing.

"I have kids," Cruz said, turning toward the doors and pressing a call button. "My youngest, Alejandro, he has anxiety. He's afraid of a lot of things. The doctor says that the only way for him to get over the fears is to push through them. Willingly expose himself to them and push through. Like climbing a hill." He gestured at the hill with the monoliths on top of it. "Eventually, the anxiety peaks, and your body will start to relax and recover."

"Yeah. That's what they say. Avoidance just makes it worse. But avoidance sounds much more attractive."

His eyes crinkled at the corners. "I'm sure it does. But you were brave and went ahead and did it anyway. And you survived."

Margie smiled back at him, her face warm. "Thank you."

The door opened and Finkle stood there. He seemed a little better than he had been when Margie saw him last. A bit more color in his cheeks. He still wrung his hands, though it was less obvious.

"Detective Pat. And…" He looked at Cruz. "Detective…?"

"This is Detective Cruz. He's helping me out today. We've taken a look around, and I wonder if you're up to answering some questions now."

He nodded and escorted them into the building. He took them to a lobby where there was some seating. They all sat down in a close grouping.

"Are you feeling a bit better?" Margie asked Finkle.

"Yes, a bit, thank you."

"Have you had a chance to pull your security footage yet?"

"I'm working on it."

She wondered whether they were ever going to see any footage. When he said that a lot of the cameras didn't work, what did that mean? Did it mean there was *no* outdoor footage? Or nothing beyond a view or two in the parking lot? And if so, how many people knew that? Had the killer known that none of his movements would be recorded?

"I told Detective Cruz that you were not able to identify the individual in the picture I showed you," Margie said. "I wonder, though, whether it might have been an employee that you don't know well, or that the water might have distorted her features enough that you just didn't recognize her."

He looked nervous. Probably afraid that she would make him look at it again to make sure that he couldn't identify the victim.

"She was a young woman," Margie said. "Mid to late twenties or early thirties. Blond, shoulder-length hair. No obvious scars, tattoos, or distinguishing features."

He considered this. "There are a few employees who could meet that description."

"Do you think you could give me their names and maybe call to make sure they are okay? You can say that there was a computer problem and you wanted to check when their next shift was. You don't need to say it's anything to do with the murdered woman or our investigation. We would just like to know that all of your employees are accounted for. The ones who could meet that description."

"Uh… okay." Finkle nodded. "I can do that." He looked at them for a minute uncertainly. "Right now?"

"You said there were just a few employees who meet that description. It wouldn't take long to check in with each one, would it?"

"No. I guess not. I thought you would have other questions, though. Then I'll call once we're done."

"Okay. Have you had anything strange happen in the last week or two? It doesn't need to be anything violent. Just whether there were any unusual occurrences. Arguments. Flower deliveries. Phone hang-ups."

"No, I can't think of anything. The education center was closed until school started again, so it's only been a couple of weeks. Everything… has seemed pretty normal. I mean, as normal as anything during the pandemic. It's a bit different with masks, social distancing, and sanitizing anything that the kids might touch during a tour. It's more work. But we're doing everything we can to keep the students safe."

"Of course. Have any of the employees taken unexpected vacations? Called in sick? Just not been available when you thought they would be?"

"No."

"Anyone sick at all?"

"Of course we've had a few people sick. But not the virus. Everyone was tested."

"No, I didn't mean that. It's more about whether everything has just been routine or there have been unusual scheduling changes."

"I can't think of anything. When you work with young people, there are always some changes. They decide they have to go away with friends for the weekend, and if you say no, then they call in sick at the last minute." He rolled his eyes. "And you know very well that they aren't really sick, they just wanted to make it to that party or wedding."

Margie nodded. "*Millennials*," she offered.

"Exactly. It isn't the way we were raised, I'll tell you. The work ethic just isn't the same."

"And you didn't have anyone do that the last couple of weeks? Since you reopened after the summer?"

"No, I don't think so. We haven't been back for long enough."

"And everyone has been working together well? Nothing unexpected? No personality changes since you were last operational?"

"Personality changes." His brows came down like he didn't like her choice of words.

"Sometimes, when people are stressed about something or have had big changes in their lives, it shows up as changes in personality or behavior. Someone very patient before is suddenly blowing their top unexpectedly. A sloppy employee suddenly seems OCD or vice versa. Someone is jumpy. Has unusual fears." She didn't look at Cruz as she said this.

Water was not an unusual fear. Well, maybe it wasn't common, but people did drown. It was dangerous, even for people who didn't think it was.

Finkle thought about this. His hands slowly stopped their wringing motions, and he smoothed his fingernails with the pad of his thumb. "Well… there was Patty."

Margie nodded, waiting. She pulled her notebook out and worked the pencil free of the coil where she had stashed it.

"She seemed overly emotional. I thought… maybe she was pregnant. Or she could just have PMS. I don't know. It isn't like you can ask a young woman these things. She just seemed like that. Hormonal."

"What is Patty's physical description?"

"She's… medium height and build. Thirty or so."

"Blond?"

"Yes, I suppose so. Light brown or dark blond."

"Do you have her number?"

He shifted uncomfortably. "In my office."

"You don't have it on your cell phone? Employees never call when you are away from the office, or you don't need to phone them to line up substitutes if someone calls you after hours to say they can't make it the next morning?"

Finkle hesitated. Margie was beginning to get impatient with him. She wasn't sure why he didn't want to call any of his employees, but he needed to get with the program. They needed to identify the woman out in the water. Patty? Another employee? Someone not associated with the park at all?

"Mr. Finkle. I want her number. Give it to me now, or go to your office and get it. Now."

He started to flush red. Not angry. A lot of men would have been furious to be spoken to like that by a woman. Or a cop. But Finkle wasn't the aggressive type. He was embarrassed or scared. He ducked his head, reminding her of a turkey.

Finkle pulled his phone out of his pocket. An older model, small screen, not one of the modern oversize ones. He tinkered with it for a moment, presumably finding the contacts app and then filtering down to Patty's name and checking her contact information.

"Do you want me to call her? Or do you want to?"

At this point, she was worried that he would completely screw it up if she let him make the call. For whatever reason, he didn't want to call his employee in front of Margie. Were they having an affair? Had he made up the part about her being moody or hormonal?

"Just give me the number, please."

He read it out to her. Margie wrote it down. "Okay. Give me a minute." She got up from her seat and walked away from Cruz and Finkle, turning her back on them. She walked far enough away that it would be difficult, if not impossible, for Finkle to hear what she was saying in a normal tone of voice. She dialed the number into her keypad and took a deep breath, unsure what she would say if Patty answered the phone. Apologize and say it was a wrong number? Explain that she was with the police and just doing a welfare check? Say that something had happened at work and she didn't want Patty to come in without knowing that there was something wrong?

The first three rings went unanswered. Most people, if they were going to answer, would do so within three rings. But sometimes the phone was across the house, or they were already on a call with someone else, or the phone started ringing on Margie's end before a connection was made. She had no idea what the cell coverage was like at the education center. She pulled the phone away from her ear for a moment to check the bars. Weak, but still connected. She put it back to her ear and waited. The tone continued to ring, and ring, and ring.

Patty wasn't there. Or she wasn't someone who answered unidentified phone numbers. Plenty of people screened by the Caller ID and wouldn't chance talking to a stranger. Especially Millennials.

Eventually, the call clicked through to voicemail. Patty hadn't recorded a message of her own, but let the default automated message answer. Margie hung up. She could try again later when they had identified the victim. Or when they hadn't.

She walked back to Finkle and Cruz. "No answer. Does she usually answer her phone?"

Finkle thought about it. He nodded slowly, hesitantly. "Yes. I think she was pretty good about it. It's hard to remember, you know."

"Yes. I'm sure you have a lot of people to keep track of. Can you give me the names and numbers of the other women who might answer the general description I gave you? Patty and who else?"

He worked through a few names, spelling them out for her and digging their numbers out of his phone.

CHAPTER SIX

When they left Finkle, Margie tried Patty's number once more. She looked at Cruz while she waited for an answer she didn't expect to come.

"What did you think of Finkle?"

"Nervous guy."

"Definitely. Very anxious."

"But… at the same time, not the type I would expect to be involved in a homicide. I don't think he's anxious because he did something. Just because he's a naturally anxious type and doesn't know how to react to a police investigation."

Margie nodded. She hadn't picked up on a lot of deception flags from him. A few, but not a lot. More hesitant and unsure of how he was supposed to act than lying or being evasive.

The call went through to voicemail again. This time, Margie left a message. Very generic, giving her name and asking Patty to call her back. No mention of police or an investigation. It could be anything from a telemarketer to a bank manager or a schoolteacher wanting more information about booking a class program. She hung up.

They were walking in the direction of the forensic techs to see if they had found anything or needed any additional assistance or direction. Which Margie was sure they didn't need. Instead, she called Detective

Jones, who she hoped would be at her desk with the computer in front of her.

Kaitlyn Jones answered, her tone cheerful but not too bouncy. "Detective Pat?"

"Hi, I wonder if you can check for me and see whether there is a missing person report filed on Patty Roscoe."

"Sure, hold one minute."

They continued to walk as Jones looked it up. She was back a couple of minutes later. "Yes. Entered just this morning."

Margie looked at Cruz. "Bingo."

"You think this is our victim?" Jones asked.

"I think it is. She's an employee at the education center out here who might have been under some additional stress lately. Fits the description of the deceased. We couldn't reach her on the phone; I took a chance it might be her."

"I'll follow up on this end. Get as much information as I can."

"Get whatever pictures you can, any background, criminal history, social networks. Who reported Patty missing?"

"Husband."

"He just reported it this morning?"

"Yes."

"Where was he last night?"

There was silence from Jones as, Margie assumed, she read through the highlights of the report that had been filed. "He figured he couldn't report it until she'd been gone for twenty-four hours. Then he decided he couldn't wait that long and made a call."

"Hmm." Margie knew that many people still thought that they had to wait twenty-four or forty-eight hours before they could report someone missing. But they usually started the process early anyway. Or started making calls to hospitals and were told by them to make a police report. "Okay. Well, start gathering what you can. Have someone bring the husband in for an interview. We'll get there as soon as we can."

"Will do," Jones agreed.

Margie hung up. She looked at Cruz. "How long would you take before you started making calls about your missing wife?"

He considered. "I'd probably be calling the last place she was supposed to be once she was an hour late. Then calling her friends, colleagues, anyone who might have known what her plans were. By the time it was a couple of hours, I'd be pretty worried. Of course, my wife doesn't go out a lot. If she was someone who was routinely unreachable for hours at a time, or who had a history of disappearing for a night here and there, then I might not call until the next day."

Margie made a mental note of these details. It was always good to see it from someone else's perspective. There were people that you would start worrying about if they were twenty minutes late for an appointment, and there were people you wouldn't start *really* worrying about for a day or two. It depended on the person. But the way that Finkle had talked about Patty, he had made it seem as if she was a usually dependable employee who had only started having problems recently.

They reached the tape perimeter, and Margie and Cruz stood outside of it, waiting for the opportunity to talk to someone. The tech who seemed to be in charge, Mitchell, according to his name badge, drifted over to them. He had a clear face shield, so Margie wasn't concerned when he lowered his mask to speak with them.

"How is it coming, detectives?"

"We've probably done about as much as we can here. How are things going with you?"

"Going to be a while yet. Calls in to see how long it would take to get equipment here to pump out some of this water and drag for any larger foreign objects. May not be feasible, but we'll see."

Margie indicated the hill with the monoliths on it and pointed out about the screens not being enough to keep prying eyes from the body, if it had still been there when visitors had started to arrive on the site. Mitchell looked up at the hill, chewing on his lower lip, and nodded.

"Hadn't even thought about that. But it was early. They got her out of here before there was a lot of foot traffic."

"That's not always the case, though. I'm just as much to blame; I never thought to look up there and see what the sightlines were."

"Next time, we'll both be wiser."

Margie nodded. "Yeah. We may have a name. It probably won't make any difference to your work, because you're not going to throw anything away that has another name on it, but our victim may be Patty Roscoe."

"Patty. Okay." He did a rapid mental review of whatever they had found thus far. "I don't think I've seen that name or any P initials on anything we've pulled today."

Margie's surprise must have shown.

"You'd be surprised at how much stuff gets thrown out in these garbages. School assignments, employee shift schedules, coffee cups and lunches with names or initials on them. But I don't think we got any Pattys."

CHAPTER SEVEN

One of the tragedies of murdered or missing cases was that the people who were closest to the victims, those who ended up reporting their friend's absence or death, were the people who were most suspect in any violence against them. Spouses and significant others, parents, children, best friends. They all worried about their loved ones, called the police to try to get some help, and ended up under the microscope themselves.

So while Margie always went into an interview with the knowledge that they might be talking to a murderer, she also kept in mind that they might be completely innocent, genuinely grieving the loss of a loved one. And, of course, many people were both the culprit and the chief mourner. They weren't exclusive.

At the police station, Scott Warner had been welcomed, given a bottle of cold water, and settled into an interview room pending Margie's return. She looked in on him before entering the room. He looked around the room restlessly, not distracted by his phone, and also not crying or banging the table, insisting that someone deal with his missing persons report. There was no outrage over being left alone in the room while they looked into his report. No obviously guilty behavior.

"I'm just going to freshen up for a minute," Margie said. "Then we'll see what he has to say."

She took a quick washroom break, splashed water on her face, and chugged a mug of coffee before re-masking and entering the room to speak with her suspect.

"Mr. Warner. I'm sorry for keeping you waiting. We have been investigating. My name is Detective Patenaude. May I…?" She gestured to the chair opposite him as if she needed his permission to sit down. Put him in a position of power. Make him feel like he had control over the interview.

"Yes, please. Have you found anything out? I called the hospitals, but they won't say anything over the phone. And I worried about what if she was brought in unconscious or had amnesia, how would they even know who she was then? Have you checked?"

"If she was taken to the hospital, she would have had her ID, wouldn't she?" Margie countered. "They would be able to figure out who she was."

He looked confused for a moment, then nodded. "Yes. Right. Of course. They would know. But they wouldn't necessarily talk to me. More and more patient rights these days, they won't tell you anything without the patient's permission, and if she is unconscious and can't give it, then what?"

"We haven't heard anything back from the hospitals yet. You'll have to wait a bit longer."

Warner sighed and nodded. He looked down at his phone, thumbing it on, looking at it, waiting for it to ring. Maybe Patty would call him to tell him her car had broken down. Or that she'd been hit on the head, but was okay. Something that would mean she wasn't gone from him forever.

"Why don't you tell me about your wife?" Margie said. "I know you've already made an official report. Filling out all of those routine questions. But that doesn't give me a real taste for the person that she is. There is so much more to a person than just the physical description and what their last movements were."

Warner nodded. "Yeah. That's so true. Patty is… a wife and mother first and foremost. We have two young children…"

"Was she a stay-at-home mom?" Margie asked, already knowing the answer was negative.

"No. But not because she didn't want to be. If we'd been able to afford it, then of course we would have. But they have a good daycare, and Patty is really good at her job. She loves teaching at the education center. She was thrilled to be able to put her degree to good use. She was passionate about the environment."

"She sounds like a really special woman. Tell me about her movements? When did you see her last?"

"When she went to work yesterday morning. I picked up the kids from the daycare after I got off work, like I usually do. She gets home after me… then we have supper, put the girls to bed…"

"But you became concerned when…"

"She didn't get back from work when she normally would. I called her cell phone a few times, but she wasn't answering. I know she doesn't answer if she has a class or tour, or if she is in a meeting with her boss. But when it got to be a couple of hours… well, she's never done that before. She's always at home, never more than an hour late. And even if she was running a few minutes late, she would have called to let me know that she was late, and when she expected to be home. She was very good about that. Better than me." His voice cracked a little.

And he was the one who was supposed to be picking up the kids. Margie didn't imagine it went over very well if he were running late and forgot to inform either the daycare or Patty.

"No calls at all? Had you talked to her during the workday?"

"Yes. Once or twice. I don't remember specifics. You know, we just check in with each other now and then. Ask the other person how it's going or call to vent about our jobs." He rolled his eyes. "Even if you love your job, there are still those days when nothing goes right."

"Of course. So, you don't know what times you talked to her?" Margie nodded to Warner's phone. "You can check your call log…?"

"Oh… I would have called her from my work phone. Not this one."

Margie let that sit for a minute before going on. "Okay. So maybe a couple of times during the day. Have you called anyone at her work? To ask what time they saw her last or when she left?"

"No. I don't know her coworkers. I know first names, of course; she talks about different people she is teaching with, or who she likes or doesn't like. In a superficial way. She didn't hate anyone, of course. Some people would just rub her the wrong way, get on her nerves."

"How about her boss?"

"Uh…" He looked blank. "I really can't tell you. I know her supervisor… that's… Sally something. And of course, the director, that guy." Warner shook his head, blinking and trying to recall. "Fink? Barney?"

"Arby Finkle."

"Yes. Him."

"Did they get along? Or did she have problems with him?"

"I think they got along okay. I know that she and some of the other workers… well, they made fun of him a little. Behind his back, not to his face." He shrugged. "Not mean-spirited or anything. Just like you do at an office. Blow off some steam talking about the stupid things your boss does."

"Sure," Margie agreed in a neutral tone.

"I guess he was kind of… I don't know. Fussy. Maybe a little…" He gave a limp-wrist gesture. "You know."

Margie looked at him, head cocked to the side slightly. "What?"

"I don't think that he was, but they talked about him a bit. About maybe he was… closet gay. Like… *Tinkerbell-Finklebell*." Again he tried to shrug it off. "Just all in fun. Not serious."

"I see." Margie didn't write anything in her notebook, but continued to look at him, waiting for more.

"I don't know. She got along with everybody okay. And she liked the job. It was important to her."

"You weren't able to contact anyone from her work. So what did you think had happened? Did you think that she was still at work, or that something had happened to her on the way home? Or just that she was out running errands and might have stopped in to see friends?"

"I thought… maybe an accident on the way home. That's why I was calling hospitals." He rubbed at the corners of his eyes. Margie couldn't see any tears, but that didn't mean that there weren't any threatening. Or that he wasn't grieving just as much as the spouses who came in weeping like fountains.

Margie nodded. "She wouldn't normally have been anywhere else between work and home? Stopping at the grocery store? Gas station? Did she ever go out with friends for a drink or coffee?"

"No. She came home. We did errands at other times. She would come home to help with the kids. Making dinner and putting them to bed."

"Who made dinner?"

He looked at her like she was crazy. "What?"

"Did you make dinner or did she?"

"Yesterday?" he asked blankly.

The night before, he had obviously been the one to make the evening meal, if he were telling them the truth.

"Normally. Did you alternate? Did you make it because she got home later than you? Did you agree on certain days?"

"Well, no, Patty was usually the one who made dinner. I was so tired at the end of the day, you know, and I brought them home from daycare, so when she came home from work, it was her turn. I just wanted to relax in front of the TV for a while."

Margie nodded. "So she usually made dinner arrangements. Or maybe if she knew she was running late, she would tell you to go ahead or would pick something up on the way home?"

He shrugged. "Yeah. Maybe."

"So, you had to make the dinner instead last night."

He nodded.

"How did that make you feel?"

His eyes widened. "How did it make me feel?" He demanded, his voice startlingly loud. "I was sick with worry! I made the kids some KD and gave them a cookie when they were done, but I couldn't eat a bite. I was just… I could barely function. I didn't know what to do. Who to call. I was alone there, just the kids and me, and I didn't know what to do."

"That must have been difficult."

"It was! You have no idea what it's like just to have someone… not come home one day."

Margie nodded slowly and made a few notes in her notebook. "We would like to talk to the kids. Where are they?"

"They're… I took them to daycare. I didn't want them around here. I knew I would be waiting around and they would be bored. And I don't want them… wondering what's going on."

"What do they think happened to their mother?"

"They don't know."

"I mean, what did you tell them? What explanation did you give them?"

"I just told them that she would be home later. They wanted her to get home, but they didn't really ask about what she was doing. Just when she was coming home."

"And when did you tell them she was coming home?"

"Soon. I didn't want to say anything specific."

"We would still like to talk to them. How old are they?"

"Two and four." He shook his head, scowling behind his mask. "They're too young to be able to tell you anything. All they know is that Mommy didn't come home last night. You talking to them… it's just going to traumatize them."

"We'll be very careful. I'll have Detective Cruz help out. He has young children at home."

In truth, Margie didn't know how old Cruz's children were. But she imagined they were young. Either way, he was a dad. He was understanding of his son's anxiety rather than being impatient and macho about it. He was clearly good with kids. He would treat Warner's children kindly.

"No." Warner shook his head. "I don't give you permission to talk to my kids. I don't have to, right? You can't talk to them without my permission."

"It depends on the circumstances." Margie made a note in her notepad. "We'll do what we can without them, but I'd like to be able to discuss this with them too."

"They're too young. They don't know anything, and you'll just confuse and upset them. I've heard of how police can plant false memories." He stared at her accusingly, as if she had already told his children that it was his fault their mother was missing. "I don't want anything like that to happen."

"I understand that. Of course we'll be very careful not to traumatize them or to plant any suggestions—"

"No. I already told you no. No way. There's no way you're talking to my kids."

His expression was fierce. Margie remembered the homeschooling dad at the park and how casual he had been about protecting his kids near the water. On the other hand, this father was not taking any chances on exposing his children to something that might be harmful to them.

She nodded and went on. "You've given a description of your wife's car in your report?"

"Yes, of course."

"Have you had any car trouble lately, anything that might make you more concerned about a traffic accident? Or maybe a stall beside the road, leaving her stranded?"

"Just the usual. You know how it is with cars. Something always needs to be fixed."

"How was your wife's mental state lately?"

"I don't know…" He thought about it. "Okay, I guess? I mean, everyone has stress in their lives…"

"She hadn't had any unusual stresses lately? Any signs of depression?

Drug or alcohol use?"

"Why? What does that have to do with anything?"

"Is it possible that your wife could have harmed herself?"

"No. I don't think so." His answer was certain at first, then less so. He stared off into the distance, thinking about it. "She had her down days, like anyone else. But she wasn't *always* down. She didn't talk about killing herself."

"Not everyone does. Has she been moody lately? More impatient? Wanting to be by herself?"

"Maybe."

"Do you have contact information for some of her friends? Her family? People who she might have talked to? Maybe even a doctor."

"She was estranged from her family. Doctors… I don't think she even has a GP. She just uses a walk-in clinic if she needs to get something checked out for herself. She has a pediatrician for the girls, but it's so hard to get a good family doctor these days…"

"Friends? She must have had someone she talked to."

"I'll see if I can get into her computer. I honestly don't even know last names, let alone phone numbers."

"You didn't do anything with them? Double dates or group things?"

"Sometimes, but Patty was always the one calling them. I'd call a couple of my friends if she wanted a bigger group, but she was the… social director in the family."

"Don't try to get onto her computer. Bring it in here. Along with any other devices she might have. Tablets, cameras, sports watch, anything that will help us to build a picture of where she was going and what she was doing. Do not try to get onto them. Leave that to us."

He was reluctant, but nodded his agreement. "Okay."

"You don't know what kind of security measures she might have. Some of these devices will wipe if you enter the wrong information too many times."

"She wasn't that security conscious. Her password is probably one of the girls' names,"

"If you could write down their names, birthdates, any important birthdays or anniversaries, her parents' and siblings' names, your phone numbers, anything like that." Margie pushed a pad of paper and a pen across the table to him. They would probably be able to access her various accounts by subpoenaing them from the service providers, but she was interested in seeing what he would write down. How much did he know? Was he the kind of person who kept track of important dates and bits of information or not? She already suspected not. Patty was the one who had managed their social lives; he didn't even bother to know the names of her friends.

She watched him puzzle over the information.

"Was Patty having problems with anyone? Any arguments? Threats? Phone hang-ups?" she asked.

"No, I don't think so. Not that she mentioned."

"You say she was estranged from her family. Why is that?"

"She…" he looked for a way to answer the question politely. "They didn't approve of all of her choices."

Margie considered. The woman's body had not had any tattoos, significant scars, or multiple piercings. Patty had married and had two children. She had a good education and was working in a good, respectable position that utilized her strengths. Any parent she could think of would have been delighted with her choices. She was not a free-spirited rebel.

"Does that mean they didn't like you?" she asked baldly.

Warner turned white. He looked at her and tried to decide how big his lie would be.

"They didn't, did they?" Margie pressed. "For whatever reason, they took a dislike to you. We're going to talk to them. And that's what they're going to say. So you may as well be truthful about it. Lying will only make it look worse."

"Okay, yes. You're right. They didn't approve of me and of her marrying me. They didn't think I had much going for me. But I've always been devoted to her and the girls. I've always worked to help support the family. I'm not some kind of deadbeat."

"Sometimes, people just rub each other the wrong way. Maybe they liked the guy she dated before you, so they were disappointed that she dumped him. People are emotional creatures more than logical."

He nodded along with her, the tension around his eyes relaxing. "I wish there was something I could do to make them like me better. But they don't, and Patty didn't want to do anything with them because of it. So we never really had a chance to make it up."

He twisted the wedding ring on his finger.

And it was too late now, whether he knew that or not.

CHAPTER EIGHT

Margie met with the rest of the team after she was finished her interrogation with Warner. They did not tell him that they knew Patty was dead. She hadn't been properly identified yet. She might not be who they thought. Once they had confirmation that it was her, and had everything they could get willingly through Warner, they would let him know and see how he responded. She suspected that he knew she was dead already. Even if he hadn't had anything to do with her death, he knew when she didn't come home that night. She had either walked out on him and the children or something bad had happened to her.

"It sounds like there might have been some issues at work," Cruz suggested, leaning forward on the conference room table. "He can say all he likes that making fun of Finkle and telling stories on him behind his back is good fun, but the fact is, Finkle probably knew about it. A guy like that might not look dangerous," he raised one brow at Margie to solicit her opinion, "but if you push him too far and he blows…"

Margie nodded slowly. "It has, unfortunately, been my experience that everybody has a breaking point. You can drive anyone to violence if you push them hard enough. And Finkle was pretty distressed today. I thought at the time that it was just the discovery of a body in 'his' park and then seeing her picture. But it could also be due to a guilty conscience."

"We should dig a little deeper there. Maybe get him in for an interview.

Check out his background, social media," Siever suggested. Margie had found his suggestions and careful documentation of their evidence to have been very helpful in the other cases she had worked on. He was a serious man, not as inclined as the others to joke and make sarcastic remarks. The kind of guy who tended to keep to himself most of the time, but was always watching and cataloging everything.

"Yeah. Definitely. Where are we on getting Patty's phone records? I'd like to start talking to some of her friends. And this should help us track down her family." She pushed the page of possible password details she'd had Warner write down into the middle of the table where others could see it. He might have denied knowing her friends' last names, but he had written down her parents' full names. No birth dates, but it was enough to get them started.

"We need to get a positive identification," Jones advised. "We're tracking down dental records. Without much help from Mr. Warner, I have to say. If we can get her electronics from him, she probably has her dentist in her contact list. He's probably right about her using one of the kids' names for her password. It's pretty common."

"Do you want to make arrangements to stop by the house and get them? I'm afraid if we wait for him, he's not going to move on it. Or he'll try to crack them at home and we'll lose important information."

"Sure," Jones agreed with a brisk nod. "No problem. I'll get over there right away."

"Okay, well…" Margie looked at the list of items to follow up on in her notepad. "We've got a lot to do, so we'll just keep moving things forward."

※

IT DIDN'T FEEL like they had accomplished much at the end of the day, but Margie knew that she had been working hard on it ever since she'd received the call early that morning. It felt like she had been working for three days straight, so when MacDonald prompted her to go home and get some sleep so she'd be able to be productive on the case the next day, she admitted she was too exhausted to do anything else on it and packed things away.

Christina had beaten her home and had already eaten supper by the time Margie got there.

"I'm sorry," Margie apologized. "It's been a bear of a day."

Christina rolled her eyes but didn't complain about how that always seemed to happen and maybe it had something to do with Margie's choice to join the Calgary homicide department. Maybe things would have been quieter if she'd taken a different position, or moved to a small town instead of somewhere busier.

"I know. I'm saying that too often. Did you have something good for dinner? Was there enough in the fridge?" Margie opened the fridge and then the freezer, hoping to be inspired about what to make for her own dinner. The only thing that looked appetizing was the ice cream, and she had to be the adult and not be a bad example for her daughter. Eating ice cream for dinner was the wrong standard to set.

Christina grunted. "This and that. There was some leftover pizza."

Margie looked in the fridge. Christina had finished it off. Which was probably a good thing. Margie should eat something that was good for her. Lots of fruits and veggies. A salad, maybe. She shut the doors of the fridge again.

"There's pasta in the cupboard," Christina suggested. "Or, you could have a sandwich."

Probably the same things that Margie would have suggested to Christina. Kids were good at reflecting back what they heard from their parents at inopportune times. Margie opened the cupboards and eventually settled on a bowl of raisin bran. Christina watched as she poured a bowl and added milk.

"That's breakfast, not dinner."

"Today, it's dinner. Give me a break this one time."

Christina was silent, looking back down at her homework.

"How's it coming along?" Margie asked. "What are you working on?"

"Just... English... math..."

"You need any help?"

"No."

"Okay."

Christina didn't look up as she scratched out some math equations. "Are you going to tell me about the new case?"

"I can't really say much about it. A body was found at Ralph Klein Park."

"Is that near one of the other ones?"

"No. It's not far from here, actually. Driving, that is. Walking, it would be too far."

"Yeah? What's it like?"

"Wetlands. Lots of ponds and water catchments and canals or streams. There is a playground with a zip line and an education center to teach kids about the wetlands."

"Cool. We could take Stella there. She'd think it was great!"

Margie thought about Stella jumping into the big basin around the education center and shuddered. She wouldn't be able to jump in to pull Stella out if something happened to her.

"There were signs up that there aren't any dogs allowed in Ralph Klein Park. We'll take her to Glenbow one of these days. And go into Cochrane for ice cream." Margie glanced at the closed freezer door. She was definitely hung up on ice cream tonight.

"Yeah! I want to do that. I was talking to Stacey about Cochrane, and she says MacKay's is awesome. They have ice cream flavors like you never even thought of there, and it's always changing, so you can try new things."

"It sounds really cool. I want to see it too."

"*Cool,*" Christina repeated with a grimace, picking up on the unintended pun.

Margie laughed. She continued to munch on her raisin bran.

"So, what else?" Christina asked.

"What else?"

"About your case. It was at Ralph Klein Park. Closer to us this time. But not anyone we know, right?" she asked lightly.

"No one we know involved in this case," Margie assured her quickly.

They didn't need more nightmares.

"Was it… like the others? Another stabbing?"

"No. I didn't see any marks on the body. The medical examiner will have to do the postmortem and report back, but it was probably a drowning."

Nothing that Christina wouldn't read in the news in the morning. If it hadn't already been reported.

"Do you know who did it?"

"No. We have some suspects. First, we need to conclusively identify the victim. We think we know who it is, but it takes some time to be absolutely sure. In the meantime, we're investigating all leads."

"You'll find him?"

"Calgary homicide has a very good solve rate. We'll find him."

"At least you didn't have to go in the water." Christina looked up from her notebook. "Right?"

"No. Not in the water." Margie couldn't suppress a shudder. "Just… close. And… over bridges." She didn't describe the walkways around the education center. She didn't want to picture them or remember them in any detail. She tried to block as much of that experience out as she could. Maybe, as Cruz said, the only way for her to get over her anxieties was through exposure to them, but that didn't mean she was going to dwell on them any more than she already had to.

"You went over a bridge?" Christina asked.

"Yes."

"In the car or on foot?"

"On foot. Actually, I had to go over one in the car too. But that was easier."

"Wow. Good for you." While Christina would laugh and tease Margie about her unreasonable fear of the water at other times, she always encouraged Margie to be brave and face her fears and try new things. Margie tried to do the same with Christina, encouraging her to do the things she was afraid of.

It was always easier to tell someone else to face their own fears than it was to face her own.

CHAPTER NINE

The next day Margie had a report from the medical examiner's office on her desk indicating that their victim had not had water in her lungs. She had not been drowned in the stream out at Ralph Klein Park.

Margie took a few deep breaths, her heart racing and stomach feeling queasy. Even though the medical examiner said that the woman had *not* died of drowning, she still couldn't help but imagine that cold, dark water flowing over her face, sealing off her mouth and nose, blinding her. She imagined sinking farther and farther down into the muck at the bottom of the stream, trying sluggishly to move, but being trapped like in a nightmare. Frozen, too afraid to even fight back against the water.

"Detective Pat…? Margie?"

Margie tried to break free of the vision. She wasn't drowning. The victim hadn't drowned. There wasn't any point to imagining it. She didn't want to see it, so why was she?

"Margie." There was a hand on her arm.

Margie opened her eyes and looked into Detective Jones's concerned blue eyes. She drew a deep breath. She could breathe just fine. She wasn't drowning. No one was drowning.

"It's okay. I'm okay."

"Are you sure? You were kind of... wheezing. Are you asthmatic? Do you need an inhaler?"

"No. I'm okay. I was just..." Margie trailed off, not wanting to have to explain it. "I'll tell you about it later. It's just... a distraction."

"You got the ME's report?" Jones nodded to it.

"Yes. Not drowning." Margie studied it for more details. "Several blows to the head. Subdural hematoma." She shook her head. "A fight... someone really got angry with her."

Jones sighed and shook her head, eyes closed. Margie thought about Finkle. Could he have snuck up on Patty? Approached her when she had been deep in thought or busy with something. Maybe not something quiet, like Margie had been picturing, but something noisy. The noise would distract her, cover up Finkle's footsteps. And then...

She couldn't see him sneaking up and bludgeoning her. That didn't make any sense. She tried again. An argument? A disagreement over something that had resulted in Patty throwing one of her insults in Finkle's face? Not behind his back, this time, but face-to-face, so that he couldn't deny it. Couldn't pretend that his staff respected him.

A slur or insult that had pricked him to act. It was too much, and he had just picked up the nearest possible weapon and slugged her with it. Repeatedly. Or he had knocked her down and continued to beat her.

In those scenarios, Patty would have to have been the last one there with him at the end of the day. So that no one else had seen or heard what had happened, or observed him disposing of the body.

Would Finkle have disposed of the body in the waterways of his beloved park? Would he have thought it fitting to return her to nature and to bury her in the water that she too had been so passionate about? Or would he think that was polluting the waters that they were trying to purify by running through the natural filters of the wetlands?

"They were both passionate about nature," Margie mused aloud. "What could they have fought about?"

"Who?"

"Patty and Finkle." Margie closed her eyes, thinking about it for a minute. It wouldn't have been because Finkle had propositioned Patty, something that happened in many workplaces. If she and the others thought that he was in the closet, then he clearly wasn't sexually harassing the women who worked under him. Unless it was to overcompensate. To make them think that he was just as big a pig as any other man who had ever abused them.

"Did we get the ID?"

"Dental clinic near her house. They're sending over x-rays. ME should have a positive ID by the end of the day."

"Good." Margie was relieved about that. She didn't want Patty's family and friends to be wondering any longer than necessary about what had happened to her. They deserved to have a little peace, knowing that she was not suffering. Knowing was better.

"Multiple blows," Jones mused, skimming the ME's report over Margie's shoulder. "Torn nails and defensive bruises on her hands. Broken finger. It was a fight. She didn't just go down with one blow."

"No." Margie pictured Finkle. Had he had any scratches or bruises on his hands? He'd been constantly wringing them. Margie had spent a lot of time looking at them, winding and squeezing each other. She was pretty sure she would have noticed if he'd had any bruising on his hands.

But then, if he'd used some kind of an object as a bludgeon, he wouldn't have bruised his hands.

There could have been someone else at work, someone who had propositioned her, or someone she had been having an affair with. Someone bigger and more explosive than Finkle.

"We need to talk to her family and friends. See if she and Warner had marital issues. See if they knew about the situation at work. Or if she'd been under more stress lately. Finkle said that she had been moody. Why?"

She remembered what else Finkle had said. He'd thought that maybe she was hormonal. Maybe pregnant. She flipped through the pages of the ME's report, scanning the rest of the information. She shook her head. No pregnancy. That was something, at least. It would have been worse—or at least, felt worse—if Patty had been pregnant when she was killed.

"I'm going to make some calls," she told Jones. "I know we don't have a confirmed ID yet, but I want to start talking to others before they know too much. People start to make things up. They start to imagine the reasons things happened the way they did. I don't want confabulation. I want the facts."

"Sure. Do you want me to make some calls?"

"We'll start with Mom and Dad. They can let us know who else we should be talking to."

"All right. The contact details we were able to pull are in the workspace. Interview room is yours as long as you want it."

Margie appreciated Detective Jones taking care of these little details and smoothing the way for Margie's investigation.

"You want to sit in with me?"

"Sure, if you want. That won't be too many people?"

"No, I don't think so. I think they'll feel better if they feel like more people are involved in seeing that justice is served."

CHAPTER TEN

Because Patty was estranged from her parents, they hadn't known she was missing before Margie's call. Margie invited them to talk to her, telling them as little as possible. Certainly not that she was with the homicide department. Let them think, at least for a little while, that Patty had just not gone home for one night. There could be a perfectly reasonable explanation for that.

Their eyes were wide and frightened when Margie met them in the reception area. She took them to the interview room. Nothing between the lobby and the interview room indicated to the couple that they were dealing with homicide rather than with missing persons. They were both housed in the same building and on the same floor. Only the room numbers gave it away to those who knew those little details.

"Mr. and Mrs. Roscoe, thank you for coming in. I'm sorry to have to involve you in this."

Mrs. Roscoe was wiping her nose with a well-used tissue. Face masks were not an option when people were crying. Margie gave them a box of tissues and a garbage can and sat at the other side of the table, her own mask firmly in place.

"Is she really missing?" Mrs. Roscoe asked. "My baby!"

"I know it must be a shock to you. This is something that no parent ever wants to hear."

"No," she agreed. Mr. Roscoe shook his head, blinking his eyes rapidly.

"When was the last time you saw or talked to your daughter?"

"Well... it's been a long time, actually. I don't know if anyone told you..." Mrs. Roscoe looked down at the table, her face pink with shame. "We were not talking with each other. Things were not good between us." Tears escaped her eyes and flooded down her cheeks. "Why couldn't we have made up before now? I don't even know when the last time we talked to each other was."

"Did you have any communication at all? Texts or emails?"

"No. I still saw her social media posts sometimes. But... well, I didn't respond to them."

"I understand. What was it the two of you fell out over?"

"Her husband. That Scott. Scott Warner. I suppose he told you all about it."

"No, he didn't have much to say about it. I think he would have preferred not to have talked about it at all. But I told him I would be talking with you, so he might as well fill me in because I was going to hear it from you anyway."

She nodded. "What did he tell you? About how unreasonable and judging we are, I suppose. That we never gave him a chance."

"Why don't you tell me in your own words?"

The couple exchanged glances. Mrs. Roscoe was the one who was more comfortable talking, but maybe she felt that her husband would sound more reasonable. Logical rather than emotional like she was.

"Just take your time," Margie urged. "I'm listening."

Mrs. Roscoe turned back to her and began reluctantly. "He just wasn't any good. I knew from the start that he wasn't going to amount to anything. I can't for the life of me imagine what she saw in the man. It wasn't even like he was good looking, so she couldn't say that it was his looks or love at first sight."

But she wasn't judging Warner.

"What made you think that he wasn't good for your daughter? They didn't have shared interests?"

"He's a bum. Patty is the one who has had to support that family from the start."

"He has a job, from what I understood."

"Yes. A job. But no education. Patty is the one who has always made the lion's share of the family's income. He should have just stayed home with the kids; then they wouldn't have had to pour money into daycare. But no, he couldn't do that either. He had to have a career. He had to show everyone that he could amount to something."

Margie made a couple of notes. "So, your concerns were mostly financial?"

"No, not just that. He wasn't a nice person. Isn't. I'm sure that hasn't changed. I didn't want him anywhere near Patty. Or my grandchildren."

"In what way wasn't he nice?" Margie didn't want to suggest that they had argued or that there had been any violence in the family. She didn't want to feed them anything. Let them offer it on their own.

"He was always talking down to her. Like he was the one who had the university education rather than her. He acted like she was… inferior. He was more intelligent, understood politics and the world economy better than she did. He thought he was naturally smart; he didn't need book learning. In fact, he was better without it. Less tainted."

"Really. A know-it-all. They can be very annoying."

"Yes. No one else ever knows anything. If you do, then you're wrong. He has to correct everything you say, and make sure everyone knows that he is the one who gets it all, that he's somehow… an advanced species over everyone else around him."

Margie nodded.

"That might be an exaggeration," Mr. Roscoe temporized. His wife gave him a withering glare. "I don't think it was that bad," Mr. Roscoe said. "At least… not that obvious. The two of them usually seemed to get along pretty well. She allowed him to express his opinions and didn't try to correct him and make him feel bad about the stuff he got wrong. She was very patient with him."

"A wife shouldn't have to be patient with her husband. Not like that. She shouldn't always have to tiptoe around his ego and make him think he's better than she is. That's just wrong."

"It seemed to work okay for them. They didn't fight a lot. Not around us."

"They were never around us," Mrs. Roscoe said. "I saw him for what he was in the beginning, and I said I wouldn't be around them."

Mr. Roscoe gave a nod and shrug. He clearly didn't find Warner quite as objectionable as his wife did. Maybe because he was a man and felt a certain kinship to him in his situation that his wife couldn't feel. Perhaps he could see how Warner might feel in a marriage with a stronger, more outspoken woman. Or maybe his wife was just better at picking up on the subtleties of Patty's and Warner's relationship.

"You must have seen her sometimes. Did you go to her wedding? See the children when they were born or at other times?"

"They had a civil ceremony and didn't see fit to invite us to that," Mrs. Roscoe said stiffly. Another problem that she had with Warner. "When the children were born... Yes, I did go by the hospital to see them when that man was not there. But the rest of the time..." She closed her eyes and shook her head slowly. "I didn't see them. Didn't babysit for them or have family dinners together." She swallowed and dabbed at tears. "I should have made up with her when I had the chance. Now... it's too late. She's gone. Thinking I didn't care."

"She knew you cared," Mr. Roscoe told her, putting his hand over hers. "She knew that the reason you didn't want her with Scott was that you did love her and wanted her to be happy."

But it had probably not made her happy to have to choose between the two of them. Or not to have her mother in her life.

"So if you haven't seen them lately, and didn't have anything to do with them regularly, then I don't suppose there is anything you can tell me about their relationship. Or whether she was under any new stresses the last little while."

"No... we just weren't a part of her life anymore," Mrs. Roscoe said. "I was... waiting for her to see the light and to leave him."

Margie sincerely hoped that wasn't what had resulted in Patty's death.

"How long had she worked at the park?" she tried. "Do you know anything about how she enjoyed that? Whether she got along with everybody she worked with?"

"She's been working there since she got out of school. She liked it. At least, she did back then. I don't know if she's had any problems since then. I guess if she's still there, she must like it. Otherwise, she would have left by now."

"Do you remember anything about her coworkers? I know it has been a few years since you would have heard anything about them, but is there anything you remember?"

"No... not really. There were always other students or recent graduates working there. Lots of young people her age. So it was comfortable for her, lots of people she could relate to."

"And her bosses or supervisors? They must have been older than her."

"She talked about them sometimes… everybody has frustrations with supervisors at work. Policies and procedures. Getting to work late. Trying to get a raise after a positive performance review. You know how it is."

"Of course," Margie agreed. "Was she not advancing as fast as she had hoped?"

"I think all kids think they're going to change the world. She thought she could walk in there and make a difference. Teach them all of the things she had learned in school. But you can't just walk into a place as the newest employee and update all of their procedures, implement all of the latest science. It takes time and experience."

Margie nodded. "After five years, or however long she has worked there, hopefully she was able to put some of her ideas into action. I guess you wouldn't know…"

The two of them shook their heads. There was a lot of sadness in Mrs. Roscoe's face. Not just grief over whatever had happened to her daughter, but the realization that she had missed out on her daughter's life the last few years when she didn't have to. If it had been Margie, she would also be wondering what would happen to the children and whether she would ever see them again. If something had happened to Patty—as they had to guess it had—then what were the chances that Warner would allow them to be a part of the grandchildren's lives?

※

Mrs. Roscoe had been able to provide some of the names of Patty's friends, at least the ones she had spent time with before getting married. And she had Patty's email address, even though they didn't still correspond with each other. Assuming Patty was still using the same email address, it gave them not only a chance to get into her email, but also her cloud storage and syncing. If they couldn't guess her password on the first few tries, they could get a subpoena for the service provider once the identification was verified.

"Do we have confirmation on the dental records yet?" she asked the team in general as she returned to the duty room after finishing with the Roscoes.

"Dr. Galt says it is a match," Siever confirmed. "He'll get us his official report later today."

"Yes!" Margie had harbored the secret worry that they were going in completely the wrong direction and they would find, on comparing the dental records, that it wasn't Patty Roscoe at all. "I mean, that's terrible, but at least we have a name now. Did we get the devices?" She looked over at Jones.

"We did." Jones pulled down her face mask for a moment and grimaced. "Hubby claimed not to know the unlock password on the tablet, but it looks to me like it's been sanitized. I'll send it over to the lab to have them see if they can recover anything. It's possible that she was just using it as an e-reader, but most people will at least put their email on the thing."

"She might have just used it as an entertainment device for the kids too," Cruz offered. "That's mostly what my wife's gets used for. Electronic babysitter when she has to stand in line for something. If the kids are going to be playing on it, you don't want them to have access to your email or schedule or anything else that they could end up messing around with."

"That's a possibility," Jones admitted. "It does have Netflix Kids and Disney+ on it."

Cruz nodded. Jones swore under her breath, not happy about this. "I've got her laptop as well. Hopefully, it has better security and he didn't guess her password before I got it from him. I don't trust the guy."

"I have a few friends to run down," Margie said, looking down at her notepad. "I'm hoping some of them were still in close touch with Patty. And then I might have another talk with Finkle. I have a feeling he wasn't totally honest with us."

CHAPTER ELEVEN

The calls with Patty's friends did not go as well as she had hoped. They were old friends, but had not had a lot to do with Patty during the last few years. They had gone different directions, had different friends, and most were still single or childless. One woman who did have a child only had a baby, none close to Patty's children's ages. So they hadn't spent much time together recently.

They expressed the appropriate shock that Patty was missing and something might have happened to her. Margie tried to gently broach the possibility that her husband might have had something to do with it with each of them, but didn't have much success.

"Do you know her husband, Scott Warner?" she asked Mindy, the one with a baby.

"Oh, we've met. I don't know him well, but he seems like a nice guy."

"You didn't ever think that he and Patty might be having problems?"

"We didn't see much of each other," Mindy reminded her. "I didn't see them together a lot. But she didn't complain about him that I heard. And when they were together, or I could hear him in the background, I never thought he was being an—well, I thought he seemed like a nice enough guy. They didn't fight or snipe at each other in front of me. He didn't tell her she was stupid or push her around."

"You didn't find him critical or argumentative?" Margie asked, thinking of what Mrs. Roscoe had said.

"Well, he was a man. Of course he was argumentative. Wanted to make sure you heard his side of the story and knew that he was the expert on everything. But that's kind of par for the course with guys like him."

"Like him?"

"Well..." Mindy looked for a word. "Kind of... guys who think they're smart? Have all of the answers, even if they change from one day to the next."

"A know-it-all?"

"Yeah. Like that. But not... I wasn't scared of him. He wasn't threatening or the kind that would get all hot and bang the table if you disagreed with him. Just... he wanted you to know how smart he was."

Margie thought about Oscar. He had wanted her to know how smart he was, too. Couldn't stand the thought that a woman might be more intelligent than he was.

※

MARGIE LOOKED DOWN at her phone. She wanted to get some more work done, but she'd been on the phone for hours. Her ear was hot and sore. Christina would soon be arriving home from school, and Margie didn't want her to be on her own for too long. She could continue her investigation from home. There were other people she could call or email, some research and background she needed to do. She still hadn't talked to Finkle again, but she suspected that he would be leaving the park soon if he hadn't gone home already, and she hadn't asked him for his personal number. With a sigh, she started to put her things away.

"Heading out?" MacDonald asked, startling Margie as he came up from behind her somewhere.

Margie caught her breath and pressed her hand over her racing heart. "Yes. I'll do some more from home, but I want to see my daughter—"

"Don't take your work home with you. Go home and relax and spend time with your family. Come fresh in the morning. You'll be more productive if you balance it out and take breaks than if you try to push through. You can't keep up that pace every day. We'll run this guy down, but it's going to be slow and steady, not a race. We'll eliminate suspects, process evidence, dig into the history. It's not all going to happen in a day."

Margie paused and considered his words. "I *have* been putting in a lot of hours on this."

"And you need to take care of yourself. You've had three back-to-back leads since you arrived here. You're going to burn out if you don't give yourself recovery time."

"Okay." Margie nodded. "All right. I'll take tonight off. I won't do anything. Just take some time with my family."

Mac nodded. "Good. We'll see you tomorrow morning, bright-eyed and ready to get back to it."

It was like physically training for a race or building muscle. Margie needed the rest days and breaks in between to be alert enough to see what was in front of her.

🕸

CHRISTINA WAS LYING on her bed, chatting on her phone when Margie got home. She rolled over and looked at her mother, eyebrows raised.

"Just a minute," she said to her friend, and covered the phone. "What are you doing home?"

"I wanted to spend some time with you. I know I've been working too late the last couple of nights."

"Nice."

"I didn't even bring anything home with me. I have a free night. I can cook while you're doing your homework, and then we can do what we want. Take Stella out for a long walk. Run some errands—"

"Go visit Moushoom?"

"Sure, of course. I'm sure he'd be happy to see us again."

Christina nodded. She returned to her phone call. "My mom is home," she said in an exasperated voice. "I have to do homework."

Margie was taken aback for a moment at this change in attitude. Then she laughed to herself. Christina just didn't want whoever she was talking with to think that she was uncool, wanting to spend time with her mother and Moushoom. Teenagers weren't supposed to care about that. They were supposed to be all about gaming and streaming video and social media. Margie went into the kitchen and looked through the fridge, this time with an eye to actually cooking something rather than just feeding a craving for sugar at the end of a stressful day. Salad, maybe a stir fry and rice. Maybe Christina would want some tofu or one of the various vegetarian meats they had purchased to try out.

If she had enough vegetables for dinner, maybe she wouldn't feel like dessert afterward. Her belt was starting to feel just a touch tight, and she didn't want to let her weight get away from her. She might not be a beat cop anymore, but that didn't mean she didn't have to keep up her fitness level. She never knew when she might have to run or get a combative suspect under control.

Christina came into the kitchen. She gave Margie a sideways hug, also gazing into the fridge. "Some noodles too?" she suggested. "We can make lo mein?"

"Okay, sure."

They busied themselves getting the ingredients out and fell into a rhythm chopping vegetables.

"How was school?"

"Oh, you know. It sucked. And then it was over."

Margie chuckled. "Who was on the phone? I don't know about any of your new friends."

"Tracy."

"Tracy. Is she the one who was telling you about MacKay's?"

"No, that was Stacey."

"Oh. Who is Tracy? What is she like?"

"He."

"What?" Margie looked up at her. "He? Tracy?"

"Yes."

"The poor guy. Who names their son Tracy in this day and age?"

"I guess there used to be a lot of guys named Tracy. Before it became a girl name. Seems like people are always giving their girls boy names, but then all of the guys with that name end up being judged as being feminine."

"Yes, it was used more a couple of generations ago. But now... I didn't think anyone would pick it for a boy name."

"Well..." Christina popped the end of a carrot in her mouth. "He's Chinese, actually, and his family adopted English names to make them fit in better. So they let the kids pick their own names. And he didn't know then that it was kind of a girly name now. He just picked it out of a book or off of a website of boy names."

"Well… it's nice he was allowed to pick his own name, but maybe they could let him pick a new one now. He doesn't have to make it his legal name if he doesn't want to, just something else for people to call him."

"I think he'll probably just go back to his Chinese name. Plenty of the Chinese kids around here go by their Chinese names and never adopted an English name."

Margie held her cutting board over the wok and slid the chopped vegetables into it. They immediately started to sizzle. "That's good. I don't think people should have to pick another name because they're from another culture. Canada isn't supposed to be a melting pot like the States. It's supposed to be a cultural mosaic. So why not keep your cultural name?"

Christina nodded her agreement. "Is that why you never changed Marguerite to Margaret?"

"It's a very common Métis name. It's not hard to remember or pronounce, so I don't see any reason to change it."

"Do people give you a lot of hassle about Patenaude?"

"I get a lot of 'Detective Pat.' It's easier for people, and I don't mind. They don't make fun of it." Margie stopped to read the instructions on the faux meat package that Christina had taken out of the fridge. "Do you get hassled for it at school?"

"No. People ask how to pronounce it or spell it, but a lot of the names are weirder than Patenaude. The Asian ones with too many consonants that we would put vowels between. It isn't like I have a name that's ten syllables long."

Margie was relieved that Christina wasn't being bullied over her name. She had been worried, going from Winnipeg to Calgary, with such different demographics, that their Métis culture would cause friction. And there would still be a few people who were jerks about it. That went without saying. But it wasn't like Christina was the only dark-skinned girl in a sea of white. The school was full of kids with all different shades of skin, from redheads with starkly white skin or freckles to ebony black with a blue sheen that she had rarely ever seen in Manitoba. Margie had been pleased with the diversity.

CHAPTER TWELVE

It was still light enough when they got to Moushoom's apartment to ask him if he wanted to go out for a walk with them. He loved to get out into the fresh air and nature whenever they could take him. The old Métis man always looked like a painting to Margie. He dressed in a mix of traditional clothes, including buckskins and a sash, and store-bought clothing like the long-sleeved boldly-colored dress shirts and dark sunglasses that he loved. Despite a long life full of tragedies and sorrow, his deep wrinkles seemed to always point up in a smile. She could have stared at him for hours and wished she had the skill to draw or paint him how he appeared to her.

"I want kisses from my two favorite girls," Moushoom declared, making them lean down to embrace him and kissing them on both cheeks, despite the pandemic. "I'm so glad that you came to live in Calgary."

"Me too," Margie told him. "It's wonderful to be so close to you."

"Do you want to go out?" Christina asked, looking through the clothes in Moushoom's closet. "You will need a jacket."

"Yes, let's go out," he agreed. He patted Margie's arm. "She is getting so big."

"Isn't she? I can't believe it sometimes. It seems like she was a little baby just yesterday."

"She is a woman now."

Christina found a jacket that she deemed suitable for their outing. It was blue with contrasting white stitching and beadwork. "This is beautiful." She helped Moushoom to get it on, then took charge of the wheelchair, releasing his brakes and pointing the chair toward the door. Moushoom folded his hands in his lap and smiled.

A few years ago, he would have insisted on getting around under his own power. He would have walked, no matter how much it cost him later. It gave Margie a little pang of pain to realize how he'd had to accept his physical limitations. He had been such a strong and active person for so many years. Now he was shrinking and becoming more dependent. That was the way of life, but she didn't like seeing him getting weaker.

She pasted a smile on her face and didn't show what she was thinking. There was nothing to be done about advancing age. All they could do was enjoy the time that they had together the best they could.

Moushoom took a deep breath when they got outside. "It was warm today," he observed. "You never know at this time of year whether it will be warm or cold."

"We had frost last week," Margie said. "And it was rainy and smoky the beginning of the week, but today was warm."

"And sometimes we have a foot of snow mid-September." Moushoom shrugged. "It has been nice so far this year."

"It has," Margie agreed.

"Where did you go this week?" Moushoom asked.

"Where did I go?" Margie wasn't sure what he meant. "Umm… I've just been here in Calgary. I went to work."

"No park this week? You were telling me all about that big park last time."

"Oh. No, I haven't been out to Glenbow Park again yet. I want to take you and Christina and Stella out there soon. When it's a nice day. We can take a tour. They have golf cart tours, so you don't have to walk and we don't have to push your wheelchair up the hill."

"I'm light."

"It's a big hill!"

"Who is Stella?" Moushoom studied her. "You only have one daughter."

"Stella is our dog."

"Oh, yes," Moushoom nodded and chuckled. "She is the dog. You didn't bring her?"

"Not today. I wasn't sure if we were allowed to bring her into the building or if you would want to go out today."

"You can bring her into the building. Some of the people there have dogs of their own."

"Great! We'll bring her next time, then."

They walked for a few minutes in silence.

"I did go to a different park this week," Margie offered. "Have you ever heard of Ralph Klein Park?"

He shook his head. "Another new one? I remember Ralph Klein. He's dead, isn't he?"

"Yes. That's probably why they named a park after him. They don't usually do it while the person is still alive."

"Is it a good park?"

"Umm… I didn't get to explore it much. It's not big, like Glenbow or Fish Creek."

"It has water," Christina offered. "Mom was saying that it is a wetlands park, so it has a bunch of ponds and streams."

"Wetlands are good," Moushoom said, licking his lips. "The white man destroyed too many of them. Why they think it's a good idea to wipe out the natural habitat and replace it with concrete, I'll never understand." He motioned to the development around them. In a minute, they would be onto the pathway beside the irrigation canal, and he would be much happier. Even though it was only a narrow strip of land, it was better than being surrounded by concrete and buildings. And on a good day, they could look out past the city to the mountains. There was too much smoke in the air for them to see anything today. But hopefully, it would dissipate in the next few days.

"One of the girls is afraid of water," Moushoom said. "Which girl is that?" He turned his head to look at Christina, pushing his chair. "Is it you?"

"No." Christina smiled at him. "It's Mom."

"You?" Moushoom looked at Margie. "Is it you? I couldn't remember."

"Yes," Margie admitted. Her face got warm, but between her complexion and the dimming light, she didn't think he would be able to tell she was embarrassed. "It's me. I know it's silly, but it's not by choice."

"We don't get to choose what we fear," Moushoom agreed. "We can choose how to behave in the face of our fears, but we do not get to pick our fears."

Margie nodded.

"You are not limited by your fears," Moushoom went on. "You live a full life."

Was it an observation or a command? Was he pleased that she didn't let her fear limit her, or was he telling her not to?

"I try to," she told him.

"Good." He reached out to pat her hand, then looked on ahead toward the green space, his expression softening, mouth going slightly slack. She didn't try to draw him into conversation, letting him think about whatever it was he was remembering or imagining.

CHAPTER THIRTEEN

Margie felt relaxed and clearheaded the next morning as she drove in to work. She was glad she had listened to Mac and put her work aside for the night. The time with Christina and Moushoom, and later on her own without any agenda, had helped. She had slept well and woke up feeling like a new person.

She listened to a classic rock station on the way downtown, enjoying the music and ignoring the DJs' chatter. Other days, when she was stressed, she couldn't stand to hear their drivel.

Margie was energized by her morning coffee and dove into her work, quickly reviewing her notes from the day before and any new information that had been uploaded into the workspace for the case. Not a lot had been done since the time she had left, which was probably good because overworking the lab or medical examiner's office was not a good idea either. Everybody deserved to get their rest.

Her eyes were on her computer screen and she didn't look to see who was calling before answering the ringing phone.

"Detective Patenaude."

"Detective! This is Carol Roscoe." Patty's mother's voice was high-pitched. She sounded panicked.

Margie winced. If Dr. Galt had issued his official identification of Patty Roscoe, as Margie assumed that he had, then she was going to have to inform Mr. and Mrs. Roscoe that their daughter was dead, as they had feared. Or maybe Mrs. Roscoe already knew. Had someone else informed her? Or had the news been leaked, and she had found out on social media or the morning news? She was definitely not in the same place emotionally as she had been the day before.

"Mrs. Roscoe. I'm glad you called," she said, in a voice intended to soothe Mrs. Roscoe. Half of the battle was making a caller feel heard. She would find out the reason Mrs. Roscoe had called and, hopefully, leave her in a better place than she had found her.

"I got an email," Mrs. Roscoe said, her voice wild, cracking up and down like an adolescent's. "An email from Patty!"

Margie blinked, staring at the screen in front of her and trying to figure out if she had heard correctly. "I'm sorry. You got an email about Patty?"

"No, from Patty. I got an email from Patty."

"I don't think that's possible, Mrs. Roscoe."

"I did!"

"What does it say?"

"There is a video recording attached. A video of Arabella."

Arabella. It took a couple of seconds for Margie to remember that was one of Patty's daughters. The older one, if she remembered correctly.

"So did this email come from Arabella?" Margie queried. "Have you ever gotten anything from the girls before?"

"You need to listen to it. Something has happened to Patty. Something... I knew that Scott was no good. I told you. I told Patty. She always said that I was wrong and he was perfectly good to her, but I knew she wasn't telling me the truth. He was mean and manipulative. He kept her from me."

Mrs. Roscoe seemed to be forgetting the fact that she was the one who had cut off communications from Patty.

"I would be happy to listen to it. Do you want to forward it to me? I'll give you my email address."

Mrs. Roscoe covered up the phone to talk to someone else, her voice going muffled. Margie could still just make her words out. "Do you know how to forward this?"

"What's the address?" Mr. Roscoe answered.

"She's going to give it to me."

The phone was taken from her. "Detective?" Mr. Roscoe asked.

"Yes, I'm here."

"What's your email address? Am I supposed to send this to you?"

"Yes, if you could." Margie gave him her email address as slowly and clearly as she could.

"Okay, I'm sending it to you now." There was a click, and Mr. Roscoe was gone.

Margie shook her head. She pressed the Send/Receive button on her email client and waited to see if it would appear. He might have taken her address down wrong. Or pushed the wrong button and it was still sitting in his drafts folder. Or it might just be taking time to process, if it had a video attached. As much as she expected email to be instantaneous, she knew that it still took time to get from one place to another.

She clicked Send/Receive again and waited.

The third time she refreshed, a bolded message appeared in her inbox. Margie double-clicked it, and then clicked on the video attachment.

The picture was fuzzy, the little girl too close to the device and not pointing it directly at herself. She was talking to herself in a whisper. Margie turned it up, plugged in earphones, and rewound to start it over again. She leaned toward the computer as if that might make the picture and words clearer.

"Mommy said do Gramma's picture," Arabella whispered. "The red button then the Gramma button. Send a message."

Margie blinked, watching it. Did Arabella have Patty's phone? An iPod of her own? A burner phone for emergency calls? Arabella was clearly talking herself through whatever instructions her mother had given her previously.

Arabella looked up, away from the phone, listening or watching something else. Her face came into focus for a few seconds. There were tears on her face. Red blotches. Her pudgy fist wiped away some of the tear tracks. Her nose blew a snot bubble. There was background noise. Margie turned the system volume up as far as it would go. She could hear voices in the background. Two voices, a man and a woman. The TV? Scott Warner and a visitor in another room? Margie tried to make out the words, but could only catch a phrase here and there. There was a crashing noise that drowned everything else out, screaming that made the hair on the back of Margie's neck stand on end, and Arabella's hands both flew up to her face, the camera getting buried in the blankets of her bed. There was a male voice shouting, Arabella crying softly to herself, and then the video ended.

Margie stared at the end frame in confusion.

"Detective Siever?" She called across the duty room to him. He looked up from his screen.

"Uh-huh?"

"I… I…" Margie stared at her screen, trying to form the question in her mind. She shook her head. "Can you help me with something?"

He got up from his desk, exhaling noisily. His chair creaked as he pushed himself to his feet. "Yeah? What is it?" he asked as he approached her desk.

"This video… it doesn't make any sense. Is it possible that… could that be Patty Roscoe in the background?"

"I thought the ME had a positive identification on her."

"Me too. That's why… I'm not sure I understand what's going on here."

He bent over and pressed play on the video. Margie switched it from her headphones to the external speaker. The bullpen quieted around them as everybody listened. Margie was even more sure the second time. It had to be Patty and her husband in the background. Arguing, and then… was it possible they had a recording of the murder?

"Where did this come from?" Siever asked.

"It came from Patty's mother. She said she got it in an email from Patty. The little girl recorded it."

"And then she didn't send it until today," Siever said. "Or else the device didn't have a connection until today, so it was sitting in the queue waiting."

"Is there any way to tell when the video was recorded?"

Using her mouse and leaning over Margie's shoulder, the other detective clicked around, examining the email and the attached file.

"I'm going to send it to forensics and get them to look at it," he said. "But it looks like it was recorded a few days ago."

"The day of the murder?"

His eyes went to the stand-up calendar on Margie's desk, counting through the days. He nodded. "Yes."

Margie swore under her breath. "That poor girl. No wonder Warner didn't want us talking to them. Did he know that Arabella overheard them?"

"Even if he didn't, they would have known their mother had been home the night before. That his story of her never coming home was a lie. Now, a few days later, he's covered. A little girl that young isn't going to be able to tell us which day she saw her mother last. And even if she could, he could just say she was confused."

"This is enough to arrest him. I'll let MacDonald know." She looked at her watch. "Warner will be at his workplace. That's good. We can arrest him while he is away from the girls, no chance of him taking them hostage."

"Have them picked up from the daycare."

"Yes," Margie agreed. "They can go to the grandparents, at least initially. Oh, I'd better call them back. Poor Mrs. Roscoe is in a state."

"I would be too," Jones contributed from where she was sitting at her desk.

"Yeah." Margie tried not to think about the sound of Patty's scream. The more she reviewed it, the stronger it would be in her memory. She needed to stay focused on her next actions rather than what she had heard and the emotional impact. Compartmentalize and not think about how this was going to affect the Roscoe family and the little girls. "Me too."

She got up and walked over to MacDonald's office in the corner. His door was closed, and she hadn't noticed whether he was in or not. She pulled out her phone and called Mrs. Roscoe back while she tried to peer through MacDonald's blinds to see whether he was in.

"Mrs. Roscoe?"

The woman cried on the other end, not managing to get out anything coherent.

"You don't have to talk right now," Margie told her. "I'm just letting you know that I got the email and have watched the video. We're going to take action on it right away. We'll arrest Scott Warner. We're going to pick the girls up from their daycare. Are you home, and are you prepared to take them for a few days?"

Mrs. Roscoe sobbed and managed a shaky "Yes."

"Okay. We'll talk later."

CHAPTER FOURTEEN

Margie hung up and slid the phone back into her pocket. She knocked on MacDonald's door, looking into the bullpen at the other detectives. "Is he in? I wasn't paying attention earlier."

She was answered by MacDonald's voice from within. "Come in."

Margie opened the door and stuck her head in. Mac was sitting at his desk, phone in hand, muffling the receiver against his shoulder.

"Detective Patenaude. A break in the case?"

"Yes. It was the husband. We have enough for an arrest."

His eyebrows went way up. "What did you find?" They certainly hadn't been expecting to come across any evidence that would be that decisive.

"One of the little girls recorded a video the night of the murder. You can hear the parents arguing in the background. Hear a physical altercation and Patty screaming."

"That doesn't necessarily establish murder. There might have been any number of fights."

"I think… when you hear the video, you will agree. Detective Siever is forwarding it to forensics, and they'll verify the data on when it was recorded to make sure it lines up with the time of death. But even before they do that, we have enough to bring him in. It proves that, at the very least, he was physically abusive."

"If you can establish that it's him on the video. Does his face appear?"

"No. But you can hear them in the background. I recognize his voice."

MacDonald nodded. "Okay. Bring him in for questioning. We'll get the details on the video verified as soon as possible."

"Great. Will do. And we're going to have the girls picked up from the daycare; they can stay with their grandma for the time being."

But when she returned to the duty room, Jones shook her head grimly.

"They're not at the daycare. Warner didn't bring them in today."

Margie looked at her phone to verify that it wasn't the weekend. "Why didn't he take them to daycare today? That means… they're with him. He must not have work today."

The other detectives on the team gathered closer to work it through.

"He's not making funeral arrangements," Margie said, thinking aloud, "because we haven't informed him that we have an ID yet. He has to pretend he doesn't know she's dead."

"So he's taking a personal day," Cruz said. "What husband wouldn't take a day or two off when his wife goes missing? It would look suspicious if he didn't."

Margie nodded. "Then he's at home. Do you think?" She was worried about the video. What if he found out about it from Arabella? What if Mr. Roscoe decided to go over there to confront him? Now that they knew without a doubt that Warner was the killer, Margie was afraid something was going to go wrong before they could take him into custody. "Do you think he's just at home? Having a lazy day with the kids?"

The detectives looked at each other. Margie was sure they were going through scenarios in their heads, just as she was.

"Cleaning up, maybe," Siever suggested. "Going over the floor with bleach another time. Making sure that anything that got broken during the fight has been disposed of. And whatever he used as a bludgeon. He's got to know that we'll want to search the house once we have identified her."

"I'll call him," Margie decided. "I'll let him know that we've identified the body of his wife. We should be able to tell by the background noise whether he's at home or somewhere else."

No one disagreed with her suggestion. He had to be notified anyway. It wasn't going to come as a surprise, though they'd see how good an actor he was when he heard about it and faked a breakdown.

Margie sat back down at her desk and picked up her phone. She breathed a few times, slowing her respiration and distancing herself from the situation. It was just a notification. She'd done dozens of them before. She was able to separate herself from it emotionally. It was her job to figure out where he was. She needed to be able to make a snap judgment.

She hit the speakerphone button before placing the call so that the others would be able to hear too. More ears were better. Warner might be able to tell that she had him on speaker, but he was going to have to deal with that. She tapped in his number and waited for him to pick up.

All she got was a long period of ringing, followed by his voicemail.

"We'd better get over there," Margie said, hanging up. She didn't want to rush into anything, but the thought of the murderer with two young children in the house set her heart thumping at a much faster speed than usual. "Maybe he's just ignoring my call, or washing the floor like Siever says, but those children are defenseless. I have to make sure they're okay."

"You want me to go with you?" Jones offered.

"Uh, yes. But separate vehicles. If he bolts, I want to be able to stay on him. One of us."

Jones nodded. They both removed their sidearms from their lockboxes without comment and vested up. Who knew if he had an illegal weapon and would decide to do something stupid like holing up in his house and trying to shoot anyone who got too close?

"You two be careful," Cruz advised, even though it was obvious that they were taking the proper precautions.

"We will," Margie confirmed.

"At the first sign of trouble, you call for help and fall back. Don't push a confrontation."

She and Jones both nodded. Margie expected him to try to trade places with Jones to go along, but he didn't.

"Cover all exits. If it is an apartment building, call for backup."

"Yes."

Margie finished getting ready. She looked at him for any further advice. He just nodded. "Okay. You got this."

CHAPTER FIFTEEN

Margie's heart was beating so fast as she drove to Warner's address that it felt like it would burst right out of her chest. She didn't feel like she had it covered by any stretch of the imagination. So many things could go wrong.

But it could all go fine too. She might just be overreacting. Warner hadn't uttered any threats when she had interviewed him previously. He hadn't said or done anything that showed a propensity for violence. He hadn't argued, called her names, insisted that they needed to drop everything else and get on top of his wife's case. While there was an estrangement from Patty's parents that he acknowledged was due to their not liking him, Mr. and Mrs. Roscoe had not suggested that they thought him capable of violence toward her or the children. She'd left the conversation wide open for them to make whatever claims they chose to. Warner had no domestic violence charges, no previous calls to the house over noise complaints or neighbor concerns. She hadn't checked Children's Services reports.

They didn't race to his house, but drove within the speed limits and didn't use any lights or siren. No need to get him or anyone else wound up. When Margie pulled to the curb near the house, Jones pulled up beside her.

"I'll go around back. Just in case. Don't stand in front of the door when you ring the bell."

Margie nodded. "Okay. Thanks. I'll give you a couple of minutes to get situated."

She watched Jones drive around the block, and used the interim to scope out the street. There was no car in front of Warner's house, and she couldn't see a garage in the back. But there might have been a gravel pad for parking; she couldn't be sure. Or the family might not even have two cars. Patty had to drive out to the park, and if Warner worked within the city or remotely, then he could bike or take the transit to work.

She didn't see anyone cross in front of the living room window while she was sitting there, but that didn't mean anything. They could all be in different parts of the house, Warner working on something for his job, washing the floor, or making other plans. He might have additional evidence to get rid of or a girlfriend that Patty hadn't known about.

Margie startled when her phone buzzed. She took a quick glance at it. Jones was ready in the back. She closed her eyes briefly to center herself, then got out of the car and walked up to the house. Standing to the side of the door, she rang and then pounded on the door with her fist loudly enough that anyone in the house would be able to hear. She didn't shout 'police.' That was mostly for cops on TV. She waited, listening for any sound from within or any movement in the window. Jones waited in back, quiet. No one trying to escape that way.

Everything was quiet. No sound of breaking glass. No footsteps within. Margie allowed herself a glance toward the street where she had expected a car to be parked. Where was he? Where would he go with the two little girls? It wasn't like he was taking them to the grandparents. He wouldn't want them anywhere near the Roscoes. She didn't know where his family was; he'd made no mention of them during their interview.

She rang and knocked a couple more times. Sometimes, residents were in the basement or the shower, somewhere they couldn't hear very well. Warner might have earphones on, listening to music as he cleaned. He could be gaming on his computer.

Eventually, Margie walked around back to where Jones was waiting. "Looks like he's out."

"Where do you think he is? Went out to get ice cream with the kids? Visiting family? Funeral home?"

Any of those were possibilities, but none of them rang true. Margie shook her head. She looked around the back yard. There was a gravel pad for parking, but no car. So, if they had two vehicles, Warner had taken the second out.

"We'll need a motor vehicles search to find out what he's driving."

Jones nodded. "Yeah. You going to put out an APB?"

"Yes… but I'd like to figure out where he's gone first. We should be able to figure this out."

"You don't think that he'd put the kids in danger, do you?"

"No. He doesn't have any reason to harm them."

Or did he? What if he did have another girlfriend and she didn't want kids? What if he'd never bonded with them in the first place and preferred to be on his own? What if the children were afraid of him and made him feel guilty whenever he looked at them?

There were plenty of reasons that he might want them out of the way. He might want a fresh start.

"I don't think so," she amended. "Warner didn't say anything that made me think he might…"

But the words sounded hollow in her own ears.

Where would he go?

If he didn't like the Roscoes, and of course he didn't, then he wouldn't take the children to them. And he hadn't taken them to the daycare.

He was not used to being home alone with them for more than an hour or two while he waited for Patty to get home from her job each day. He would quickly find out that single fatherhood was no walk in the park.

Margie's brain caught on the phrase. *No walk in the park.*

She didn't think that he had taken them out for ice cream, but what about a walk in the park?

She walked back around the front of the house, Jones trailing her and asking something Margie didn't hear. She looked up and down the street. A neighborhood playground? No. He wouldn't need the car then. Somewhere farther away. In her memory, she saw Patty Roscoe's body in the water. She flashed on the children dipping minnows from the water from the little floating dock, their father standing back, watching them with unconcern.

They could fall into the water. Even though it wasn't deep and there was a lifesaver float right on the dock to be used if someone went into the water, something could still happen to them there.

And if a father's intentions were violent rather than just unconcerned that anything could happen to them…

There was a certain symmetry in the children drowning where their mother's body had been dumped—a way of giving them back to her.

"They've gone to the park," Margie told Jones. She was sure of it. She could feel it in her bones. "I'm going to head over there. We'll need a warrant for the house in case I'm wrong. Can you get that moving?"

"Yes, but I'm coming with you. You're not going on your own."

Margie nodded. "Yeah. Okay." She was probably right. That was just the kind of thing that a TV heroine would do—racing toward disaster, all by herself. No one to back her up.

"Do you know where it is? Have you been there before?" she asked Jones.

"Never been there before. But I studied the maps and the layout as part of the investigation. I can get out there."

"Okay. Just in case we get separated in traffic."

With a nod, the two of them separated to go back to their cars. Margie took one more look at the house for any sign that there was someone home, watching them through a window. But she didn't see any sign of life.

She checked through her GPS destinations and brought up the one for the park again. She knew where it was, but she didn't want to get it wrong. No wrong turns today.

CHAPTER SIXTEEN

Margie was impatient with the traffic lights on the way to the park, but she didn't want to use her lights and siren. They didn't know for sure that anyone's life was in danger. It was only a gut feeling that Warner was taking the children to the park. Even if they found him there, they couldn't assume that he had any intention to harm the children unless he took some action to indicate that he did. They would arrest him for his wife's murder, but that was all they could do to start with. MacDonald had said to bring him in for questioning. Hopefully, before they got very far, they would have confirmation that it was his voice on the recording and that the time record on the video put it in the window of time of Patty's death.

As she got out to the highway, she could see Jones's vehicle behind her. They were going to get there. They were going to arrest Scott Warner. They were going to take the children to their grandparents.

It would be a happy ending.

Not for Patty, but for everyone else. Her killer would be brought to justice. Her family would be reunited. They would be safe.

Margie couldn't see Warner at the creek where Patty's body had been dumped. She continued to drive around to the public parking lot but, rather than stopping, drove up over the sidewalk as close as she could to the education center, looking for Scott Warner's figure with the two little girls.

She only had a vague picture of the little girls in mind, built from the blurry video of Arabella. Warner hadn't brought them with him the day he was interviewed. He hadn't shown her any family pictures. He hadn't wanted the police to have the opportunity to talk to the girls about what had happened to their mother.

Maybe he knew that Arabella knew something. Maybe he knew only that the girls knew their mother had come home, that they hadn't gone to bed waiting for her to return home.

She got out of her car, looking around. People were walking around, enjoying the mild weather—many of them stopping to look at the two vehicles driving up on the sidewalk. The cars were not marked squad cars, so people were probably pretty confused as to why the two women would drive their cars right up to the education center. Until they saw the women's vests and gun holsters. Then they'd have a pretty good idea.

Margie led the way around the education center, ignoring the queasiness and the pain in her chest as she climbed onto the walkways to go around the building. She could have told Jones to go around that side and gone around the other side of the education center on solid ground herself. But she hadn't been able to see Warner or the children in the playground on the other side of the education center. She had the little floating dock in her mind. That was where the children would be. That was what Scott Warner had in his mind. He would take them out there, show them how to dip their little nets into the water, and dump the contents into a bucket.

He would wait until they were happy and distracted. And then he would strike.

She could hardly breathe as she rushed along the walkway, up the stairs to the next level, and then out to the little bridge and pathway that would take them around the hill with the art installation and to the dock. Jones hurried behind her, asking questions that Margie couldn't hear or answer. It took everything she could to get over the grille on the bridge to where she felt safe.

CHAPTER SEVENTEEN

Warner was right where Margie had expected him to be. Standing on the floating dock with the two children kneeling in front of him, just like she had pictured. She had to blink her eyes a couple of times to clear them and make sure she wasn't really seeing the homeschooler dad or another small family group. Was she only seeing what she had thought she would see?

But Jones was swearing under her breath, hurrying along behind Margie.

"I'll fall back and flank him," Jones suggested. "You engage with him, talk to him, get him distracted. Keep him looking in your direction as much as possible. I'll get in behind him, closer to the children. We'll try to cut him off from them."

Margie nodded. Her brain objected that it wouldn't work, but she had to do what she could. Without a good plan of her own, she fell back on Detective Jones's.

"Mr. Warner," she called out, projecting her voice. She had a tough, no-nonsense, don't-mess-with-me cop voice. That, combined with a glare she had perfected as the mother of a teenager, was usually enough to get a suspect's attention and make him think twice about what he was doing.

He turned toward her, away from the two blond little girls with pails. Margie kept moving, walking on the path going past the dock, making him turn his body to keep facing her. His expression was one of shock. Eyes wide, skin pale, his mouth a slash of color that stood out in stark contrast to his skin.

"What are you doing here?" he demanded in an, aggrieved tone.

"We were looking for you. You weren't at your house, so I thought maybe you were here."

"What made you think I would be here?"

She didn't point out that since that was where his wife's body had been dumped, it seemed a logical choice. She didn't want to wind him up more, escalating the fear and anger he was already feeling. He felt vulnerable. He hadn't expected them to know that he was there. He had thought he would be safe and anonymous. He could bide his time until just the right moment, when no one would see or understand what he was doing. He had counted on being unknown and able to choose his timing.

"I'm glad we found you, Scott." She used a warm tone and his name. Make him feel seen. Make him feel validated. Important. "This has been a tough week on you."

"You're not kidding!" he agreed with a bark of laughter that was anything but amused.

"How are you feeling? Is there anything we can do for you?"

"*Why* are you here?" he asked again, shaking his head slightly.

"We just want to make sure that everyone is taken care of." She had planned to mention the girls, to ask him how they were doing, but she didn't want him to focus on the girls again. She wanted him to stay looking at her, talking to her, while Jones slipped between him and the children.

"You *know*." His tone was flat. Certain.

"What do we know?" Margie cocked her head as if she were curious. As if she didn't know what he was talking about.

"I had no idea. No way of knowing that she had given Arabella a phone." He shook his head in irritation, but did not turn to look back at his daughters. "I knew she was playing with one, but I thought it was Patty's old phone that didn't work anymore."

"What did she do with the phone?"

"Don't mess with me! I know that you know. The minute I saw that email go out to Patty's mother, I knew I was sunk."

Margie took a step closer to Warner, to keep his attention as much as to get close enough to do anything. Jones was staying quiet, trying to remain invisible and not to attract Warner's attention with her movements.

"How did you know about the email?" she asked Warner.

"I monitored Patty's email so that I would know if she was contacting her mother. Her friends. Trying to keep secrets from me. I would know if she was seeing someone behind my back."

Margie nodded slowly. "So you set something up so that you would be notified or copied any time she sent out an email."

"Of course I did. Anyone in my position would have done the same. I was protecting her. Protecting my family."

"Protecting them from what?"

"That mother of hers hated me. Right from the start, for no reason at all. How is that fair? How do you start off hating the person your daughter is dating without even knowing anything about them? Nothing at all!"

"That must have been hard for you."

"I was doing everything I could to keep us together. You don't know what it was like. How exhausting it was to keep on top of everything she was doing, to make sure that she was safe. That our family was safe from any outside forces. You have no idea how hard that is."

"No." Margie took another step toward him. They were almost close enough for her to grab him now. Just a few more steps, reaching out quickly, and she would have him. She didn't see a weapon, but that didn't mean he didn't have one. If he were doing everything he could to protect his family, then she wouldn't be at all surprised if he were carrying a knife or a gun. Or both. Gun violence was less common in Canada than it was in the States, but it wasn't nonexistent. People still shot each other. With registered or unregistered weapons. Warner didn't have a firearms license, but that didn't mean he hadn't acquired a gun somewhere.

"What happened? What was it that drove a wedge between the two of you?" she asked with as much compassion as she could muster. "Was it just her mother? Or were there other things? Money? Other pressures?"

"Her mother was a thorn in my side. She said that she wouldn't have anything to do with Patty while the two of us were together, and it was tearing Patty up. I thought that as the girls got older, it wouldn't be as much of an issue. She would establish a mother-daughter relationship with them, and her connection to her mother wouldn't matter so much. But I think the opposite was true. The older the girls got, the more she wanted to make up with her mother. I told her she couldn't. She couldn't be the one to give in first. And the only thing her mother would be happy with was the two of us getting divorced." He gave Margie a fierce look. "And we weren't getting a divorce."

Not for anything. He would kill her first.

Margie cast around for something else to ask him. But at that moment, he realized that Jones was there, working her way between them, cutting the children off from Warner.

Making a noise like an enraged bull, he threw himself at Jones. She wasn't expecting it, but she was well-trained and solidly built, and she absorbed the initial impact.

"Mr. Warner, you are under arrest for assaulting an officer of the law," she told him in a calm, clear voice, grasping his arm.

But somehow, he slipped out of her grasp. Having failed in pushing her farther away from his family, he tried the reverse. Before Margie could take one step forward to stop him, he had rushed at the girls, sweeping them out into the water. There were a couple of strangled screams of surprise and fear before they went under the surface of the dark water. Margie ran toward them, her mind a horrified blank, unable to process what had happened or what she should do about it. Warner charged her, bowling her over. The collision knocked the wind out of her, and she was left on the ground, her head spinning. She stared up at one of the towering monoliths, then forced herself to move. Roll over. Regain her feet and her balance, look around for Warner. But the babies were behind her, and what was she going to do about them?

"Go!" Jones shouted at her. "I've got the kids. Go after him!"

Margie's movements were slow, like swimming through concrete. She saw Jones pick up the lifesaver and toss it into the water. As she turned away to look for Warner, she heard a splash and knew that Jones had jumped in.

CHAPTER EIGHTEEN

Warner was on the run. Margie shut everything else out and focused on gaining on him. He couldn't be allowed to get back to his car and make an escape. He had killed his wife, had intended to kill his children, and she was not going to let him get away. She didn't know if he had planned to kill himself too, but running suggested to her that his instinct to preserve his own life and liberty was still strong.

Her feet crunched through the gravel of the pathway. Warner was headed for the education center, toward the big pool and the walkways elevated over the water. Margie's mind rebelled against the idea of running toward them. The last thing she wanted was to end up plummeting into the water. But she had a job to do. She was a cop and she couldn't let her phobia control her decisions. She had been told more than once that the only way to overcome her fear was by exposing herself to it. So in reality, running toward the water at a breakneck pace was good for her.

She had a stitch in her side. She had let her running habit fall by the wayside when she had moved to Calgary. If she wanted to stay in shape, she would have to get up earlier in the morning to run, and morning was not her best time. But she was getting out of shape, and should at least consider it.

Warner entered the walkways. He slowed down, but was still moving at a pretty quick clip. Margie put on a burst of speed to catch up with him and stepped onto the walkway herself. Her heart was in her throat. She could barely breathe. Her vision was narrow so that she could only see what was in front of her. She knew the way out. She needed to keep pushing forward, and then she would, in a couple of minutes, be on solid ground again. She could tackle Warner in the parking lot. Cuff him and take him into custody. It would all work out just fine.

She was no longer running, but was pushing herself to move as quickly as she could. The walkway felt narrow and unsteady. She knew she was suspended above the water, and her brain was telling her that at any minute, she could die. She went up the stairs to the second. She listened, but could no longer hear Warner's footsteps clanging ahead of her. He must already be off of the walkways and into the parking lot. That meant that she didn't have much farther to go.

A blow hit her from the side as she turned a corner. She was stunned and thrown off balance. Where had it come from? She grabbed onto the rail to steady herself and to try to reorient herself. She could see the water below her. Just her and a thin grille topped with a railing to keep her separated from it. Whose idea had it been to put young children and the frail and infirm so close to danger? Why had they thought it such a good idea to build out on the water instead of on solid, safe land?

She caught a flash of his face in front of her—an angry, maniacal grimace. "Leave me alone! You think a woman is going to get the better of me? Never!"

Before she had a chance to anticipate what he was going to do, he slammed into her again, the weight of his body throwing her against the low barrier. His hands grasped her elbow and knee, and he lifted her off of the ground. Using their momentum, he had her up and over the railing before she could catch hold of anything.

She was airborne, arms and legs flailing frantically for something to stop her fall. Then she was in the water. It drove all of the air out of her lungs when she hit the surface and then sank beneath it. Shockingly cold. The water enveloped her. She couldn't see. She held her breath and flailed and hit bottom. She was disoriented, feeling the mucky, slimy floor of the pond bottom beneath her. Had her brain blocked out the sensation of falling through the water? It seemed as if the journey to the bottom of the pond had taken only an instant.

She tried to push herself up, her hands sinking into the mud and not propelling her toward the surface. She tried to swim up toward the surface, and her hands broke out of the water.

Margie repositioned herself feet downward, and tried to stand. The muck prevented her from doing it very gracefully, sucking her feet and ankles down, but the water was not even to her waist. Margie took in gasps of air and tried to settle her panicked body and brain. She could breathe. She wasn't drowning. But she was in the middle of the pond, sinking almost to her knees in muck.

She looked around, trying to figure out the best way to get out. The education center towered above her, and the walls were sheer rock, too steep to climb.

Someone was yelling at her. Margie blinked foul water from her eyes and tried to focus on the voice.

"…okay?" she heard from somewhere up above her. Margie tipped back her head to look at the figure standing on the edge. Finkle, his hands making anxious movements.

"I'm okay," she confirmed, still gasping.

"Can you turn around? Or are you stuck?"

Margie lifted her feet one at a time, pulling them out of the sucking mud and looking for somewhere more solid to put them down. The water was frigid. She was already shivering.

"Over to your left, you see the rock steps going down into the water?"

Margie saw a stonework of long, shallow steps. A couple of other workers stood there gaping at her.

"Just make your way over there," Finkle told her in a calm, even voice.

Margie waded through the mud, one painstaking step at a time. It would undoubtedly be faster to lie down on the surface of the water and swim across, unimpeded by the mud, except that she had never learned to swim. Even floating was an issue for Margie, especially with her face in or close to the surface of the water. When she finally got close enough to the steps, Finkle was waiting there, still encouraging her in a measured, reassuring voice. Finkle reached out a hand for her. His grip was strong. With his help, she was able to drag her feet one last time out of the mud and crawl back onto solid ground. It was an effort to break the surface tension. And then she was above the water.

Finkle patted her on the shoulder. "You're good. Keep going."

At the top, back on firm ground, someone wrapped a blanket around her.

"Ambulance is on the way. Just sit down here and stay warm."

Margie shook her head. She felt better standing. Like she was a grown-up, not a little kid. She wiped foul pond water from her face, looking around. Jones was a short distance away, mothering the two children, all three of them soaked. But they seemed to be in better shape than Margie, who was shaking like a leaf and having problems catching her breath.

"Are you okay?" Jones asked, looking over at her.

Margie cleared her throat. "I wasn't planning on going into the water."

"No," Jones gave a little laugh. "None of that was planned."

"Where did he go?" Margie looked at Finkle. "Did you see where Warner went? What direction…?"

"Back into the city. Headed north. Couldn't tell you more than that."

"They've got hawks out," Jones said.

Margie didn't understand at first. Jones pointed to a black helicopter in the sky some distance away. Helicopter Air Watch for Community Safety—HAWCS. The police services helicopter.

"Does that mean they know where he is?"

"I don't know. Need to get back to the radio in my car to touch base. I don't think either of our phones are going to work. They called 9-1-1," Jones motioned to the various education center workers who were standing around, some helping and some just watching. "And the chopper was scrambled pretty quickly. I called in the APB on Warner's vehicles as we were driving over, so they knew what he was driving. But they'll be waiting for an update from us."

"We'd better do that, then." Margie attempted to squeeze some of the water out of her clothes and headed to the cars. At least they weren't very far away. Jones left the children under the supervision of one of the teachers and followed.

They stood outside of the vehicles, dripping everywhere, while Jones called on her radio, asking to be put in contact with the homicide department and with the HAWCS and other police on the ground. In a few minutes, they were all on the same channel, exchanging what information they could.

Margie bent her head close to listen. "He's in Erin Woods? I know where that is. That's not far from my place."

"You want to go over?" Jones asked. "I'm not sure how close we'll be able to get to the action, but you're going to have to go home to get changed anyway."

Margie nodded. "Yeah. Let's do it."

"More than likely, they'll just tell us to stay out of the way. But you can at least see HAWCS up close."

"Yes."

"You know your way around there? How to get there? Do you want to meet up in a particular place if we get separated?"

"I don't know my way at all." Margie reached into her car to grab her GPS. She tapped in Erin Woods and waited for something to come up on the screen. "Uh… the Community Center. How about that? We'll meet there, or get as close to it as we can."

CHAPTER NINETEEN

There were squad cars everywhere. The big armored rescue vehicle used by the CPS Tactical Unit was stopped in the middle of the Community Center parking lot. Both still dripping, Jones and Margie were directed to the tactical unit leader who got what details he could from them as to what had happened at Ralph Klein Park.

"So, what is your evaluation of his state of mind?" Sergeant Burns queried. "He's on the run, so you would think he was concerned with self-preservation, but if we've got a man who might be armed and who really doesn't have any reason to live, we need to know that before going in."

"Do you know where he is?" Margie asked, trying to discern from the activity around her just what the status of the pursuit was.

"He ditched his vehicle and took off on foot, so he can't have gotten far." HAWCS continued to buzz around overhead, looking for him. "We'll have scent dogs in a few minutes and they'll find him. But how he's going to behave once he's cornered, that's always a concern."

"He killed his wife. We have the proof and he knows it. He knows he's going down for it. He's looking at years of incarceration. He went to the park to drown his children. What I don't know is whether he planned to kill himself, or to disappear and start a new life somewhere else."

"So he doesn't have anything to lose when we catch up to him. Death or prison. Those are his only options."

Margie nodded. She looked at the armored Tactical Unit members. "Be careful. I don't think he's armed, but there's no way to know for sure. I don't think he's going to come easy."

Sergeant Burns nodded briefly. He'd probably already guessed that, but it was vital for him to have as much information as he could get.

"Is there any way we can help?" Margie asked.

"You don't have a relationship with this guy?"

"I've interviewed him before. He wasn't antagonistic then. But today..." She looked down at her dripping uniform. "I don't know whether he intended for me to drown, but he did throw me over a railing into the water."

"So, no," Burns said dryly. He looked at Detective Jones. "And you?" He observed her soaked uniform as well.

"No. Although I can tell him that his kids are okay. If he thinks he succeeded in drowning them, he might be more desperate. If he knows they're okay..."

Burns scribbled notes into a notepad. "Whoever tracks him down can pass that along. You're right; it might be just enough to make the difference between him being taken into custody quietly and suicide by cop."

He didn't tell them anything else they could do, so Jones and Margie stood around awkwardly, watching the rest of the officers who were involved moving from one position to another and reporting to Burns. The dog handler arrived with a German shepherd at his side and, after a few minutes, the dog was put onto the scent he was to track. Margie watched him put nose to ground and cast around. She imagined Stella trying to do the same thing. Stella sometimes thought she was a hunting dog, but she wasn't very good at it. She could track a quarry a few feet, but then she lost the scent. The shepherd with the dog handler seemed to be up to the job. In a couple of minutes, he was pulling hard on the harness, following Warner's trail from the car he had ditched. He led his handler to the far corner of the school field, which then joined with a pathway, out of their sight. Margie looked at Jones, then around at the houses close to the Community Center. There were a lot of residents looking out their windows or doors or hanging around the sidewalk. They looked up at HAWCS and took pictures of the tactical vehicle with their phones.

"The Twitterverse is buzzing," Jones observed. "Let's just hope that Warner isn't following it."

Wherever Warner was, crouched between houses or hiding under someone's car, Margie didn't imagine he was tapping on his phone, checking out all of the social media.

Would he hide? Would he try to walk out of the area? Get on a bus and escape the police net? She really wanted this guy. She wanted to make sure he was put behind bars for as long as possible.

She tried to squeeze more water out of her chilly, chafing clothes.

"You should go home and change," Jones suggested.

"I know. But I want to see how this all ends up. It won't take long, right? Just a few minutes?"

"You never know. Sometimes a standoff can go on for hours before the person finally gives up to the police."

"I'm going to stay for a while, at least. I really want to see them catch this guy."

CHAPTER TWENTY

They heard the dog barking in the distance. They all stood as still as statues, waiting for gunshots and explosions. Margie could hear Sergeant Burns's radio crackling, the reports coming in one on top of the other. He had been spotted entering the back yard of a house across from Erin Woods Park. The Tactical Unit worked to surround and contain him. Still no shots fired. Margie breathed shallowly, not wanting to miss anything. Over the radio, she heard the shouted command for him to come out with his hands up. Warner yelled back, wanting to know the status of his children and of the police women at the park.

Margie and Jones listened to the information being relayed back to him. Would their reassurances be enough to deescalate him? Was he past that, too desperate to be calmed down?

No shots.

He exchanged words with them another time. And another. Margie started to breathe normally again. He was having a conversation. He had not attacked or made threats. He hadn't said he had a weapon and charged one of the team.

It was working. They could all breathe again. Margie would be filling in paperwork for days, but they would have him. The children were safe. The other people in Warner's life that might have crossed him one too many times were safe.

Eventually, a voice came over Burns's radio.

"We're clear. Suspect in custody."

❧

MARGIE FOUND she didn't care about the paperwork. She was happy to go home to change and then drive back downtown with towels on her car seat and report back to the office to be debriefed and get started on the pile of reports that would need to be filed.

"The Roscoes have the children," Cruz told Margie. "They were taken straight there. Children's Services will follow up to evaluate the home and finalize the placement, but they will be safe with family tonight, not in foster care."

"But they don't know the Roscoes. So it's still going to feel strange and foreign to them."

"Better to be with family, though. They can start settling in and getting healed, instead of being disrupted with a series of placements and maybe getting separated. And I suspect they know Grandma and Grandpa better than we think."

Margie raised her brows. "Oh? I didn't think Mrs. Roscoe was lying when she said she hadn't had any contact with them."

Cruz pointed to Margie's computer screen, where the video Mrs. Roscoe had received from her daughter's email account was still frozen in a small square in the corner of the desktop. Margie pressed the 'play' triangle, and it started from the beginning, Arabella talking herself through the instructions that her mother had given her. Tapping on the picture of Grandma.

Cruz nodded. "She knows who Grandma is. Her mother showed her pictures and talked to her at least enough to recognize the picture and know who it was. Maybe they didn't have any direct contact, but the little girl had been told who she was, and that was who she was supposed to send the recording too. She knew that Grandma would do something to help them when she received the video."

CHAPTER TWENTY-ONE

*I*n a few days, Margie was with her own grandparent, secure in the knowledge that Warner was behind bars awaiting trial and Patty's daughters were safe. Moushoom had been quick to agree to go with them to Glenbow Ranch Provincial Park for a golf cart tour, and after that, to MacKay's for ice cream.

"You are in for a treat," he told them, eyes shining. "MacKay's is a tradition."

And traditions were important in Margie's family and community.

"I didn't think you'd know about them," she told him, glancing at him in surprise as she navigated the highway between the Park and Cochrane. Ice cream was just two kilometers away.

"I took your mother there when she was a little girl," Moushoom said. "We were just visiting then, I hadn't moved to Calgary yet, but MacKay's was there back then, and it was one of our favorite outings."

Margie's mother had always loved ice cream. Margie looked at Christina and grinned. It was a family trait.

Jones had told Margie that MacKay's had dozens of flavors, but she had still not expected the densely-written chalkboard she saw when she got there. She and Christina stared at it with their mouths open, marveling at all of the options.

"Bubblegum," Christina pointed out almost immediately.

Margie remembered blue stains on many of Christina's collars when she was a little girl, when blue bubble-gum ice cream had been her favorite treat. So sticky and messy. At least now, as a teenager, Margie wouldn't have to worry about Christina staining all of her clothes.

"What is 'barn door'?" Margie asked no one in particular.

A helpful patron described the ice cream concoction that included marshmallows, chocolate chips, chocolate chunks, Reese's peanut butter cups, fudge brownie bits, cookie dough, nuts, Oreo cookie crumbs, and coconut.

"Oh, my."

It wasn't going to be an easy choice. They had the cherry custard and cotton candy, two flavors she had enjoyed as a child when camping by the lake.

"Maple bacon," Christina murmured reverently.

"I thought you were vegetarian now."

Christina opened her mouth, considering. "I don't think maple bacon ice cream counts," she said finally, without bothering to give an argument as to why that was.

"I know what I am having," Moushoom announced.

Margie looked at him. She was expecting to have to read the board to him. But either his eyes or his memory was better than she had expected.

"What are you having, Moushoom?"

"Nanaimo bar."

"Oh…" That was tempting. But if Moushoom was getting it, then she was sure he would allow her to taste a bit of his custard and chocolate concoction. Sharing ice cream during a pandemic might not be such a good idea. She'd get a spoon and have a taste before he started it. That way, neither was contaminating the other.

They were getting to the front of the line, and Margie still hadn't made up her mind. She skimmed over the board once more.

"What is 'shark attack'?"

"Blue raspberry ice cream with red raspberry jam ripples," the young woman at the counter advised. She didn't have to check. She probably told ten people an hour all day long. Behind her face shield, forehead and temples glistened with sweat despite working with frozen desserts all day.

Margie's mind went back to Warner attacking her at the park and throwing her into the water, thinking she wouldn't make it out alive.

No, it wouldn't be shark attack. Not this time.

RALPH KLEIN PARK

The Ralph Klein Park is much smaller than the previous two parks in the series, but this little place packs a punch with manmade wetland features, public art installations, a community orchard of apple and pear trees, a unique playground with a zip line, and an education center.

Ralph Klein Park is on the east side of Calgary, and like Glenbow Ranch Provincial Park, opened in 2011.

It is named after former Calgary mayor and Alberta premier Ralph Klein, who lived to witness its opening and passed away in 2013.

Did you enjoy this book? Reviews and recommendations are vital to making a book successful.

Please leave a review at your favorite book store or review site and share it with your friends.

Don't miss the following bonus material:
Sign up for mailing list to get a free ebook
Read a sneak preview chapter
Other books by P.D. Workman
Learn more about the author

Sign up for my mailing list at pdworkman.com and get Gluten-Free Murder for free!

Join my mailing list and

Download a sweet mystery for free

PREVIEW OF SHE WORE MOURNING

ZACHARY GOLDMAN MYSTERIES #1

---

*More Parks Pat Mysteries are planned.
While you are waiting for them, why not check out
Zachary Goldman Mysteries?*

CHAPTER 1

ZACHARY GOLDMAN STARED DOWN the telephoto lens at the subjects before him. It was one of those days that left tourists gaping over the gorgeous scenery. Dark trees against crisp white snow, with the mountains as a backdrop. Like the picture on a Christmas card.

The thought made Zachary feel sick.

But he wasn't looking at the scenery. He was looking at the man and the woman in a passionate embrace. The pretty young woman's cheeks were flushed pink, more likely with her excitement than the cold, since she had barely stepped out of her car to greet the man. He had a swarthier complexion and a thin black beard, and was currently turned away from Zachary's camera.

Zachary wasn't much to look at himself. Average height, black hair cut too short, his own three-day growth of beard not hiding how pinched and pale his face was. He'd never considered himself a good catch.

He waited patiently for them to move, to look around at their surroundings so that he could get a good picture of their faces.

They thought they were alone; that no one could see them without being seen. They hadn't counted on the fact that Zachary had been surveilling them for a couple of weeks and had known where they would go. They gave him lots of warning so that he could park his car out of sight, camouflage himself in the trees, and settle in to wait for their appearance.

He was no amateur; he'd been a private investigator since she had been choosing wedding dresses for her Barbie dolls.

He held down the shutter button to take a series of shots as they came up for air and looked around at the magnificent surroundings, smiling at each other, eyes shining.

All the while, he was trying to keep the negative thoughts at bay. Why had he fallen into private detection? It was one of the few ways he could make a living using his skill with a camera. He could have chosen another profession. He didn't need to spend his whole life following other people, taking pictures of their most private moments. What was the real point of his job? He destroyed lives, something he'd had his fill of long ago. When was the last time he'd brought a smile to a client's face? A real, genuine smile? He had wanted to make a difference in people's lives; to exonerate the innocent.

Zachary's phone started to buzz in his pocket. He lowered the camera and turned around, walking farther into the grove of trees. He had the pictures he needed. Anything else would be overkill.

He pulled out his phone and looked at it. Not recognizing the number, he swiped the screen to answer the call.

"Goldman Investigations."

"Uh… yes… Is this Mr. Goldman?" a voice inquired. Older, female, with a tentative quaver.

"Yes, this is Zachary," he confirmed, subtly nudging her away from the 'mister.'

"Mr. Goldman, my name is Molly Hildebrandt."

He hoped she wasn't calling her about her sixty-something-year-old husband and his renewed interest in sex. If it was another infidelity case, he was going to have to turn it down for his own sanity. He would even take a lost dog or wedding ring. As long as the ring wasn't on someone else's finger now.

"Mrs. Hildebrandt. How can Goldman Investigations help you?"

Of course, she had probably already guessed that Goldman Investigations consisted of only one employee. Most people seemed to sense that from the size of his advertisements. From the fact that he listed a post office box number instead of a business suite downtown or in one of the newer commercial areas. It wasn't really a secret.

"I don't know whether you have been following the news at all about Declan Bond, the little boy who drowned…?"

Zachary frowned. He trudged back toward his car.

"I'm familiar with the basics," he hedged. A four- or five-year-old boy whose round face and feathery dark hair had been pasted all over the news after a search for a missing child had ended tragically.

"They announced a few weeks ago that it was determined to be an accident."

Zachary ground his teeth. "Yes…?"

"Mr. Goldman, I was Declan's grandma." Her voice cracked. Zachary waited, listening to her sniffles and sobs as she tried to get herself under control. "I'm sorry. This has been very difficult for me. For everyone."

"Yes."

"Mr. Goldman, I don't believe that it was an accident. I'm looking for someone who would investigate the matter privately."

Zachary breathed out. A homicide investigation? Of a child? He'd told himself that he would take anything that wasn't infidelity, but if there was one thing that was more depressing than couples cheating on each other, it was the death of a child.

"I'm sure there are private investigators that would be more qualified for a homicide case than I am, Mrs. Hildebrandt. My schedule is pretty full right now."

Which, of course, was a lie. He had the usual infidelities, insurance investigations, liabilities, and odd requests. The dregs of the private investigation business. Nothing substantial like a homicide. It was a high-profile case. A lot of volunteers had shown up to help, expecting to find a child who had wandered out of his own yard, expecting to find him dirty and crying, not floating face down in a pond. A lot of people had mourned the death of a child they hadn't even known existed before his disappearance.

"I need your help, Mr. Goldman. Zachary. I can't afford a big name, but you've got good references. You've investigated deaths before. Can't you help me?"

He wondered who she had talked to. It wasn't like there were a lot of people who would give him a bad reference. He was competent and usually got the job done, but he wasn't a big name.

"I could meet with you," he finally conceded. "The first consultation is free. We'll see what kind of a case you have and whether I want to take it.

I'm not making any promises at this point. Like I said, my schedule is pretty full already."

She gave a little half-sob. "Thank you. When are you able to come?"

―――

After he had hung up, Zachary climbed into his car, putting his camera down on the floor in front of the passenger seat where it couldn't fall, and started the car. For a while, he sat there, staring out the front windshield at the magical, sparkling, Christmas-card scene. Every year, he told himself it would be better. He would get over it and be able to move on and to enjoy the holiday season like everyone else. Who cared about his crappy childhood experiences? People moved on.

And when he had married Bridget, he had thought he was going to achieve it. They would have a fairy-tale Christmas. They would have hot chocolate after skating at the public rink. They would wander down Main Street looking at the lights and the crèche in front of the church. They would open special, meaningful presents from each other.

But they'd fought over Christmas. Maybe it was Zachary's fault. Maybe he had sabotaged it with his gloom. The season brought with it so much baggage. There had been no skating rink. No hot chocolate, only hot tempers. No walks looking at the lights or the nativity. They had practically thrown their gifts at each other, flouncing off to their respective corners to lick their wounds and pout away the holiday.

He'd still cherished the thought that perhaps the next year there would be a baby. What could be more perfect than Christmas with a baby? It would unite them. Make them a real family. Just like Zachary had longed for since he'd lost his own family. He and Bridget and a baby. Maybe even twins. Their own little family in their own little happy bubble.

But despite a positive pregnancy test, things had gone horribly wrong.

Zachary stared at the bright white scenery and blinked hard, trying to shake off the shadows of the past. The past was past. Over and done. This year he was back to baching it for Christmas. Just him and a beer and *It's a Wonderful Life* on TV.

He put the car in reverse and didn't look into the rear-view mirror as he backed up, even knowing about the precipice behind him. He'd deliberately parked where he'd have to back up toward the cliff when he was done. There was a guardrail, but if he backed up too quickly, the car would go right through it, and who could say whether it had been accidental or deliberate? He had been cold-stone sober and had been out on a job. Mrs. Hildebrandt could testify that he had been calm and sober during their call. It would be ruled an accident.

But his bumper didn't even touch the guardrail before he shifted into drive and pulled forward onto the road.

He'd meet with the grandmother. Then, assuming he did not take the case, there would always be another opportunity.

Life was full of opportunities.

———

She Wore Mourning, book #1 of the *Zachary Goldman Mysteries* series is available now at pdworkman.com

ABOUT THE AUTHOR

Award-winning and USA Today bestselling author P.D. (Pamela) Workman writes riveting mystery/suspense and young adult books dealing with mental illness, addiction, abuse, and other real-life issues. For as long as she can remember, the blank page has held an incredible allure and from a very young age she was trying to write her own books.

Workman wrote her first complete novel at the age of twelve and continued to write as a hobby for many years. She started publishing in 2013. She has won several literary awards from Library Services for Youth in Custody for her young adult fiction. She currently has over 70 published titles and can be found at pdworkman.com.

Born and raised in Alberta, Workman has been married for over 25 years and has one son.

Please visit P.D. Workman at pdworkman.com to see what else she is working on, to join her mailing list, and to link to her social networks.

If you enjoyed this book, please take the time to recommend it to other purchasers with a review or star rating and share it with your friends!

facebook.com/pdworkmanauthor

twitter.com/pdworkmanauthor

instagram.com/pdworkmanauthor

amazon.com/author/pdworkman

bookbub.com/authors/p-d-workman

goodreads.com/pdworkman

linkedin.com/in/pdworkman

pinterest.com/pdworkmanauthor

youtube.com/pdworkman

Milton Keynes UK
Ingram Content Group UK Ltd.
UKHW022008091024
449514UK00007B/93